THE
SYNDICATE

CYRUS BOZORGMEHR

First published in 2017 by Metamorphosis

ISBN 978-1-911195-52-8

Also available as an ebook
ISBN 978-1-911195-51-1

Designed and typeset by K.DESiGN
www.k-design.org.uk
Cover design by Berni Stevens

To Mado and Zara

PROSPECT

Idealism's a funny thing. It's like this grinning paradox of cosmic mischief where we oust the moneylenders at dawn, nail ourselves to a cross by noon, and then morph slowly into Pilate by sunset.

But I digress. Let's dial this right back to an English idyll – a bastion of pride, privilege, and the volatile rustlings of puberty.

Athos Freeland stared out on a distant prospect of Eton College and wondered for the thousandth time what lay beyond the spired womb. There was something so reassuringly familiar about his surroundings – an antique continuum of pastoral plenty, and yet its very embrace seemed like slow suffocation with a silken scarf.

His formative years had differed from those of his contemporaries, the majority of whom had been ensconced in boarding schools since the tender age of eight. Athos had trodden the ever so slightly edgier path of urban privilege at a private day school in London and absorbed some of the big city's intoxicating miasma by osmosis. Yet somehow that made him an interloper here, in much the same way the aristocracy once frowned upon trade. To have even the most basic understanding of the English upper class, one must see London's garden squares and stucco frontages as somewhere between a necessary evil and an opportunity for mildly illicit indulgence. It was the countryside that really defined the aristocratic psyche – a world of nobly frayed tweed, the sweet scent of perfumed manure, a dog blanket, and a vast encumbered pile of stately stone. If you didn't go traipsing through the mud in a worn Barbour to shoot dinner, you would never truly understand, and in so many ways the stable boy had more in common with the lord than the merchant.

But this wasn't about alienation or anything as identifiable as that. It was like standing at the crossroads between the high road and the low road, where the low road involved drinking in this garden of earthly delight and the high road wasn't located on any available map. The low road wasn't a place of vice or lapsed high-mindedness either, no matter what mythology says – it was just safe, familiar, and seductively unchallenging. Athos longed for an alternative though, and as the pirate radio station he was tuned into crackled with renegade bass, he wondered in what dimension he too might be hanging an aerial off a tower block and chatting into the mic without seeming like an outrageous parody of a public schoolboy gone street.

It was 1989 and the subcultural wave of acid house was cresting. An electric freedom had come unearthed and the perfect storm of a new sound, a new chemistry, and a new empathy was spiraling across the country. Barriers crumbled as black and white, rich and poor, gay and straight hit the same groove and a magnetic possibility ricocheted through the synapses. Football hooligans were hugging on the terraces instead of smashing each other's faces in, crews that once stared menacingly at one another across a dingy club were joining forces, and unity was the new tribalism. Ecstasy, in every sense of the word, engulfed them all.

Athos was plugged into the matrix through his radio, and yet the white noise that kept bustling in over the beats acted as a constant reminder of how far he was from the epicenter. Which in geographical terms may have just been a few miles, but every inch was a turn of society's wheel away. There were some older boys who had been, or at least claimed to have been, to one of these fabled gatherings, and as he loitered around them hoping for some unlikely bond, he consoled himself with the purchase of some shit weed and yet another listen to Bob Marley's *Legend*.

Eton doesn't do dormitories. It wasn't entirely clear why not – it may have simply been able to afford not to, or it was trying to nurture individuality and personal responsibility with none of the barracks-like tomfoolery that dormitories might engender. Personal responsibility did however come with a maid who was good enough to wake the boys up in the morning, sparing them the clumsy indignity of a bell and ensuring laundry came back folded.

Athos had formed a particularly strong rapport with the maid on his floor, an elderly Scottish love called Edith, who hid his porn and cigarettes when Mr. Franklin the housemaster went on patrol. The results of the private room policy were twofold: one was the enhanced scope for introspection, and the other was to turn the whole fucking house into the boys' realm. Give them a dormitory to despoil and they might check their ambition at the door. Give them isolation and an easy way to verify if the housemaster was in bed and they would occupy the building. Young boys in groups need to pirate a domain together, and if one isn't supplied, they'll simply raise the stakes.

Mr. Franklin's house was a byword for debauchery around the school, and Athos embraced that reputation with gusto. From the moment Franklin's light was seen to go out, twenty or so boys crawled out of the woodwork and ran riot in the corridors, raiding kitchens, smoking out of random windows, writing appalling folk songs, and occasionally breaking out streetside in a triumphant pair of pants. An unusual community of all-nighters had begun to form that cut across the most intransigent school barrier of all: age. Most of the Night's Watch were between sixteen and eighteen, but Athos and his best mate Harry Bradley staked their claim as thirteen-year-olds, and after being ignored for a mere matter of months, they found themselves able to cook a 3 a.m. bacon sandwich in the senior common room and share the occasional spliff. It was a strange community of misfits, no doubt, and the more Athos found himself accepted by eighteen-year-olds, the more he thought he could take on that all-elusive "outside world."

And yet his most meditative space was the Porson Library, a dusty old repository of classical literature tucked away at the base of a tower. He came not to corrupt its taciturn walls but to immerse himself in history. Not the history contained in those antediluvian volumes, mind, but the presence of the books themselves and all their cloistered lore. The Thames too had a hypnotic appeal – a deep channel into Blake's green and pleasant land and an opiate-like timelessness that

Coleridge or Wordsworth would instantly have recognized.

There was a tension there – he was arguably the biggest rebel in his year, and yet he seemed to be mainlining the school's history to fill some rootless void. This conflict may well have continued through the next five years, but it turned out that the school – well, the school didn't really see him as a fitting inheritor. Apparently, not doing any work, getting into the occasional fight, and smoking like a chimney weren't seen as just the usual japes, however cheery his insouciance might be.

It was Franklin who really loathed him – a rather petty man who himself seemed overawed by such a grand institution. Franklin didn't get Athos in the slightest, and as he saw relationships develop with older boys and heard music he didn't understand, he began to see Athos as "the other" – something both his polyglot background and newly shaved head did nothing to dampen. Athos was a "bad seed," who needed uprooting before he took the whole flower bed down with him. Ironic really that, while Athos got on famously, if cheekily, with the truly ancien-régime masters of Eton's heritage, it took someone who didn't truly belong themselves to orchestrate his downfall. That's the thing about Eton: it is at once a conveyor belt of polished conformity and a celebration of eccentricity; the trick is to rescue individuality from the paradox.

THE BILL

"FREELAND!"

It was a jangling wake-up call. Fuck. He picked his jaw up off the desk and adjusted to the classroom's unforgiving gaze. He'd nodded off somewhere between the accusative and genitive, and as he grasped for a reflex declension, he wished he was still dreaming. Without so much as a knock, a prefect had swept haughtily into the room to deliver a summons. That's how being in trouble worked at Eton: if your card had been marked and authority wanted a stern word, you'd be notified by a mortifying interruption to the pre-lunch lesson. Someone just stormed in, bypassed the teacher, and dragged you off to see the headmaster in a curious inversion of hierarchy. The teacher nominally in charge of the class had no say in the matter and was roundly ignored by the prefect – a situation in which an eighteen-year-old boy trumped a middle-aged man for temporary generalship. Maybe that kind of setup was what led to such a natural sense of entitlement.

Athos groaned and trotted off after the prefect. This must be the hundredth time this had happened, and despite the inevitable sense of dread, he had struck up a rather warm relationship with a couple of the prefects. This particular beacon of scholarship, a Henry Rutherford, had a soft spot for the wayward Athos, and as they stopped outside an imposing wooden door, they were engrossed in conversation. All around the door was graffiti sanctioned by history – names carved into the stone of boys who'd gone before. They could be anywhere from a century to four centuries old, and there was something both haunting and gently comforting about the silent solidarity. Henry caustically noted that it was usually prisons that inspired such scratched bids for immortality, and while the comparison of boarding school to prison is an old adage, the tension between individual and institution is a primal source of energy. As the door swung open to reveal a stern set of pince-nez, Athos wondered how many mischief makers had once stood in his place.

"I do despair of you, Freeland. You're here today for persistent tardiness. It's hardly the crime of the century, but your stubborn refusal to engage with this school in any kind of acceptable way simply can't continue."

"Yes, sir. Or rather, no, sir."

"Damn it, boy, you do have real potential, but you absolutely insist on squandering it. There will be – there must be a reckoning very soon if you do not change course."

"Sir, I'm hoping to focus my energies into producing a play in the autumn. I do strongly believe that having a creative outlet will help stabilize some of my other behavior."

The headmaster nodded and cracked the beginnings of an approving smile. He recovered his poise swiftly though.

"I think we'd all like to see your 'energies' guided towards the arts and away from the public house. But it's rather late in the day, I must tell you. Your housemaster is not optimistic about your future here. Plays are all well and good, but they are known as extracurricular for a reason. Surely even your grasp of Latin can fathom the meaning of the word 'extra.'"

"Yes, sir. I do understand that I have to shape up on the intracurricular front."

"Your tutor doesn't hold out much hope for you either."

Athos made a note to self that his tutor was a bandwagon-jumping prick. How could he possibly have formed such an opinion when Athos had been to so few of his tutorials?

"We have a month left before the summer holidays," continued the headmaster. "Decisions about your future will be taken then, so I suggest you consider very carefully whether you wish to remain a pupil here."

"Yes, sir. Thank you, sir."

"And do something about that ghastly haircut. You look like some sort of inmate."

'Yes, sir."

NO SMOKE WITHOUT FIRE

"So what do we think? *The Tempest* or *Catch-22*?"

"Well, Harry, old boy – having read neither of them, and with remarkably little desire to do so, I'm going to vote *Catch-22*. It's twentieth century and it's American, which in itself is probably going to be more up our streets. And there's something about performing Shakespeare at Eton that just seems… well…"

"Yes, I take your point. I had a glance at *Catch-22*. Definitely more our cup of tea, I think. All a bit avant-garde, and the protagonist has an even sillier name than you."

"So it's settled then. Bloody brilliant – we've got a project on."

Now, one might argue that this admirable foray onto the boards was a crimson fucking herring. Becoming the poster boys for mid-twentieth-century drama wasn't going to get Athos any nearer to his goal of breaking out of the bubble, and nor was it going to guarantee him a place at Eton next year. He had managed to invest the play idea with extremely unrealistic expectations of its potential for character rehabilitation, and as he worked with Harry on booking a theatre and getting some sort of cast together, he signally failed to do much else. As the weeks unfolded, he began to subconsciously view the production of *Catch-22* as a sort of touchstone – a dream that he could actually achieve instead of staring out of the window listening to pirate radio and conjuring a fantasy world. And it would also magically reform him in the eyes of the law – a thesp, for fuck's sake.

The gentle thwack of bat on ball and Pimm's on ice ushered in the honeyed months of summer. The sun oozed lazily over Windsor Castle's bristling battlements, and going for a cheeky spliff became something of a romantic odyssey – as Athos, Harry, and a small crew of die-hard marijuana enthusiasts clambered over fences and wove through weirs to find a small slice of paradise. Summer brought a new innocence: that spellbinding amnesia that bewitches us into thinking it was always thus – we had been in Arcadia all along. The combination of these THC-loaded nature rambles and taking on a play free of any teacherly control saw Athos finally reach something resembling peace with himself, and he reluctantly put his acid-tinged ambitions on hold. He had a project after all.

One fine summer's eve (do we ever remember the miserable ones?) the likely lads trundled back to the house and rolled in by the back entrance. Spirits were running high and a cheery uproar was ringing out the chimes. A wrestling match here, a food fight there; the smiles bounced off the sober green walls, and with the playfulness rising, someone, somewhere had a fucking brainwave. Fire extinguishers. Great big juicy red ones stuffed with water rather than foam. And they were dotted around the house like a fucking Easter egg hunt.

It remains unclear who the instigator was, or if indeed the situation was that Newtonian. Perhaps the application of causal logic had no place in the chaos equations of testosterone unbound, but whether a butterfly flapped its wings or not, the jets of water began spraying wildly.

It was like a scorching summer's day in the Bronx, with the neighborhood kids let loose on the hydrants, except with a bit less Kool Herc and a lot more pasty Englishmen. But the vibe ran universal – that midsummer soak of liquid freedom.

It all descended into farce, of course, and before long every extinguisher on the entire premises had been drafted into the fray, emptied, and left prostrate on the floor. With the extinguishers, er, extinguished, wiser heads emerged from the orifices they'd been tucked into. Hmm. This pile of red metal bodies and sopping wet walls didn't look too good.

Etonians are famed problem solvers, and in that moment everyone pulled together to demonstrate the kind of cool head and tactical genius that saw nineteen alumni become prime minister. They put all the empty extinguishers back where they had found them and hoped no one noticed. It was a masterful plan undone only by its utter strategic failure.

The fact that the carpets squelched when you walked across them and the overpowering smell of damp that permeated the corridors seemed rather trivial to those involved. One hesitates to speak of ringleaders because the whole thing was so organic, and boys of all ages, stripes, shapes, and interests had answered the call of the wild. It was the stuff Edwardian school songs are made of, and yet, by dinnertime, a hushed pall had set in over the house.

The first sign of trouble came hot on the heels of after-dinner prayers – one of those quaint conventions in a sea of agnosticism. This was usually an opportunity for Mr.

Franklin to hold forth on important matters of tedium, but tonight he was looking like a dyspeptic character from a Dickens novel.

There was something unconvincing about him even when he was trying to intimidate. You could just imagine him practicing his admonishments in front of a mirror while his loyal wife urged him on. But there was no getting away from the fact that power did rest within his rather underwhelming person, and it seemed like he was onto the water-fight crew. Damned if anyone could work out how – the extinguishers had been put back, for fuck's sake.

The mystery would have to wait, for he had a pronouncement to make. All privileges were to be revoked until a confession was made.

Mr. Franklin only really thought in linear terms, so the idea of the waterfight being a spontaneous eruption with no guiding hand was beyond him – a lesson Athos would never forget when dealing with authority. He wanted to know who was responsible, and being met with an admirable wall of silence, he went for a combination of carrot and stick. No privileges until the culprit was found, but if the miscreant fessed up, no punishment would be meted out and the matter would rest there.

Mr. Franklin was nobody's fool. If no one confessed, his authority would be sorely tested. There was only so long you could deprive fifty boys of their freedoms without provoking mutiny, and if the instigator stayed schtum, things might end up more dangerous for master than boy. So he declared an amnesty, and with consequences out of the picture, Athos went full Musketeer and stepped up for the team.

Athos reasoned that he may as well take the rap for this. After all, Franklin's opinion of him couldn't sink much lower, and better the black sheep wear the black armband than let it sully a fresh white coat. Athos loved this kind of chivalrous shit, and he quietly basked in the gratitude and admiration of his peers as he began the long walk up to the scaffold. But knowing the hangman had been given the day off, he could see nothing but an upside to the situation. He knocked on Franklin's door and stepped inside.

ROOTS AND REVOLUTIONS

The last day of term was a flurry of tentative sunshine, tenuous promises, and turbulent anticipation. Weeks of adventure lay ahead, and the memories that summer etches into teenagers' souls remained to be written. A whole swathe of Athos's older friends were taking their final leave before gap years beckoned, and it was hugs and vague promises of keeping in touch all round before parents began to arrive. Athos was pretty chuffed that he'd made it through unscathed despite the headmaster's dire warnings, and for a second he was happy to forgo the holidays entirely and crack straight on with the play. He still hadn't actually read *Catch-22* but had managed to pen a whole different meta-play in his head – a play about doing the play that was his strongest totem of identity. If he couldn't access the big wide world, then he would create a whole new one.

His parents were far from the norm at Eton, and a million miles away from the county set. His father, Phillip, had been a journalist and mid-level diplomat, while his mother, Leila, had been a ravishing lady of leisure. The two had met in late 1960s' Iran, where Phillip had been posted, and they had lived a life of swimming pools, cocktails, and intellectual salons, safe in the bosom of an increasingly repressive regime.

We always wonder how we would behave if we found ourselves at the sharp end of dictatorship, and the Freeland story was instructive. Iran was the West's primary ally in the region at the time, a state of affairs that seems almost impossible to comprehend when examining the tortured alliances of today's Middle East. It was open season for oil men, hoteliers, investors, and a whole generation of wealthy Iranians who had been educated abroad and sought to instill a forward-looking cosmopolitanism. Parties grew increasingly lavish and decadence aligned itself with culture. Money was flowing free, and it seemed for all the world like a golden age of progress with echoes of the Roaring Twenties.

But the '20s were flanked by two world wars and in hindsight seem like an urgent jazz riff sandwiched between the geopolitical pillars of disaster. And so it was in Iran – nothing like the scale of world wars, of course, but national traumas all the same.

When the elected prime minister, Mohammed Mosaddeq, took the wildly popular decision to nationalize the Anglo-Iranian Oil Company (modern-day BP) in 1952, he set off a chain reaction that would come to define Middle Eastern politics.

Britain was still smarting from the loss of India and the slow dissolution of Empire. She hadn't yet been humbled by the Suez fiasco, and the government took this outpouring of popular will as a direct threat to their interests. The British had learned during the Second World War that the United States was an excellent proxy, and what muscle Britain couldn't deliver, the Americans might be persuaded to cough up. America still hadn't fully embraced its imperial role and with the Cold War heating up, they were just beginning to grasp the global game of chess. Britain were old hands at the table, having ruled an unreasonably large chunk of the world, and its panjandrums were thoroughly schooled in the murky waters of backstairs maneuvering. And that included "encouraging" the United States where it suited them.

Having tried economic sanctions, Britain had a brainwave. In 1953, they whispered the word "communism" into the ear of the incoming Eisenhower administration and convinced the US that this oil nationalization was a Soviet power play. Well, that did it, and before you could say "freedom and democracy," the CIA had come up with a plan to topple Mosaddeq in a coup d'état while leaving their client-king, the Shah, intact. Britain got some of "its" oil back while surrendering the whip hand to the Americans, the Shah turned into a paranoid wreck awed by US power, and the Iranian people lost all faith that they could control their own destiny.

As the '60s and '70s ticked on, the Shah leaned ever further towards the American way of doing things while building the third largest secret police network in the world. Society was rigidly controlled, and even as autocracy mounted, around the swimming pools of North Tehran it seemed for all the world like halcyon days of prosperity and liberalism. That's the thing: if the state is letting you drink vodka martinis and wear bikinis while disappearing religious activists, that can feel remarkably liberal – especially if you don't know about the latter. What wasn't to love?

Plenty as it turned out. The Shah's police state was reaching a tipping point and the firesale of assets to Western interests alongside the importation of Western cultural norms alienated huge swathes of the population. You couldn't tell while sipping champagne and discussing Pollock in the gilded enclaves of the capital, but discontent was stirring and repression was only pouring fuel on the fire. Revolution was in the air, and there were only two banners strong enough to unite under: religion and ideology – or, in this case, Islam and communism. No other belief systems had the same roots or currency, and in such a totalitarian atmosphere, building a consensus-based political philosophy was impossible. Blunt instruments would have to be fought with blunt instruments.

The rest is history: cue revolution, hostage crisis, an Islamist purge of their erstwhile commie allies, and, unbelievably, it seemed to take the Freelands completely by surprise. Shocked to discover that their luxurious lifestyle and laissez-faire cultural sensibilities weren't shared by people from villages and industrial towns, they vacillated wildly and hoped for the best. As the merchant classes smelt the impending cordite and exported cash furiously, the Freelands and many others on the fringes of aristocracy simply dithered until it was too late. By the time the penny dropped, all their assets had been seized and they just about managed to escape with their lives and their baby boy to England – sinner and saint of this whole sorry mess.

Leila's father had been a flamboyant n'er-do-well, who'd knocked up his young bride before settling into a temperamental routine of cards and opium addiction. Once she'd wrapped her head round parenthood, Leila's mother had thrown over her rather pointless first love and taken to the social carousel with a glint in her eye and a thirst for the good life. A dazzling beauty with a formidable personage to match, she finally wedded a certain Dr. Assemi – an Anglophile with a countenance of creased kindness who'd set up shop in London and done pretty well for himself.

He accepted Leila without question, but with half brothers and sisters tumbling out of the fecund new union, she decided to strike out on her own. It was all rather awkward being ten years older than her nearest half siblings, so she'd thrown herself into Tehran's metropolitan life with a precocious independence. But suddenly, in the wake of revolution and without a penny to the Freeland name, there was nothing for it but a return to the fold.

In today's world of industrial-scale displacement, capsized rafts, sprawling camps, and desperate human misery, it's difficult to sympathize with the plight of a refugee sipping questionable wine aboard a 747. But crisis is relative, and while the landing was materially soft, the scars ran deep. Phillip plunged into a pit of despair – half mourning an idyllic life and half terrified of how he might reinvent himself in England. Rather than tapping up all his old contacts, he retired behind a veil of depression and Leila stepped up to back the family's bone.

Reluctant to take any handouts, and keen to establish independence from her family, she found herself in the tricky position of being formally qualified for nothing and middle-aged to boot. She ducked and dived to make ends meet – working briefly in the rag trade, a Swiss perfume company that swiftly folded, a clunky computer firm, an estate agent's, and a shoe importer before finally managing to cobble a mortgage together and begin life in the newly ascendant British tradition of property flipping. An enterprising, charismatic sort, Leila evolved into a style consultant – often for Iranians who'd got their wedge out in time. The shift in relative status was bittersweet, but for a while there, the family stabilized.

With no inheritance left to bestow on Athos, they piled on the education. For years, Phillip painstakingly instilled in Athos everything from Greek mythology to mathematical puzzles. Depressed he may have been, but he certainly didn't show it, and with Leila holding the economic fort, he doubled down on highbrow house husbandry. Learning was made genuinely fun, and those years were as cathartic for Phillip as they were formative for Athos. But the era of the gentleman amateur had to end at some point, and from then on, only the best would do. And to Athos's parents, that meant Eton.

Thing was, they only just barely had the money to pay for it, and Leila had to hold the financial foundations together by her fingertips. Much of this was lost on Athos, as he'd never been made to feel like he was lacking anything – he wasn't from the school of "immigrant family done good," where a child grows up knowing the family has all its hopes pinned on him. Phillip and Leila had purposefully spared him that kind of burden, focusing all their hopes on a liberal education. Concepts like reason, democracy, argument, and persuasion had been introduced early on with the firm belief that such a mindset – free from the dictatorial strictures of "do as I say" – would yield a progressive, rational mind.

It sort of worked – but it sort of didn't. When a six-year-old sees the word "No" as a starting point for negotiations, it almost doesn't matter how erudite the ensuing debate is; willfulness and entitlement will be at least one of the results. So when they sent him to Eton with every penny invested and every dream cashed into chips, they never really managed to communicate the gravity of it to him, and as a result he viewed the whole experience through a deeply self-involved prism.

But as they arrived to collect him for the carefree summer ahead, Leila was sobbing violently into her handbag, while Phillip's stiff upper lip quivered in the breeze. Athos stood on the pavement with his bags packed, and as he saw their faces through the windshield, he couldn't for the life of him work out what was wrong.

REBOOT

Those fucking fire extinguishers. His stomach bounced around the inside of the car like a burst balloon. How had it come to this?

It seemed that his parents had received a call from the Lower Master – a sort of bureaucratic deputy to the Head and nominally in charge of the younger contingent. Much of the usual flannel had been dispensed with, and the upshot was that Athos's invitation to return in the autumn had been revoked. Nothing so drastic as an expulsion, you understand – just a wonderfully British set of euphemisms that came to the same thing.

In any context, this would have been severely upsetting news, but the Lower Master had gone on to decry a litany of sins that included the destruction of school property with fire extinguishers. And the betrayal in those words was savage. All that talk of an amnesty had been a trap, and the cowardice Franklin had shown in not even telling Athos his fate was staggering. What example did it set about adulthood and personal responsibility if a fifty-year-old man couldn't look a fourteen-year-old boy in the eye and tell him straight?

That was the summer royally fucked though. Forget a Don Henley-soundtracked voyage of Mediterranean abandon, clumsy fumbles on the beach, promises of undying friendships, iced inspiration, and eternal blue skies. The altogether more mundane quest for an alternative educational establishment would dominate.

Tutorial colleges – also known as crammers – are a sort of Champions League for the public-school dropout. Athos was accepted without much question by WPM off the Gloucester Road, and neither he nor his parents held out that much hope for its pedagogic embrace. The fees somehow matched those at Eton, a fact justified by small class sizes and claims of excellent teaching, but the assumption that the whole place was some sort of transitory Borstal for dysfunctional rich kids was difficult to avoid.

And yet, to Athos's amazement, that characterization turned out to be lazy at best. There was a far more diverse pool of students than public-school scallywags, and despite the financial barriers, a far wider spectrum of backgrounds. You could smoke, you could go to the pub, your free time was your own – there was literally nothing to rebel against, and being treated like an adult was a remarkably effective method of encouraging engagement. This again was a lesson Athos would internalize: that rules breed rebellion and trust breeds responsibility.

The teaching too was extraordinary. It rapidly became apparent that the kind of educator such a college attracted was someone who was highly qualified, knew their shit, had no desire to be trapped in a formal institution, and wanted a higher salary than a state school could proffer. Oxbridge double firsts abounded, but with none of the rigidity that phrase suggests. Shakespeare was taught with references to Aleister Crowley, *The Magus*, and 1960s' literature, and with a far more sophisticated reading of the source than the bloated Victorian norm.

King Lear, for example – filial ingratitude or parental abuse? *Hamlet* – terminal indecision or poison in his ear? What did his father's ghost achieve by emotionally blackmailing a scholar into soldierly revenge, except the loss of his kingdoms and the total slaughter of his family?

Suddenly this was the Bard alive, exploring complex moral questions and shifting shades of gray. Not a lifeless "betterment" that landed somewhere between a psalm and a grammatical primer. History too stopped looking like a relentless assault of dry facts and jumped off the page in three dimensions – a fascinating tapestry of social evolution, cyclical forces, multilayered causality, and the macro manifestations of humanity. Athos had always been clever, but he had stopped giving a shit about learning a while back, preferring the monuments of scholarship to its actual pursuit. But suddenly, his thirst to discuss and debate was overwhelming.

He still didn't do any homework, of course – that smacked of Stakhanovite excess. But this is the beauty of the humanities: there's no such thing as a right answer. Athos was lucky enough to attend school in a pre-Blairite world – before investment in public services was yoked to an obsessive drive to measure the immeasurable.

Blair and his team of hotshots reasoned that if they were to keep an essentially rightwing country happy under a Labour government, they would have to arm themselves with an arsenal of statistics to justify public funding. More money for the NHS? Targets would be needed, metrics would be established, oversight would be expanded, and a new managerial layer would be required to implement it all. So the next time someone asked where the money went, you could show them a phalanx of graphs and tables. It might have worked to a limited extent in the NHS had bureaucratic inflation not sucked funding from frontline services. But education?

How do you measure learning in binary terms? It's simple – you can't. Not in the arts anyway, where argument is all and multiple choice misses the point. Not in the sciences either, after a certain stage. But Athos was encouraged to think independently, experience the questions being asked, and harness answers from argument. The fascistic impact of league tables and a reductive approach to intellectual endeavor were yet to kick in, and conveniently, that meant you could still wing it as long as you read the book or looked at the painting.

Athos found himself transported into a different educational realm – one of DIY philosophy and genuine enlightenment. The backdrop of the Cromwell Road may be rather more prosaic than the Perpendicular Gothic wrapping Eton's pedigree, but there could be little doubt that he'd had the best of both worlds: a taste of academic theater and now some actual learning.

Socially too, things were beginning to change. Already there was something more cosmopolitan at work, and he soon struck up core friendships with a bunch of pot-smoking adventurers. They set up a forward HQ in a local bar called

The Precinct, which came recommended by its pool table, menu, and trust that its patrons were all over eighteen. It was the middle of a weekday after all – wouldn't an under-eighteen be at school?

At least two of his close friends lived more or less in their own flats, propped up by allowances while their parents enjoyed more exotic climes. We're not talking Cristal and private jets here, but a couple of hundred quid a week – enough for weed and takeaways. The real prize was independence – suddenly you had a school that didn't care what you did in your free time, a bar you could hang out in, and flats to chill in. At the age of fifteen. A fucking triumph …

But that siren call of renegade bass still rang. Acid house parties had effectively been neutralized – at least temporarily – by shrill tabloid hysterics, a ludicrous overreaction by the state, and a titanic police operation. Amazing how dancing and environmentalism seem to attract such disproportionate disapproval, where legions are deployed, phones are tapped, randy undercover officers are embedded, and teenagers are beaten senseless. It's almost as if those two strands of human existence are threateningly primal. Dancing and tree hugging? An existential threat? Really?

But while the orbital warehouse events were in a lull, the club scene in London was jumping. And he now lived in fucking London. It would have been a shameful dereliction of duty if he hadn't told his parents he was off to stay the night at a friend's, met up with his fledgling crew, and headed down to one of the clubs. Music was in flux, house now had a breakbeat over the top, reggae and hip-hop flavors were in the mix, and from across the Channel a new strand of Belgian tribalism was abstracting the living fuck out of modernism. Techno was here. Hardcore was here. Rave was here.

INDEPENDENCE

By day, Athos immersed himself in a kaleidoscope of ideas. Anton Wilson, Leary, Castaneda, Mckenna – the cosmonauts of consciousness, the paradoxes of quantum physics, the politics of altered states, the rewiring of reality, the nascent whisper of cyberspace, and the limitations of three-dimensional perception.

And by night, he, Tim, Ben, and Jason – his closest friends at college – would head down to The Temple, a sort of shrine to post-'60s hippydom, where world music, bongo drums, and decent drugs forged a community of art students, squatters, and "types," while maintaining a bizarrely civilized set of opening hours: 8p.m. to midnight on a Saturday night.

There was an elephant in the room though. Class A drugs. For all his psychedelic research, he was still intellectualizing rather than experiencing them. Truth be told, he was shit scared.

His posse was an interesting mix of misfits. Tim Aitken was the one with the flat and had been kicked out of some other public school for cannabis-related crimes. His parents may have vacated the Big Smoke for a small Provençal village, but they had left a smattering of guardians in the shape of Tim's eleven older siblings. Ma and Pa Aitken either had an admirably carnivorous sex life or a Puritan sense of duty to the marriage bed – Athos couldn't for the life of him figure out which. But twelve kids. Jesus. The Middle Ages would be proud, and as for Tim, being the youngest had taken its toll, and his tolerance for henpeckery was tightly wound.

Ben Abrahams was a wry smile incarnate. His father was Chelsea's premier second-hand car dealer, and the family hailed from South East London. All the characteristics of the trade were amplified in Mr. Abrahams: he was larger than life, possessed a magic ability to convince people to buy things they didn't want, retained a cheery cat-and-mouse relationship with the tax authorities, could offload any item of questionable provenance within twenty-four hours, and was on drinking terms with most of the London gangland families. Having been through about seventeen schools, including several in Spain during one of his father's routine misunderstandings with the law, Ben had a rather hardened view of mollycoddled public schoolboys, and Athos had to prove his worth before the two could be friends.

And finally, Jason Bourne, whose mother was – I shit you not – a spy. No one actually ever introduces themselves as such, but he was pretty confident he'd rumbled her talk of "diplomatic postings" and "security consultancy in Whitehall." He didn't quite know how to feel about having a secret agent as a mother, not least because his father had been bypassed in the personality handouts. Dad had taken the very unusual step of insisting Jason be homeschooled for the first ten years of his life and the insularity had begun to show, spiking into reckless acts of property destruction and a suicidal courting of danger. The scars were only deepened by the train set his father seemed to love more than his son, and throwing a kid into the social minefield of an 11+ classroom after years of the station master's hollow gaze was a tough ask. Jason hadn't coped well and here he was. As for his mother – well, she kept a distant if coldly loving eye on his progress. Which, to be honest, worried them all.

Twixt The Precinct's pool table and Tim's flat was their domain and they lorded over it like acne-ridden kings. Gloucester Road had a slight murk to it – that feeling one gets near a train station. It never quite rose to the red lights of Earl's Court, where a strident gay community, an inebriated Australian community, a transient hustler community, and a rising Sloane community made merry. West London in the '90s still had healthy pockets of vice rubbing shoulders with bastions of conservatism – Earl's Court Road suddenly jinked into the millionaire Boltons, Chelsea's cousin Fulham was a right den of old-school grit, while Holland Park percolated into the badlands of Ladbroke Grove. This cheek-by-jowl melting pot of synergy and friction gave the city an edge, a throbbing pulse, and a volatile energy.

Gloucester Road however didn't really fit any of these categories. It was far enough away from the charred B&B facades of Cromwell Road to not feel too much like an open-air hostelry, but the preponderance of bureaux de change and pubs that made you wonder who drank in them gave it a strange lack of cohesion. Minutes away were the more solidly stylish realms of Kensington and South Kensington, but the very nature of Gloucester Road always made you puzzle over the people you met there. Those that passed through

The Precinct were a funny bunch – nearly always from an unidentifiable ethnic background, with an impenetrable accent, and an air of money mingled with slight desperation. It was an interesting study in outsiderism, and the low-level shadiness proved an intriguing teenage cocoon.

Khallid, a tenant of The Precinct who lasted about six months before disappearing without trace, had done the lads a massive favor. He had set them up with a reliable hash connection. Up until that point they had run the gauntlet of Portobello Road to score – basically looking for black people to ask. It was cringingly awkward – they radiated uncertainty, fear, ignorance, and a patronizing excitement at being in the "ghetto." The success-to-skank ratio was about 50:50, but perhaps the standout moment was when they pulled aside a towering mass of dreadlocks and haltingly asked him if he was selling any hash. Drawing himself up to his fullest height, their target gave an imperious flick of his locks and looked at them in disgust. "Don't stereotype me," he boomed, and strode off.

There was a lesson learned there for Athos. One of his heroes was Martin Luther King, but he'd never realized until that moment that it was possible to be totally antiracist while unwittingly being a bit racist. You couldn't admire the struggles of the Civil Rights movement while assuming every black dude with dreads in London sold weed. That kind of pigeonholing would have to go if he was ever to become "real."

Plenty of opportunity to learn though. Khallid had introduced them to a guy called Errol who lived in a

Kensington bedsit – back in the days when Kensington still had bedsits and not million-pound "pieds-à-terre." He must have been around fifty years old, hailed from Trinidad, was of rather substantial girth, had gone bald somewhere along the line, and stuck monastically to a uniform of stained white T-shirts and baggy tracksuit bottoms. The bedsit was sparsely furnished and wreathed in the brown floral patternry the 1970s have yet to apologize for. Carpet and wallpaper could have done with a change, but it was always immaculately tidy and Errol took his hosting duties very seriously.

He didn't have a landline number and mobile phones still had a yuppie mystique to them, so the boys would just go round there unannounced whenever they needed a smoke. Seems like such poor form in today's world – you don't knock on a drug dealer's door without phoning first unless you want to get shot or blacklisted. Errol was an absolute godsend. A warm welcome fifteen minutes' walk away from The Precinct, fair deals on hash, an early glimmer of skunk, a cup of tea, a place to skin up, and a wonderfully random relationship with a middle-aged man.

Errol didn't seem to mind having a load of sixteen-year-olds coming over and using his house as a chill space. He was remarkably tolerant of them, and it wasn't until years later that it occurred to Athos that he would happily spend time alone with Errol without the slightest thought that it could be construed as odd. Because it wasn't. In a *Daily Mail* reality, Errol would be a predatory pedophile or pushing drugs on kids – but he was neither. He was just a lonely bloke trying to make ends meet.

Perhaps his only slight quirk was an insistence that he was a stock-market genius, with a Derek Trotter-like certainty that this time next year he'd be a millionaire. He would get rather carried away with tales of his future glories, and after a couple of beers would occasionally and only half-jokingly start referring to himself as "Errol the King." Every now and again, he would ask the boys if they wanted to invest and guarantee themselves a spot by his side when the markets bucked to his will, but they always managed to sidestep the issue. He gave the distinct impression of doing the boys a favor, never sounded in need of the money, and registered an avuncular disappointment at their lack of ambition when they said they couldn't. He was only suggesting a stake of two hundred pounds each as well, which in itself seemed suspiciously low. That alone made Athos think it might be either a scam, or more likely a delusion, as million-pound profits didn't come from two-hundred-pound stakes. He'd have taken him more seriously if the benchmark was twenty grand.

So life was good and all the pieces had fallen into place. And yet Athos couldn't help but feel he had moved from one bubble to another. Yes, this bubble was a bit more worldly, but it still felt limited. The key to any successful bubble is comfort, and this one had everything it needed to not warrant further exploration. And that for Athos was a problem – one that manifested itself in very odd ways.

Like, what the fuck was with the blazer and chinos he had started sporting? Make no mistake, this was considered terminally uncool even at Eton. Green jeans, lumberjack shirts, and Doc Martens had been all the rage there, and there was literally no discernible excuse for Athos's curiously conservative choice of attire. Worse still, he had taken to wearing them to places like The Temple, where most people went for the "Moroccan carpet with sleeves" look, or the "baggy trousers with Special Brew accessories" collection.

Tim, Ben, and Jason could hardly bear the embarrassment – he was actively sabotaging their attempts to blend in, and while they might admit everything about Athos's character and even the way he wore the offending articles contradicted their symbolism, the first impressions thing was a bust. And anyway, if you wanted to nail a unique look, London offered a million and one ways to be conventionally unconventional. Why, oh why a blue blazer and chinos?

No one, least of all Athos, could articulate why, but a psychoanalyst would probably put it down to two main currents. One was using the uniform as an umbilical cord back to the one place that told him he wasn't wanted: Eton. The other, and to be fair much more prominent reason, was rebellion. Athos had subconsciously realized that dressing and acting like everyone else created yet another bubble. If he had worn baggy trousers and Public Enemy T-shirts at Eton because that was two fingers up, then surely it made sense to wear something equally contrarian in a London context. If everyone else was dressing down, dressing hippy, dressing cool, then fuck that shit – have some navy blazers, motherfuckers.

Yes, he was challenging these new tribes, but not to antagonize them or define himself in contrast to them. It actually was acceptance he craved, but he was determined to be accepted on his own terms rather than because he wore appropriate camouflage. If people could get past the blazer and chinos, then that would be real acceptance. And despite such a quixotic approach, this tactic worked remarkably well. Having a pretty decent-sized character helped – if he'd been a shrinking violet or on the bland side it would have been game over. But he wasn't. He was large. And that swung it.

THE TEMPLE

Saturday night in Shoreditch. Fuck me, that sentence carries a different meaning twenty years on. Long before the hipsters, the labored quirks, the silicon roundabouts, the hot-desking craft ales, and the eruption of international nightlife, Shoreditch was a right shithole. Every other building was boarded up, import-export offices smeared their monikers over dirty windows, the scent of decay was palpable, and the feeling of having wandered into no-man's-land was unmistakable. As he and his mates walked up Hackney Road, Athos couldn't help thinking that even the street names screamed transit rather than destination. The Temple was held in a former town hall, which seemed apt, as it arguably had a far more community-spirited ethos than the committees that once jockeyed within its walls. Behind an imposing facade of exhaust-stained neoclassicism lay a linoleum world of possibility, transformed by strategically painted bedsheets and boundless optimism.

There were two very distinct camps within the tie-dyed town hall. One came until midnight, drank some beers, smoked some weed, banged some drums, and then fucked off home with their thirst quenched. But then there was another camp: a little bit older, a little bit rougher, a little bit readier, and with an elemental glint in their eyes. And over the weeks, Athos started to lose all interest in the former –

been there, done that – and focus his attentions on the latter.

Ever since his bid to breach the age taboo back at school, Athos had learned a thing or two about getting a bite from much older, much cooler people than he. There were a couple of basic precepts. One: find something transactional that benefits the target person and will therefore necessitate at least some contact. This allows for a conversation – albeit limited – but without feeling clingy or forced. Two: use these windows of functionality to inject fragments of character that cumulatively prove you're worth knowing. It really is that simple. If you try to strike up a friendly conversation or show off in their vicinity, you'll crash and burn. Similar rules apply to meeting someone famous. Gush and beg for an autograph, and it's embarrassed exits all round. Play it cool, drop a punchline, and suddenly you're on equal terms.

The purchase of marijuana is an excellent way in which to create these apertures, and has the benefit of offering scope for return visits. And so it was in this case. Athos pinpointed who he aspired to hang out with, played it cool, bought some weed, and then some more the next week. And the week after that. Each time, he'd show a little bit more of himself, and within about six weeks he could happily chat to them without pretext. He began to divide his time between his college crew and what might be described as his "outside the bubble" crew, whose world so intoxicated him.

The more he spoke to them, the more he would hear the word "taz." He didn't have a fucking clue what it might mean, but rather than ask, he applied his analytic skills. At first, he thought it might be some shamanic potion or a freshly synthesized psychedelic, but the repeated contextualization of it as a place led him back to the drawing board. Google didn't exist in those days, but he did scour the *Time Out* nightlife listings to see if it might be a club. Bless.

He started to build a piecemeal picture of what "taz" might refer to – much like a man refusing to ask directions might guess his route from the sun's position. It pretty much had to be some kind of underground rave. The conspiratorial tones in which it was discussed definitely suggested secrecy, but that could simply have been the nagging human fondness for cliques at work. One thing was clear: invitations weren't being broadcast, and it felt like the address for a resistance meeting being given out at a communist rally in Eastern Europe. If the word "taz" had put on a pair of stockings, covered its curves in honey, and mouthed "come here, big boy" at him, Athos couldn't have been any more determined to leap into bed with it. Secrecy is the ultimate yin to desire's yang.

Jason, Ben, and Tim were rather less obsessed with this mission. Life was good – they could go out, have a belting night, wolf down a takeaway, and jump a cab home to chill in peace. So when Athos came to them with his rather predictable plan of seeing if they could all go to this "taz" thing too, they were unenthusiastic. They didn't really care about taking things any further, and if they were honest, were not remotely convinced that they wanted to be going anywhere those other guys were going. The appeal simply wasn't there. Over the next four weeks, Athos tried to talk them into at least giving it a go, but they wouldn't budge. Slight fissures started to appear as frustration mounted on both sides. Athos despaired of their lack of adventure, and they despaired of his choice of grails.

As the divide grew between Athos and the others on the most appropriate way to live life to the full, he grew closer to his new mates at The Temple. Numbers fluctuated on any given Saturday, but they could best be described as a happy-go-lucky crew of squatters who had tuned out of mainstream society and had been waiting ever since for something worth tuning back into.

There were a few standout characters, the first of whom was Steve. Steve was short and rake thin with a gleaming bald dome, piercing blue eyes, and a radiant smile that beamed generosity of spirit. He might best be described as the conscience of the group, and could always be relied upon to rein in the drunken excesses of his mates if they looked likely to upset or intrude upon anyone else. Athos had gravitated towards him early on because Steve didn't really do hierarchies of cool – he was just a visibly kind soul.

Offsetting Steve was Havoc. He would generally be the one Steve was trying to rein in, as his penchant for super-strength lager, cheap spirits, edgy banter, and punk diplomacy rolled through social situations like an alcoholic hurricane. He was clearly a hippy at heart, and couldn't possibly have been further from anyone Athos may have had firsthand experience with, but Athos loved the challenge of establishing a rapport with him – something best nailed through dark comedy.

Claire was an interesting soul, to be sure. She was rowdy as fuck after a few drinks, and vibrated with a raw sexual magnetism that was almost intimidating in its self-confidence – I say almost: it kept tongue-tying Athos. Just as beguiling was her degree in nuclear physics, and Athos loved the fact that stoned conversations about the meaning of life had to keep at least some scientific basis around her or a withering stare would shut the wafting down. She was the one Athos spoke to least, as he wasn't sure how to get past the attraction thing, but she did keep catching him shoot her not quite subtle enough glances.

Then there was Tank. The name had a double meaning: yes, he was built like a brick shithouse, but as a restless engine of ideas, political philosophies, occult musings, and scientific minutiae, he was also known as "Think Tank" – or Tank for short. He rather enjoyed having his true self hidden behind a meat-head exterior, taking a real delight in upending people's preconceptions of him.

And finally, there was Chris. Chris didn't like people in blazers. Chris didn't like people with posh accents. And most important of all, Chris didn't like Athos. What gave it away remains a mystery, but one school of thought traced it to the sentence "Fuck off, you posh cunt" when Athos tried an ill-advised joke at his expense. He'd overplayed his hand on that one, and while he couldn't for the life of him remember what he'd said, the prickly forcefield coming off Chris certainly kept reminding him of the consequences. It wasn't a deal-breaker on hanging out with the group as a whole, but there was tension, and it wasn't clear that a resolution would even be possible given their respective characters.

Athos was spending more and more time with them at The Temple, almost to the point of rudeness to the three friends he'd come with. Their ambition seemed so limited to him, and he seemed like such a social-climbing twat to them. But as Athos discussed physics with Claire and the Dead Sea Scrolls with Tank, he knew there was no going back. And underpinning it all was the inexorable gravity of "taz." It had stopped actually mattering what it was – whether it was a DJ residency somewhere or a hedge people smoked weed in – it was what it had come to symbolize.

Projection is a powerful trope. It invests people, places, and things with meaning, energy, and a significance they don't always objectively merit. Consciousness finds ways to externalize emotion and manifest feeling in physical entities that turns abstractions into "things." That's what we do – that's what mythology is, what religion is, what archetypes are, what unrequited love is, and what art is: mediums through which to perceive, embrace, or fight our emotions through the allegory of form and function.

"Taz" was a blank canvas to Athos, and yet it was a castle in the clouds, a sword in the stone, a Shangri La of possibility. As the murmuring multiplied in the shadows, he began to project with an almost dangerous intensity onto it. It symbolized his quest to find something beyond the bubble, and he'd started to wonder if fate had ordained him to reach this point ever since that pirate signal. Fate, destiny – these were some pretty dramatic expectations. What if "taz" was shit?

And then one Saturday night in December – the winter solstice, no less – the die was finally cast. The "taz" whispers were at fever pitch, and there was an overwhelming anticipation as The Temple played its final tune. As the sound system faded to black and people began to filter toward the exits, Steve casually asked if Athos was coming with them to "taz." And Athos casually answered yes. He told his college friends he'd call them tomorrow, and they shook their heads at his giddy glee as he sped off. So "taz" it would be. By tomorrow he'd either be a new man, or be needing a new mirage. Onwards.

IN THE ZONE

"Here – put this in your mouth."

Athos didn't have time to question it, and it seemed like the right moment had arrived. He slipped the small square of white blotting paper into his mouth as they vaulted the Tube barriers and went subterranean.

It was a short hop on the Northern Line from Old Street station to their destination: Kings Cross. The last train acted as a sort of art installation that encapsulated the detritus of the urban maelstrom, and just as it had begun to suck some of his passion away, they rattled into their stop.

Clambering out from the musty tunnels, they surfaced into a large, open-air crack den, skipped past the gentlemen of the night, and padded on towards the decaying industrial wasteland that lay behind the station. The smog held a gentle haze and the refracted light draped a veil across them as they trampled over storm drains and skipped round obsidian puddles.

Tank had a well-thumbed copy of the *A–Z* and led the way like a slightly suspect scout. A couple of corners were cut in swashbuckling style, and as they rounded the third, the vista opened into a grand processional avenue. Or a deserted backstreet anyway. The lampposts flickered uncertainly, as if they had lost some sense of self when their light was no longer needed – no longer a link in manufacturing's chain.

It was an open question as to when the last living soul had actually walked up this road – maybe an enterprising junkie looking for an al-fresco fix – maybe a rushed blowjob in a haunted doorway. What was certain is that functionality was long gone; here lay the skeletons of imperial glory – the rusted engines of progress holding their unloved heads high. As they quickened past the nihilistic graffiti scrawls – so aesthetically void that they spoke for the times – more and more people emerged from the shadows. A web of loosely knit humanity converging like grainy fractals on a shadowy strange attractor.

Towering above them was a yellow-brick cathedral that clung to its former glory like a weather-beaten old man wondering where all his dreams had gone. They swept past some randomly placed bollards and, with Athos's pulse clanging, were waved inside by a cheery-looking chap clad head-to-toe in a white jumpsuit. A huge arch loomed, and Athos caught a flash of a post-Enlightenment tabernacle, where human innovation was holy and the divine had shares in the railway. They passed silently under the arch, and just like that, he stepped inside the matrix.

The first thing that hit him was the bass: muffled and menacing. Then the tops: crisp and urgent. And finally the midrange: a warm redemption. He stared around dumbstruck. The cavernous space throbbed with energy – flaming torches lined the walls like a pagan ceremony, and thousands upon thousands of bodies writhed in ecstasy. Lights flashed, nanoseconds froze in the strobes, and as he drank it all in, a drumroll soared to the vaulted roof and burst with Promethean release.

He had totally forgotten he'd taken that trip Havoc had given him – there had after all been a cornucopia of distractions – but as he saw geometry swirl, he realized he was through the looking glass. There were no hallucinations, no theatric visitors from another dimension – just a stunningly detailed retina on the fabric of reality. It was like the world seen through a microscope – where cell structure sharpens into vivid focus, lucidity gleams, and interconnectedness crystallizes. Reality distilled rather than reality warped.

He lost the others but was way past caring – this was no time for such workaday concerns. He made his way towards the center of the throng, and with every step he took, arms shot out to pat him on the back, eyes smiled in solidarity, and teeth flashed their bountiful welcome.

He danced. Oh by fuck, he danced, weightless in the moment as his limbs dissolved into the music. Like a group of discordant metronomes on a springboard surface, all his constituent parts coasted into perfect time until they were beyond control and into instinct's flow. He had never felt such a union of self with surrounding, and as he stopped to draw breath, one overriding epiphany rushed in. This singularity had spontaneously formed in a sea of chaos.

There was no identifiable structure to the event. No one wore the symbols of authority; there was no clear guiding hand. People were stuffed to the rafters, and intrepid climbers hoisted banners from the column tops; there was no stage, no podiums, no performers, no self-satisfied grins, and no glory. The music must be being played by someone, but try as he might to identify a fulcrum, Athos could see no star but thousands.

Break-dancers spun one way while fire jugglers fanned out the other, and every time, the crowd would part as if directed by a holographic conductor. This was chaos theory in action: random elements forming patterns whose feedback loops oscillated into something mirroring order, but with none of its labored mechanics. The best description he could muster was universal rhythm – an intuitively self-organizing system composing reality in its own image.

He resolved to find the others and cantered off purposefully. Tucked away in the industrial apses, sculptures loomed and canvases splashed color, while rippling laughter chorused through the cracks. The main arena must have once been a huge factory floor or a vast storage depot, but on the fringes, the supporting cast of spaces shimmered with life. Poems were read, debates raged, and voices peaked – Athos didn't have a clue what they might be saying, but he almost didn't need to at this stage. They had "trying to build a better world" written all over them. Of course, they could have been discussing the football and he could have taken some really good acid – but that's the funny thing about good acid: it amplifies the essence of reality rather than obscuring it with its own agenda, which is what shit acid unfortunately does.

He was still trying to wrap his head round how this could be such a friendly, peaceful environment without any kind of protective force when he came across the others. It was hearty backslaps all round.

"Fucking amazing," gushed Athos.

Knowing winks and bear hugs ensued.

"Ha ha ha ha," laughed Claire. "Welcome aboard."

"But… but… What the fuck? Who the fuck? What is this place?"

"Taz, innit."

"Yeah, but does all this get tagged as 'taz'? How does a word get chosen to represent all this? And how does anyone think, 'You know what – let's go with taz'?"

"You're standing in a Temporary Autonomous Zone," chuckled Steve.

"A what?"

"A Temporary Autonomous Zone. Does pretty much what it says on the tin. It's temporary – in that we aren't all going to stay here forever. It's a zone, cos, well, it is. But the key word is autonomous – there is no external state control. This is our domain – all of ours. Every single beat, every single piece of sound equipment, every single light, every flash of feeling is generated by the community right here, right now. It's as much yours as mine – you're as in charge as I am – and the beauty is its Heisenberg nature. We're all in charge and none of us is in charge."

Athos didn't have a comeback to that, and after a reflective moment spent spiraling toward the vanishing point, he ventured a question. "So is this a protest?"

Tank laughed. "I'll take this one. No, it's not a protest. And no, we aren't fighting for anything. This transcends all that bollocks. This is an ephemeral micro-society that harnesses ideas around primal ritual to create a portal of magic."

"Beer's cheap too," interjected Chris soulfully. "And you can take drugs as blatantly as you like."

"And that," agreed Havoc.

"But who makes the rules?" stammered Athos.

"Let's take this from the top," said Claire with the air of a governess giving her charge a final chance. "No rules. No authority. No structure. No committee. Just anarchy in its purest form."

"So this is what anarchy looks like?"

"Yep. Real anarchy. Not all that shit you see on the news. This is proper anarchy: self-governance through an absence of government; order through an absence of formalized order; security through the absence of a security force; just human beings trusting one another and working for a whole greater than the sum of its parts."

"It's inherently unstable because it's a vortex opened up within a dominant social framework and our conditioned responses to it," said Tank.

"You what, mate?"

"So it's necessarily temporary," continued Tank. "We aren't sat on some commune milking goats here – we live in fucking London. It's not about permanence – it's about the moment. It's not about virtuously building a new utopia – it's about the present, the now, the surrender of ego, and the momentary access to what lies beyond. Make it permanent and ego will start to reassert itself. This pours so much energy into a single vector that it channels a collective consciousness. Cosmic as fuck."

Night teased into day and the narrow windows that sat

under the roof began to angle in rays of sunshine. On the dancefloor, the intensity of the midnight hour settled into a steady flow, and the pockmarked bricks of the old factory smiled down as if happy to be in service once more. The lights looked a tad lost as they clung to their nighttime liturgy – so spellbinding in the darkness, so anodyne in day's denuding gaze. As the beats slowed imperceptibly toward midday, the crowd began to thin, but Athos, Claire, Tank, Steve, and Havoc sparkled the afternoon away in furious conversation, setting the world to rights, then tearing up the template and writing it anew. Chris, meanwhile, was asleep in a bass speaker, and no one could resist a smile when a passing rudeboy upbraided him for "lowering the tone."

As the sun began to set, Athos reluctantly remembered that he was sixteen, lived with his parents, hadn't called them since he left the day before, and was staring down the barrel at some heavyweight drama. But he couldn't leave this enchanted place. Not yet anyway. By midnight, there was a smattering of hundreds left and bonfires sprang up around the back of the building. Warming himself as his appetite for solid food gnawed back, he gazed into the embers.

Patterns wove in and out of shape, well-known faces metamorphosed into ancient archetypes, and a sacred mathematics reinforced the lesson: order through chaos, progress through entropy, and a universal algorithm that kept time through the symphony. Every answer provoked a flurry of new questions: Could reality really have a code? Could God be a mathematician? Was metaphysics an untapped branch of science? Before he knew it, Monday morning had dawned, the music had gone off somewhere along the line, and all that was left was the pack-down.

It seemed that whoever was left standing was part of the team. Athos, Steve, Tank, Claire, Havoc, and a rather stained Chris grunted speakers off stacks and hoisted amplifiers into trucks. The once-flaming torches were plucked off the buttresses by people more adventurous than they, and with all remaining hands on deck, the equipment was packed away neatly in under an hour. There was just one thing left to do. Black rubbish bags suddenly surfaced and every single person grabbed one to set about litter picking.

There is no accounting for the moments that mark us, and the litter picking was the crowning light on an illuminating weekend. If you were to think of the least-glamorous activity a group of pirate renegades could possibly be involved in, picking up crumpled beer cans, cigarette butts, and the occasional condom would have to top the bill.

No one was organized enough for gloves, and the matter was so seriously viewed that getting right on your knees and scrubbing ash stains out of the concrete was par for the course. As Athos started to hit a physical wall of exhaustion, he drew on every reserve of energy and spurred his arms onward. This from someone who two short years before had casually chatted up his school maid. It was an ascetic ritual to end a weekend of remixed rituals, and the pride with which they all beamed when they'd finally buffed the space spotless broke new spiritual ground for Athos.

They had taken a space without consent to celebrate the human spirit. The space belonged to them by natural law as no one else was using it, but the responsibility that underpinned that right was to leave it as they had found it. It was the first time Athos had ever seen a responsibility as a badge of honor rather than a millstone around his neck. Maybe this was what community felt like.

"Right," chirped up the guy in the white jumpsuit who had ushered them in nearly forty-eight hours ago. "Cup of tea back at the bunker then?"

THE BUNKER

The outside world. Ouch.

The irony was palpable. Here was Athos quietly congratulating himself on having broken out of one bubble just as the trauma of leaving another took hold. Outside the TAZ, life had thoughtlessly continued. He was holding onto the solid weight of an amplifier rack in the back of the truck as it trundled recklessly around corners, and from the small window cut into the box, he could see the world go by. It looked like a Lego megalopolis populated by the broad strokes of a science fiction novel, and while the acid had long since worn off, his perception of the world around him had changed, perhaps forever. He couldn't quite put his finger on it, but the angles had edged a degree or two.

Alongside his altered perspective there crept the arrogance of purpose. All these people: where were they going in such a hurry? It was the rat race writ large: an endless procession of drones rushing through the motions of aspiration. Capitalism's pawns who had fallen for the ultimate confidence trick: investing the machine's contrived cogs with meaning in a futile bid to find self-worth in exploitation. As the world jerked by like a silent film at the wrong speed, Athos couldn't help but contrast his newly found enlightenment with the crystal-meth Monopoly board outside the window. Sorry dupes, the lot of them.

There must be some evolutionary reason for that kind of moral certainty – maybe seeing the world in black and white rather than empathetic shades of gray drives a restless need for change. That's the thing about being young and newly blessed with purpose: it does drive evolution. Smash it all down in your teens, cling onto the past in middle age. If we were all born with the multilateral considerations of a forty-year-old, we may never look beyond the safety of the status quo. Even the forty-year-olds who stood on the precipice of progress were there because youthful single-mindedness hadn't succumbed to the slow erosion of certainty.

Cars honked, buses lumbered, pedestrians squawked, and the soundscape dulled into homogeneity. They approached the river, crawled over Waterloo Bridge, and came to a halt in a tiny slip road behind the giant gyratory that distributed traffic out from the incoming bridge. It seemed a mighty strange place to pull over and park, and for a second he wondered if they had a flat tire. Then the roller on the back of the truck juddered upwards and he saw a smiling face beckon out the fifteen or so of them who had been cocooned in the box.

The guy in the white jumpsuit leapt into something resembling action. Reaching into a cardboard box, he pulled out a fistful of hi-visibility vests and began distributing them. This was getting increasingly random, and for a second Athos wondered if he'd signed up for some weird sexual role play involving a niche builder fetish. He held the faith though, and followed the brisk trail through an underpass and out into the middle of the roundabout, where a huge office building stood, moated by three lanes of remorseless traffic. It seemed an odd choice of destination, both for its resolutely corporate feel and its totally counterintuitive degree of exposure. A small, wiry figure with an aquiline profile and hair by the National Grid pulled out a bunch of keys the size of a football and jiggled one of the offerings into the door.

Some light began to glimmer as they walked into what can only be described as an atrium. The building was deserted, and fragments of its working past littered the sight line. Desks, chairs, and filing cabinets lay sybaritically around the floor as if they'd been on a solid bender, while computers aired their circuitry to catch a tan. The skinny guy led them purposefully across the assault course and towards an area sealed off by red-and-white tape and a large "Danger" sign. Ducking under the tape, he held it up until everyone had passed through. Retaking point, he led them down a set of stairs and then another until they were a good couple of floors below ground. Picking up a candle from the floor, he led them down a long, dark tunnel. This was getting really fucking weird.

Thirty-one steps later, they drew to a halt in front of an imposing steel door. Out came the comically large bunch of keys again, and after some teething problems, the door swung open and striplights came on like dominoes. Athos looked around. He wasn't in Kansas anymore.

If a Bond villain was a bit skint and just starting out on the very early stages of world domination, this was what his lair might look like – albeit with some homely touches. Huge maps lined the walls with pins stuck in them, and desks were piled with papers, bits of broken electronics, soldering irons, books, magazines, industrial catalogues, and unidentified rucksacks. One corner was bristling with hard hats, harnesses, and rigging equipment, while in another a bank of computers whirred softly. The third corner housed a makeshift kitchen, and completing the rectangle, the fourth bulged with sofas, tables, a lava lamp, and a bong collection that would have turned the Freak Brothers green with envy.

Play it cool, Athos reminded himself, still dimly aware he was wearing a hi-vis. He resisted the temptation to blurt out, "Wow, what the fuck is this place?", and determined to go with the flow while piecing together the answers through a Holmesian eye for clues. A few fading acid house flyers were clinging onto dirty bits of Blu-Tack, a Cure poster sat at a jaunty angle, and most random of all, the word SYNDICATE was painted on the back wall in massive letters.

The walk from the truck had been rather taut and the mood suddenly lifted as everyone around him decompressed into the room. Steve, Havoc, and Chris flopped onto one of the sofas and began press-ganging one of the bongs into service, the white jumpsuited guy put the kettle on, Tank started making a sandwich, Claire looked thoughtfully at the esoteric map collection, two unidentified fellow travelers went to sleep, and the skinny dude with the keys strapped himself in behind the wall of computer screens.

Athos milled about, slightly lost, before realizing he had to pick an area and engage or he'd look weird. The bong seemed like a reliable place to start, and after a couple of hits the tea spilled into view. Small talk about emergent skunk strains and whether Tetley's whipped PG Tips settled him in, and before long, Athos was totally at home and taking this unexpected turn of events in his stride.

The white-jumpsuited guy turned out to be called Leary. Blessed with a disarming Irish brogue, he was as close to a formal host as they had. Having made the tea and done a round of the room making sure everyone was happy, he joined the sofa-bong posse and started telling gloriously improbable stories about his lapsed-Catholic Auntie Sheena and her run-ins with Special Branch. Apparently Sheena was quite the Republican firebrand, though she would always fight the good fight in a state of cheery intoxication – something that bamboozled her adversaries far more than the kind of po-faced agitating they had trained for. After one particularly epic story that involved an umbrella, three nuns, a replica AK-47, the Secretary of State for Northern Ireland, and the cast of an amateur light opera, a voice called out from across the room.

"Can anyone give me a hand for a second?"

Athos sprang to his feet. "Yep, no worries."

"Cheers, mate," said the skinny bloke as Athos approached. "I'm Hermes, by the way. Nice one."

"Hello, mate. I'm Athos. Erm, thanks for having me over."

Ironically, both wondered for a split second how the other had ended up with such a pompous name, but the task at hand resumed dominance.

"If you could just help me lift these terminals up onto the table and then wire them all up like this one here, that would be wicked."

It didn't take long, and there was a mildly pregnant silence as they both focused on the physical process. This may not seem like it warrants saying, but they hadn't been to bed since Friday and it was now Monday evening, so the concentration on an apparently simple task was intense, to say the least.

"More acid?" inquired Hermes.

"Twist my arm," smiled Athos and he accepted the proffered square.

With the moving process complete, Hermes edged back behind the pilot side of the desk. Just as Athos was about to politely leave him to it, Hermes kicked a chair towards him and raised an invitational eyebrow. Athos didn't need a second hint, and he gladly decanted himself into the chair and edged over to the screens. Codes rolled across the black background, and suddenly the words "Access Granted" flashed up on the screen. Hermes's fingers darted across the keyboard like a concert pianist on amphetamines, and a series of black-and-white diagrams appeared. Having invited Athos to join him, he didn't offer much in the way of either interaction or explanation, and as the novelty began to wear off, Athos found himself wishing he'd stuck with Bong Corner. Making a last-ditch attempt to rescue the bonding session, Athos played his only card, feeble as it was.

"So, erm. What exactly are you doing?"

"Joyriding," came the response.

This did nothing to lift the fog. At the risk of sounding stupid, Athos felt he had to go all in.

"How do you mean, 'joyriding'? Are you loading up a driving game or something?"

Hermes snorted, half in derision and half in avuncular amusement. "Ha! No, not that kind of joyriding – I mean data. Taking a few unsuspecting systems out for a spin."

Apparently that settled the matter. It really didn't though. "Eh?"

"What does joyriding mean to you?"

"Stealing a car and then ragging it senseless for the buzz."

"So how might that apply to data?"

"I haven't got a fucking clue"

Hermes sighed as if this level of obtuseness was a scandalous inconvenience.

"OK – see this here. This is the London Underground computer network. These diagrams on screen not only show a network of service tunnels and disused sidings, but which areas are manned and when. So say you wanted to break into them to have a look around or set up a TAZ – this gives you everything you need. And anyway, it's a right fucking laugh rummaging through data sets you aren't allowed to see."

"But how – I mean. How can you see that from this computer here?"

Hermes tapped the phone on his desk. "Modem. I can contact their computer system through this telephone line. Any computer system that is itself connected to the outside world can be reverse engineered. Say you want to explore a prison. The phoneline is like a virtual ventilation shaft, and by picking the lock on the grate, you can get inside. Once you're in, the blueprints for the entire building come up and you can navigate wherever you like.

"Anything someone with access to the prison's computer system can do, you can do too. You can look up prisoner information, find out what cell a prisoner is in – hell, you can cross-reference which prisoners share a birthday, if you like. And as more and more stuff gets computerized, you'll soon be able to change release dates, raise alarms, change names, and disappear a set of records, all without setting foot in the actual prison."

"And nobody knows you're doing it?"

"No risk, no buzz. The key is to balance a bit of exploratory mischief with a low enough profile that you don't raise flags. So don't log in as the administrator at 3p.m., when everyone's at work and the alarm triggers. Do it at 3 a.m., when you'll actually get away with it."

"OK, so hang on – how did you get the password in the first place though?"

"Good question," smiled Hermes. Maybe this guy was worth persevering with. "There's a few options. If you can get into the actual building on a blag, you can upload a program into a terminal that opens a back door into the network. Design it right, mask it properly, and you can control that terminal remotely.

"Or you could turn up pretending to be from the software company they use, tell them there's a security issue, and hand over a disk saying it'll close the loophole. Hey presto – same result. Always loved using fear of a break-in to get people to unlock the door – if that isn't art, I don't know what is.

"You can also learn about someone with access to the system. Find out what their pet goldfish is called, and bang – that's their password. And finally, if you're really fucking good, you don't need any of that – you can just clean hack the system. And I'm really fucking good. Modest too. Now open your mouth and let me look inside."

It took a moment for that last line to sink in. Bit of a punch to the solar plexus, to be honest – Athos was lost in a world of schematics, information banks, and fake cleaners, and an enchanting world it was too. How did the opening of orifices enter the equation?

Hermes chuckled mischievously. "Chill out, sunshine – this is neither sexual, dental, nor downright mental. There's method here, trust me."

Not going to lie – Athos was struggling with the trust factor, but it seemed like it might create an even weirder situation if he didn't open his gob. After all, he was locked in a basement under a roundabout with a bunch of complete nutters. He cracked it open gingerly.

Hermes then proceeded to emit a bleeping noise akin to a metal detector. More unsettling still, the bleeping rose and fell in intensity as he inspected different areas of Athos's mouth. As his pupils bore in on the left-upper molars, the beeping crescendoed to a piercing shriek, and just as Athos was starting to panic, Hermes patted him on the cheek, gently closed his jaw, and looked approvingly at his thoroughly discombobulated patient.

"Security clearance granted," he said in a robot voice.

Well, this was all a bit Mad Hatter's Tea Party, wasn't it?

THE SYNDICATE – PART 1

Against all odds, there had indeed been method to Hermes's madness. Turned out that his rather distressing foray into amateur dentistry had actually been a test of whether Athos had swallowed the trip he'd just been given. As an ad-hoc method of verifying someone wasn't a policeman, it was undeniably original, and when Hermes finally explained the rationale, Athos didn't have the heart to suggest that he could have spat it out while Hermes was turned to the screen – why spoil a beautiful moment of trust?

"See this," said Hermes as a click pecked insistently. "This is the Metropolitan Police mainframe. Intelligence Division."

The Intelligence Unit was the frontline for anti-terrorism and anti-subversion. The line often blurred between their mandate and the activities of MI5, who were busy scavenging fresh purpose from the ashes of the Cold War, but, well, MI5 had a better-protected computer network, so the police it was.

"Their security is properly Mickey Mouse, bless 'em. First cracked it about three months ago, and it was a lesson in the flimsiness of intelligence, I can tell you. I honestly thought breaking in here would be like wandering around a lurid multiplex of conspiracy, but it turns out that the whole house of cards is built on conjecture, sketchy informants, and clumsy surveillance. Fair play to the police though – they've done a blinding bit of branding. If people knew how threadbare their grasp on criminality really was, they'd be fucking terrified."

"Is there anything on there about the TAZ?" asked Athos.

"Why do you think we're popping in for a visit? I check it every few days to see what they know, how they know it, what conclusions they've reached, and if they have any kind of operation planned."

Athos leaned in excitedly. "So what does it say? What have you got?"

"Nothing yet about this weekend, but here's a briefing document from a fortnight ago. Fascinating how they see the structure of a TAZ as a greater threat than what actually goes on. What's really doing their heads in is how large groups of people can converge in one place. To the conventional mind, there's only one way to get thousands of people to an event and that's by advertising. Flyers, posters, radio, billboards, magazine listings, and all the rest. None of those apply here – not least because it's not profit driven. If thousands of people come – great. If three lost tourists and a border collie turn up – that's still a TAZ in action. So the standard model is redundant, and they just can't get their heads round it. They're convinced they're missing an answer, when in fact, they've just asked the wrong question."

"Are they missing something?"

"Well, yeah – but don't ruin the mystique. Bottom line, it's mostly word of mouth, but we have a forum tucked away in a corner of cyberspace that acts as a hub for information: dates, locations, people offering to chip in time, equipment – whatever."

"And they don't know about that?"

"Pfffftttttt. Please. As if I'd be that sloppy."

"Interesting though," mused Athos. "So their primary fear is how thousands of people can congregate at one time and place without using established communication mediums?"

"Yep. And what might happen if a radical political group did the same. Must keep 'em awake at night. If there's one thing I've learned about the state though, it's fear of the unknown that drives repression. Why did they go all out against acid house when it was just people dancing? Cos they didn't understand the mindset and worried about the numbers. And all that moving of bodies – it must look like a brainwashed cult to an office in Scotland Yard. I honestly think they believed it was a moral crusade to protect the country's youth before the virus spread."

Athos was entering neural overload territory. There was so much food for thought here that his mind had turned bulimic. He strategically played out a ten-minute extraction process from the lock-in with Hermes and then headed back to Bong Corner. Chris was making steady progress through a bottle of whiskey and had started rapping "Straight Outta Compton" with the kind of authenticity only a drunk white Englishman can manage. Claire was stroking Leary with a cagey flirtatiousness and Havoc was lining up assorted powders to maintain the vibe before tiredness sank them all. Athos went in heavy on the light-blue-colored line and settled in to talk some shit. He was about an hour into a conversation about whether Neanderthal man had taken mushrooms or not when he realized he still needed to fill in a few gaps about where the fuck he was and put the question out there.

"So what's all this about then?"

Leary chuckled. "Fair question. This is the Syndicate HQ. We're a pretty loose-knit collective of people, who help create environments interesting things can happen in. That can be anything from art exhibitions in abandoned Tube stations to the whole idea of the TAZ."

"Where did the TAZ concept actually come from?"

"It's a sort of mix between acid house and anarchism – the phrase Temporary Autonomous Zone comes from a book by this Sufi bloke called Hakim Bey. The idea being that instead of getting trapped in the revolutionary cycle, you create free spaces outside any control structure and use them as a rolling experiment in creativity and community – making damn sure the whole thing isn't defined by what it's against, but by what it's for."

Sounded pukka. This called for another line of the blue stuff.

Athos nodded, "So basically, it's a really intense moment of freedom."

"Exactly. And it can take loads of different forms – but these ones use music, dancing, art, and celebration as a medium. Which is where the acid house influence comes in."

"OK, so if it's defined by what it's for and not against, what is it actually for?"

"You felt the vibe this weekend, didn't you? Not sure it needs to be broken down and analyzed any more than that. It speaks for itself – at least, it bloody well should, or you're doing it wrong."

Athos was quick to agree before anyone thought he didn't get it. And d'you know what? Now that Leary put it that way, he genuinely did get it.

And just as he got it, another penny dropped. He was bang in trouble and needed to get the fuck home before the police were called. He stood up to hug everyone goodbye, realizing he'd be in no condition to work up an excuse on the train home if he left it much longer.

"Come back in the week, if you want," said Leary genially. Keep the hi-vis – that's so you blend in as a workman if anyone sees you walk in. Ironic, eh? Neon yellow as camouflage. But seriously, please don't forget. No one bats an eyelid at people in hi-vises, but if you were seen in the middle of the roundabout in civvies, someone might get suspicious."

Good to know the hi-vis thing had logic behind it. He had wondered.

"When you get to the front door, you'll see a fire hose on the left. Reach behind it and you'll find a bell. Ring it five times and we'll let you in. Be lucky."

Athos struck out into the unforgiving world. Those three lanes of gyratory traffic he had to negotiate were a pretty apt metaphor for his headspace. He crossed the moat and stepped back onto the mainland.

An hour later he was home, and, not unexpectedly, his mother was in floods of tears. As his key turned in the lock, she rushed to the door and enveloped him in an urgent embrace. At which point the four stages of parental post-panic syndrome were initiated. Stage 1 is relief and the quickest to pass, generally lasting about thirty seconds before jackknifing into incandescent anger. Stage 2's duration was contingent on the behavior of the offender and the quality of his excuse, but seasoned professionals would either go with a web of total bullshit or else abject remorse. Stage 3 was disappointment and a lofty appeal to that sense of moral duty parents fondly imagined their teenagers possessed. And finally, Stage 4: acceptance and a reinstatement of all rights predating the incident.

Athos was hoping to nip matters in the bud during the opening salvos of Stage 2. As a general rule, the most effective approach to mendacity was sticking as close to the truth as possible. It adds a certain verisimilitude to the telling, giveaway tics stay dormant, and it's far easier to field an unexpected question either on the spot, or weeks later. Then, just as you reach the compromising bit, you spike off into fiction before returning to the truth as quickly as circumstances allow. Reliable as it was, this method wasn't going to cut it here. Not after two days and nights AWOL.

Going big was the only option: take a shocking central premise, work in some scene-setting detail, and generate a story so improbable that you reverse the psychology. The desired effect is *no one would come up with such a ludicrous tale and expect to be believed, so maybe it's actually true.*

Athos launched into a suitably preposterous yarn involving hospitalization, an arrest based on mistaken identity, a human rights lawyer, and racial profiling at the hands of the state. It was touch and go for a while, but as he piled on the spurious detail and eked out a couple of tears, the cavalry came charging and put any last doubts to the sword. The needle was threaded, the field was his, and sympathy was rescued from ignominy's jaws.

And yet as he closed his self-satisfied eyes that night, he couldn't help feeling that this was getting a bit ridiculous. You couldn't go around instigating a new dawn of anarchy on the weekends and then lie your way past your mum on a Monday. He had to get a grip here. It was one or the other, and pretty soon he'd have to man up.

URBEX

He sleepwalked to college the next day and kept a low profile. Tiredness bred an uncharacteristic silence, but there was a deeper rupture brewing. After a weekend of wild pagan liberation and science fiction-style bunkers, a tutorial college in Gloucester Road seemed agonizingly anemic. There was no doubt that he'd been the youngest person in that bunker, if not the actual TAZ itself. And yet that hadn't even occurred to him until now. Nothing about that weekend had made him feel out of his depth and nothing about the way the others had behaved towards him suggested they either knew or cared about his age. This was a world where the usual identifiers were laughably irrelevant – you know, stuff like surnames, real names, age, occupation, etc. Back at college, Athos found himself wincing at any conversation that fell short of revolutionary, and grew increasingly tortured by the brazen normality on display.

"Yeah, we're going to go clubbing this weekend. It's going to be crazy," said one classmate.

Athos shook his head mournfully. If it didn't involve the subversion of control structures, rollercoaster rides through the recesses of consciousness, and breaking into police mainframes, then it was fucking amateur hour.

Tuesday and Wednesday saw him recharge after the emotional outlay of the previous weekend, but by Thursday, he was restless, truant, and heading toward the bunker.

He had been forced to bin his hi-vis in case it prompted awkward questions from his parents. It would have been a rookie mistake to try selling the arrest story while clad in unexplained neon, so he had chucked it. It wasn't difficult to find a hardware shop and buy another one though, and by one o'clock he was reaching behind the fire hose looking for the bell.

The door was opened by a dusky face he wasn't familiar with. The gatekeeper eyed him doubtfully, but with both hi-vis and secret bell ring in the equation, the interview wasn't overly taxing.

"Sorry – who are you?"

"I'm Athos. Sorry, I was here last weekend after the TAZ? I'm a friend of Tank and Steve. I met Leary and Hermes here the other day?"

"Seen – yeah, safe," came the response in a hybrid London accent."I'm Jayden – nice one geez."

They made their way to the basement and through the steel door. The bunker was a hive of activity – no trace of any bongs, definitely no casualties on sofas, and the focal point was the two wall-mounted maps.

"Hey, Athos," called out Leary."Come join us, brother."

Athos walked over rubbing his hands as if to say, "Bring it."

"We're looking for a venue for the next TAZ. Identifying a few options on the map, and then we can get a couple of reccy teams together. What you saying? Are you in?"

"Roger that," said Athos.

"You public school lot will roger anything," chimed in Chris, who surveyed from a detached distance.

Athos ignored him, and was relieved to see that everyone else did too. That's the funny thing about snobbery: it cuts both ways. So many people think that they are stereotyped by "posh cunts" while applying an equally arbitrary set of stereotypes right back. Write off whole segments of society and all you do is limit your scope for new experience. So fuck Chris, basically.

Athos edged further into the map huddle. There seemed to be three main spheres of operation under consideration: Shoreditch, Hackney, and Silvertown. All three specialized in rundown industrial areas, and all three were depopulated on a weekend. A central tenet of the TAZ concept was that rebellion didn't enter the mindset, and the choice of venues reflected that. Had this been a shouty incarnation of unruly youth, they may have sought more provocative locations, but rather than chase conflict, they concentrated on getting through the weekend unnoticed.

The great thing about history is that it offers the chance to build on it – even if we do have a tendency to look that particular gift horse in the mouth. Subcultural history was no different. Punk's naked anger was certainly of its time, and in many ways a direct repudiation of the fluffy floral utopiansim of the hippy generation. Acid house was arguably the apex of Thatcherism – the "on your bike, get up and go" mantra through a yellow smiley prism. Surely taking empty spaces, bypassing regulatory red tape like licenses, and then charging twenty quid on the door was the very model of an enterprising small business. What Thatcher hadn't bargained for was the overwhelming wave of love that subverted neoliberal doctrine for diametrically opposite ends.

In 1991 and 1992 though, a different set of contextual stimuli were in the mix. Subcultural sensibilities were leaning back towards the idealism of the '60s, and there was a renewed interest in consciousness, eastern spirituality, magic, cutting-edge science, and the strangely reconcilable celebration of communal and individual alike. Unlike the '80s, which fetishized outward individualism, both the '60s and the '90s held inward self-discovery as a sacred mantra. Lessons had been learned though, and there was an edge this time round – punk's legacy lived on through a more streetwise form of cosmic adventuring. The sanctification of materialism during the '80s, and the shameless worship of the shiny sparked a backlash that would go on to shape the next wave.

It's an open question whether the crushing recession that took hold at the turn of the decade forced a reevaluation of the materialist doctrine, or whether the pendulum would have swung back anyway. But even if the recession didn't trigger it, it sure as hell reinforced it. The braying of bankers barking sell orders into absurdly sized mobile phones had lost its luster, and England was simultaneously more skeptical and more spiritual as it sought soul rather than just naked wealth. Sumptuous skyscrapers suddenly seemed like hubristic follies, and the empty phallus astride Canary Wharf was the ultimate symbol of the shift.

The recession had struck closer to home too. Athos's grandparents had seen their relatively comfortable townhouse drastically downsize into a one-bedroom flat. Dr. Assemi had been convinced by a particularly oily financial advisor that property was the way to go. So he bought big in a dramatic entry to the game – right as property prices collapsed. His grandparents found that they could neither rent nor sell their new portfolio. Worse, they had borrowed as much as they had invested, and the payments grew crippling. Then the repossessions started. After an inevitable period of denial, they finally accepted their new circumstances, auctioned off their antiques, and settled into suburban pottering. God knows why they'd done it in the first place. If you're in your 70s and have a healthy bank account, why not just enjoy it? Why tempt fate for profits you'll never get to spend?

On the bright side though, as they pored over the map in the bunker, the economic meltdown made for a squatters' market. So many businesses had gone bust, so many industrial estates forsaken that their biggest challenge was an embarrassment of riches.

It was agreed that they would split into three advance parties and scope out the respective options. Athos found himself signing on for the Shoreditch mission, and minutes later, he, Jayden, and another Syndicate member by the name of Trade leapt into a battered Ford Capri and sped off with an asthmatic screech. Athos had to ask. He just had to. Who the fuck calls themselves Trade in any walk of life, let alone someone immersed in anarchist principles? Jayden hooted with laughter at the bluntness of the question and stepped in to answer on Trade's behalf.

"City boys got nothing on your man here. Buy, sell, borrow, steal, cajole, negotiate, leverage, ransom, upsell, downsell – you name it, T's in there with a handshake before anyone else knows what's going on. I've seen this geezer sell everything from windscreen wipers to a consignment of Russian tanks."

"Those were the days," nodded Trade. "Picked 'em up in a scrapyard for pennies and sold them to the Afghans. Oh to have seen the look on the Russians' faces as the Mujahedeen turned up in a squadron of Soviet tanks.

"Should've retired then and there, but I ended up balls deep in a very costly love affair. Loved everything about her. Her smell, her taste, her snow-white complexion, and how alive she made me feel. If she was gone for more than an hour, I'd plunge into depression, and before long she was my whole world. Call it lust, call it infatuation, call it obsession – but in the end, she cleaned me out."

"What was her name?" asked Athos.

"Cocaine," laughed Trade. "Co-fucking-caine. Still, retiring would have done me no favors anyway. Took a while to get back in the game, but I prefer to duck and dive for the cause these days."

The car pulled up in a quiet street lined with warehouses. Jayden pulled a pair of bolt croppers out of the trunk with as innocent a facial expression as such a guilty act could permit. Their primary target was an old dairy that had fallen victim to the Nietzschean rise of the supermarket. The buying and selling of produce was a relatively civilized affair once upon a time. Every link in the chain respected the importance of the other, and the underlying economics of food production imbued the dinner plate with a certain dignity. Farmers thrived, markets thrived, importers thrived, exporters thrived, and then, almost without anyone realizing it was happening, the supermarket mainlined a massive dose of steroids and bulldozed through this ruddy-cheeked idyll.

It was an extraordinary coup, and as power concentrated, supermarkets called the tune. Fuck farmers, fuck markets, fuck greengrocers, fuck the dignity of your dinner plate – we're in charge now. Margins were squeezed beyond reason, and the entire farming sector became a mechanized supply chain rather than a sustainable ecosystem of independent businesses. This particular dairy couldn't afford to keep sacrificing a living wage for the dialysis of turnover, and so, like a thousand others, it mooed its last pint.

See, that's the thing about taking over buildings with histories like this and creating a nexus of positive energy. If you can get past notions of property law, it starts to look like a public service and a tribute to all those who once infused the dairy with pride, before drowning in the corporate tide. Right now, the place was a broken dream, a symbol of independence lost. Turn it into a TAZ for a weekend and it would resurrect for a final fanfare.

They high-mindedly cut through the padlock, nobly looked around to see if they'd been spotted, and then virtuously crept into the abandoned building. It seemed downright churlish to call it breaking and entering. Set at the back of a crumbling yard was a long, rectangular building that looked like it could take about three thousand people. They checked for power, and having no luck in the sockets, probed onwards in search of a junction box, finally finding it next to a poignantly upended milk float.

Suddenly they heard footsteps. Shit. The police were unlikely to go for a potted history of supermarkets as justification for being there. They edged into an alcove and held their breath. The footsteps grew louder. Then louder again. Then they stopped dead. As Athos took a timid suck of oxygen, a head suddenly shot round the side of the alcove and shouted "Boo!"

All three of them had a cardiac episode. Whoever the fuck this bloke was, he had them dead to rights. He looked bizarrely buoyant though, as if brimming with zest for the good things in life. Here, they thought, was a man who knows how to locate the bright side.

"Don't suppose you're artists are you? Are you trying to squat the place?"

No foreplay then.

"Well …" said Trade.

He left matters there though. It was a tough one to call. This bloke was hitting almost unseemly levels of joviality, considering he'd just caught them mid-crime. Was it all a sadistic trap, or should they take the smile at face value, go with the artist thing, and see where it went?

"Because if you are, I think we can come to a very amicable arrangement," continued the cheery bloke.

This wasn't getting any less weird. The implication was

that he owned the building, but considering he looked about twelve, they needed further evidence of this. And what exactly might an "amicable arrangement" look like?

Trade reckoned he'd heard enough to gamble. "We've been known to paint the occasional canvas. We weren't trying to squat though – we thought it might make the perfect exhibition space for our conceptual stuff. We just wanted to have a proper look before contacting the landlord about rental."

Athos could only admire such skillful footwork. A delicately judged balance of semi-honesty, whoppers, and some light fluffing.

"I bought the place at auction last week actually. Sorry, terribly rude of me – my name's Wilkinson, Nick Wilkinson. I love the exhibition idea – site-specific works and all. But are you sure you don't want to look after it for a year or two? No rent necessary – just a couple of small stipulations."

Here we go, thought Athos. "What kind of small stipulations?"

"You take care of utility bills and guarantee to have at least two public exhibitions a year here. Also, I'm closing on a couple of similar buildings two streets down, so if you have any friends who might be interested in a similar arrangement, send them my way."

Jayden peered at the bloke skeptically. "I don't get it though – what's in it for you?"

"I like to think of myself as a patron of the arts." He smiled. "I won't be developing any of these buildings for a few years yet, so if they're just going to sit here, they may as well be put to good use."

They agreed to think about it and took their benefactor's card with a promise of a follow-up call. Back in the Capri though, they reviewed what the fuck just happened. It was a puzzler, but with all things considered, they opted to avoid the dairy and Mr. Wilkinson altogether. The TAZ concept relied on secrecy, and landlords knowing anything whatsoever about what they did was a risk – however affable they might be.

Still in a slight daze of surreality, they drove back to the bunker empty-handed. All was not lost though. Tank and Leary had a place in Hackney Wick ready to go.

LIBERTY

Taking stock, it had all been a bit of a whirlwind. Ten days previously, Athos had never set foot in a TAZ and was still guessing what the word might mean. Here he was now, having informally joined something called The Syndicate, stayed up for days, taken any chemical he could lay hands on, hung out in a basement under a roundabout on the South Bank, broken into empty buildings, met some lunatic who sold tanks to Afghans, broken into police computers, and grown increasingly convinced that a new age of enlightenment might be at hand. Pretty solid work, to be honest. There really was no turning back now. This shat all over a few spliffs and a couple of tentative sorties to The Temple. There was a new temple in play – and it was on the move.

Momentum grew. The weeks blossomed into months and Temporary Autonomous Zones sprang up in all four corners of London. It was like looking at a thermal map of the city, where fiery nuclei burst into being, held for a moment, and then disappeared into the speckled abyss.

Athos had finally made a clean break with formal education, and after a half-hearted attempt to see his 16+ exams through, he departed both his college and his parental home to dedicate himself to the cause. Having straddled both worlds in halting fashion, the decision to cut the cord and trust his instincts proved cathartic. His parents didn't take it well, not because they were still fixated on education as the sole guarantor of a future, but because they couldn't understand what the hurry was. In their minds, holding on until eighteen and covering all bases with a qualification seemed like common sense. But Athos couldn't wait.

When a random series of elements converge into a current of energy, there's no slowing the juggernaut until it's convenient to climb aboard. It was the very essence of present, where past and future lose their grasp and self-questioning is swallowed by the swell. The brain's relentless rationalization of variables had proved humanity's most powerful evolutionary tool, but even as extraordinary results manifested through tools, farming, civilization, law, politics, and the ascent of complex economics, the soul was being imprisoned in the underworld. The rise of monotheism was but one example, codifying spirituality, stamping out mysticism, denying sexuality, and sacrificing experience on the altar of doctrine.

Somewhere along the line, ideas around desire, dance, sensuality, trance, natural energy, and altered states of consciousness came to be seen as profane – human weaknesses that needed constant vigilance. The subconscious became the ultimate threat to order, while the strictures of the rational mind were invested with righteousness. There's an argument to be made that the recasting of reality into a set of self-denying precepts precipitated our divorce from the natural world. As "civilization" expanded, we began encoding the world around us into structures that facilitated the establishment of order – the alphabet being a prime example. When our very medium of communication is an abstract set of twenty-six symbols that bear no relationship to the world they map, it builds a barrier between ourselves and nature, locking our existential interface into an artificial construct. Perhaps these processes have fueled progress, but we lost magic along the way.

So it was now or never. You can't bridle chaos once it's on a roll – jump aboard, or forever hold your peace. Athos evacuated the parental embrace, moved into a squat off Portobello Road, and threw himself into the now. He'd come a long way since he'd profiled Rastas for weed, and Portobello was nothing short of the promised land for who he was becoming. Heavily influenced by West Indian culture and the pressure cooker of race relations, the Ladbroke Grove area had an irrepressible energy to it. Elderly rudeboys smoking dog ends zigzagged from pub to bookie, while flamboyant bohemians, gaunt poets, penniless artists, louche hippies, clued-up wideboys, swaggering ragamuffins, and two-tone soul dealers cruised its wandering spine.

Above all, Portobello Road was a market – not just for battered antiques but fruit and veg, cheap household gear, and the latest rags, so every ingredient of a proper melting pot was on display. Costermongers rhymed Cockney to reggae beats, pork pie hats flew at rakish angles, graffiti writers rode rampage, and B-boys bounced in Trellick's brutalist shadow. The icing on the cake was Carnival: that crucible of cultural connection, concrete calypso, and volatile sunshine. Raves, festivals, concerts – they all have their own special energy, but Carnival pushed so many envelopes, pulled at so many threads, and wove so many new fabrics that as a forerunner of the Temporary Autonomous Zone, it had actively helped redefine what it meant to be a Londoner.

It was a halcyon period, and the TAZ concept spread like wildfire. Before long, average weekend numbers were in the upper thousands and venue finding became more of a challenge, not least because architecture itself was so critical. Every incarnation of the TAZ felt different because it was shaped by its environment: long, linear spaces with huge production lines still resident, circular fortresses, catacombs, train yards, old breweries, abandoned printing presses – the ghosts of a faded past.

There was only ever one arena, one sound system, one dancefloor, and in order to prevent any kind of ownership, the constituent parts came from a broad spectrum of participants. Some would bring lights, others would haul in sound equipment, artists would breathe visual life, poets would write all week, musicians would offer to play, and the underlying principle of a self-organizing organism held fast. Every individual was a contributor, a stakeholder, and a vital part of the experience, whether they brought a set of Technics or an infectious smile. Neither lived without the other.

Unlike the traditional concert dynamic – stars on an elevated stage and an audience looking up beholden – the TAZ drew its power from inverting that relationship. The DJ would always be hidden behind a wall of speakers to prevent them becoming a visual focus, and rather than everyone facing the same direction at all times, crowd-flows undulated and orientations morphed through the night. The physics reinforced the conceptual, pockets would appear and disappear, there was no front, there was no back, there was no side – just a fluid whole that used perpetual motion as a bulwark against formal structure.

Athos had settled right in. He'd always thought he'd been unaffected by his parents' dash from impending revolution, but he'd been conning himself. The whole blazer and chinos thing after Eton, the frustrated sense of unfulfilled promise while he'd been there – it was simple really: he'd been looking for somewhere to belong, and finally he was home. Yes, the Syndicate had a tendency toward self-righteousness, but then so did he, and despite the agonizing they put themselves through over the tiniest details, that rather turgid worthiness was offset by heroic bouts of hedonism.

Banter and irreverent comedy were the lifeblood that fed the moral machine, while breaking into buildings, hacking computer networks, and plowing through indecent piles of drugs kept the adrenaline pumping. He'd woken up in the most random places, had the most unlikely affairs, made the most improbable getaways, and met people he'd never have dreamt of in his former life. Everything had been building towards this point, and he let rip, surfing every curl that came his way with an increasingly confident hand. There was no pretending, there was no belonging, there was no ardent existentialism – there was just day rolling into night, and a big fat mischievous grin laced with promise.

The bunker at Waterloo Bridge continued to avoid any unwelcome police attention. Hermes's window into official thinking certainly played a part, but if ever there was a golden example of hiding in plain sight, this was it. Everyone involved self-policed to a certain extent, aware as they were that by planning the context in which a TAZ could manifest, they had a greater degree of influence than those who came on the weekend. That was a threat that needed managing, but they relied on one another to stay honest. More and more people stayed on to the end of the TAZ so were welcomed into the Syndicate, and as the diversity of backgrounds and skill sets expanded, the possibilities multiplied.

The absence of a symbolic language helped insulate the TAZ from the outside world. The press were dimly aware that something resembling acid house was active, but with no flyers, no posters, no logos, and no words, it remained something of a chimera. And yet even as this principle kept prying eyes out, internal debates kept flaring up over the rights and wrongs. The issue was fundamental because every instinct of a human collective is to project identity through symbols. Corporate logos are just the most recent embodiment of this need for communal expression, and ever since the first cave paintings, man has created emblems through which identity can be proclaimed.

It was seriously tempting to come up with a symbol for the TAZ, but there was a dogged resistance from those who saw it as the first step toward branding. It was a strange situation, suppressing a primal need in order to protect a primal experience, and the realization that both sides of the debate had a point didn't make its resolution any easier.

Almost a year to the day since Athos had first entered the zone, a new figure began to emerge at the heart of the movement. Michael Templemann was a well-known name to most, having written a series of books about everything from shamanism to Marxist theory, and his appearance at a TAZ one day created a stir akin to celebrity. If Madonna had walked in, no one would have batted an eyelid, but Templemann's books had inspired a whole generation. His combination of comparative spirituality and radical social philosophy felt particularly relevant to the emergence of the TAZ, and having a forerunner of the movement give his seal was a special moment.

Michael loved what he had seen and began to return regularly, often joining the Syndicate during the week for impromptu symposiums on everything from Jungian theory to structuralism. Clad in "foreign correspondent" khakis, he had a soft, welcoming manner and a mesmerizing way of speaking – blowing your mind with penetrating insight while giving you a cuddly verbal hug. He was a bit older too and so rapidly acquired a kind of "tribal elder" status where people used him as a sounding board and sought his advice.

Alongside these philosophical gatherings, another school of thought was emerging. Best described as the "Illuminati Model," it posited that a small cabal of disproportionately powerful individuals controlled the tectonics of global events. In this worldview, governments were smokescreens for a corporate oligarchy and political figures were either dupes or accomplices. These shadowy power brokers started wars, deposed governments, enslaved populations, and controlled the media. Events bent to their will, central banks were a front, and no establishment figure was credible, lest they be yet another head on the Hydra. Some called this group the Illuminati, others the Bilderberg, while others still claimed the Rothschilds had run the world since the eighteenth century.

This proved a deeply seductive vision, partly because it reinforced a masochistic sense of powerlessness, and partly because it simplified the financial, political, and social complexities into a clear narrative. It was also anchored in a recognizable form of dualism, with clear baddies to blame.

The leading proponent of this worldview was a brooding ex-punk called Tony. Covered head to toe in tattoos, he held court on the fringes of the TAZ and warned darkly of Illuminati plots. Having thought at length about Tony's theory, Athos found himself in something of a quandary. He did agree that governments were beholden to corporate interests and the military-industrial complex. He also agreed that the democratic process seemed to offer the same wolf in two sheep costumes rather than any serious choice of models.

But having been at Eton with one of the Rothschilds, he was pretty sure they were just rich rather than the architects of a dark conspiracy, and that firsthand knowledge set him thinking. From what he knew of tomorrow's elite, nothing could convince him that any of them could pull off this kind of empire building. If he'd learned anything, it was that most individuals in power are pretty unremarkable, and it was systems that drove the macro behavior of societies. Yes, there are the occasional great men of history, but even they ride a systemic wave – whether climaxing or collapsing. In Athos's experience, most people were, well, normal, but it was easy to see how others might project an almost superhuman level of omniscience onto those in power.

He was in a minority though, and the Illuminati worldview gained real currency in the TAZ as time went on. Tony became something of a guru and held court to ever greater numbers. He even started a free magazine that was handed out at the TAZ detailing how the latest world events had been guided by the puppeteer's hand. Tales of false-flag operations, actors posing as bomb victims, media lies, and political manipulation proliferated, and he coined the catchphrase "Look Beyond," which urged people to disbelieve whatever they saw in the mainstream media and focus on "truth." Which Tony apparently had a monopoly on.

The intellectual difference between the two camps was defined by method as much as conclusion. One felt restlessly self-questioning to the point of inertia. The other had far more certainty and far more self-belief, despite having remarkably little evidence to support any of its positions. A true visionary might have seen a struggle for the TAZ's soul beginning to ferment, but Athos was no visionary, and anyway, he was focusing all his energies on the pirate radio station they'd set their minds to starting.

POLICE AND THIEVES

"A bit to the left."

Hermes jiggled the antenna and stood back to admire his handiwork. "Right – let's try it now."

They were stood atop a Hackney tower block with commanding views of several other tower blocks. Leary raised an arm in acknowledgment and fished in his pocket for his prized new possession: a Motorola phone. He flipped it open, wondering if that frisson of excitement would ever get old, and phoned Havoc in the next building. "You got a signal?"

"Ninety-four point one is a GO," came the reply. "Congratulations, Apollo twenty-three – we are live on air."

Back in the makeshift studio two buildings away on the same estate, "Energy Flash" was spinning on the turntable, all driving bass and odes to a darker ecstasy. They were transmitting live and direct to the world – or if not the world, then at least a fair chunk of East London. The thrill of the signal was heady indeed and the knowledge that they had a direct link to any radio in a three-mile radius was spine-tingling. For Athos, it was a moment to savor after all those long nights at school staring at his radio, wondering if dreams came true.

It hadn't been difficult to recruit DJs for the station – anyone who'd brought a bag of records to a TAZ in recent weeks had been encouraged into service, and they had managed to pull together a suitably eclectic set of genres, from reggae to soul to techno to the first rumble of jungle. There had been an extensive debate over whether they should also have some spoken-word segments – a sort of countercultural Radio 4. Alas, and with a heavy heart, most people finally agreed it probably wouldn't go down all that well. Not yet anyway. Let the tunes do the talking on this one – it would have been the equivalent of turning the music off in the middle of a TAZ and having a debate on stage. You always have to be careful not to neuter the visceral side of an experience by over-talking it.

There was another area of disagreement. Should they overtly align the radio station with the TAZ? One camp was all for it – think of the possibilities, they urged. As a medium to expand the message, bring in new people, and act as a rolling manifesto for the TAZ, it was undeniably potent, but there was a strong counterargument.

For starters, this was classic McLuhan territory: the medium WAS the message. And that was powerful enough. Second, it could only inflame tensions with the police, who had grown testier over recent weeks. At pretty much every TAZ since the summer, the police had turned up at some point, but due to the critical-mass theory of spatial hijack, they had never been able to prevent one.

Every week, a new telephone number would appear in the hidden corner of cyberspace where Hermes cultivated his forum. What with this being the early '90s, not everyone was aboard the personal computer revolution quite yet, but enough people had access to a terminal to seed a surrounding cluster. With the telephone number circulating, at 11 p.m. Saturday night, a greeting message with an address would be recorded and the phone switched off. Crucially, this was not the actual location of the TAZ – had that been put online it would have led to disaster. People would have come in dribs and drabs, and by the time unusual activity had been reported to the police, the TAZ wouldn't have fully formed. If numbers inside were small enough, the whole thing could be shut down with relative ease.

So the address given out would be a public space close enough to be convenient but far enough away to not flag the venue itself. By midnight, a few hundred people would have descended on the meeting point and a hidden spotter would judge when there were enough bodies. Radioing back to base, he would call in tactical support, and the battered Ford Capri would drive to the meeting point, flash its lights, honk its horn, do a U-turn, and start driving back to the site. The assembled throng would jump in the nearest car, whether they knew the occupants or not, and a convoy would snake its way to the Zone.

The result of this rather circuitous subterfuge was that somewhere between eight hundred and a thousand people would all enter the space at exactly the same time. This created critical mass – a volume of people so large that the crowd could not then be evicted by conventional means. The police could, and often did, cotton on to what was happening both at the meeting point and during the convoy, but what could they realistically do? The kind of backup they would need didn't arrive in minutes. No wonder the state was growing increasingly nervous about the TAZ. Rendering its security apparatus powerless on a biweekly basis was such a direct threat to the rule of law that something had to be done. It just wasn't clear what yet.

So the conclusion was that the radio station should steer clear of all things TAZ. But what with the universe's impish sense of humor, the very next weekend saw the theory spectacularly unravel.

It was Saturday night in Lewisham and the clock had just struck ten. The Syndicate had taken the space at around seven, and trucks stuffed with equipment began to arrive shortly thereafter. There must have been about fifty people working at breakneck pace to get everything ready for midnight, and the building hummed with energy. Trusses were hoisted, lights were rigged, speakers were connected, paintings were mounted, switches were flicked, cables were flown, and everything started to take shape. Then, without warning or fanfare, three of the Met's finest came strolling into the middle of it all. For a moment, neither the short arm of the law nor the miscreants themselves had any idea how to react. There was a silent stand-off while options were frantically calculated. But three helmeted plods do not a raid make, so what gave?

Well, some sloppy fucker had left a door open, and they had just randomly wandered in on patrol. They left just as quickly, but everyone knew this wasn't over and the clock was ticking to a flashpoint. They were off to assist their careers in a northerly direction and the population of the warehouse into the back of a riot van.

Ten-thirty passed. Then eleven o'clock passed and the meeting point location went out on the phonelines. This would be down to the wire. If they could just make it to around 12:15, they'd be home and dry – critical mass would've been reached and they'd live to fight another day.

Enter the police commander of Lewisham, who had obviously been rousted reluctantly out of his bed. It was 12:05. And he had a rather large entourage with him.

As soon as a senior officer puts his credibility on the line by making a personal appearance, they can't be seen to back down, so this was going to be a fraught negotiation process. Tank was about to open the bidding with the commander, but Leary held him back.

"Let me have a crack," he said. "You're such a big fella that it might put the shits up them."

Police negotiation is all about being the reasonable face of something that instinctively frightens them. If you can be sober, smiley, helpful, responsible, respectful, but quietly insistent that everything is under control, you're halfway there. And always skillfully turn them so they can't see the inevitable "hardcore" shouting "Fuck off, you pigs" and discussing the merits of bacon. Fear is the driving force of almost all overreactions, so diffusing it is key to a mutually beneficial resolution.

And by fuck was Leary reasonable. He wrung out every last drop of Irish charm and dropped the timbre of his voice to an almost Wogan-like sooth. But the commander seemed remarkably impervious to his charms and even more to his logic. He was, however, prepared to have a bit of a pavement debate about it all. The gathering was clearly illegal, unlicensed, and all the rest of it, but with the convoy having arrived during the melee, a tense situation was developing. A couple of hundred of the new arrivals circled round the back of the building and managed to penetrate the sanctum, but just as others began to follow, a phalanx of police vans steamed in and began blocking off roads.

At this point, there was only one real card to play, and it had the merit of being the only logical choice. Surely the commander could be persuaded that it was in his interest to let the event go ahead – contained, safe, and without thousands of people who'd now missed the last train pouring out onto the streets. I mean, honestly: you've got thousands of people laden with alcohol and drugs, and with their spirits up. Where would you rather have them: in one place all night before going their separate ways tired and happy in the morning, or rioting in the streets?

"Who's in charge?" he asked. Shit. This was going to be one of those tricky ones.

"Erm. No one's in charge," said Leary. This wound the commander right up. "We don't actually have a leader or a boss as such," smiled Leary." But I can pretty much speak for what's going on here."

The commander peered at him suspiciously. This was either a feeble lie or a hippie shambles. Everything has a leader. Just ask Mr. Franklin.

"Who is your security firm?" he asked.

"You're looking at them," replied Leary with a comforting" You can count on us officer; we're actually very similar;

some of our best friends are policeman; if only we'd met in different circumstances" kind of grin.

The commander did the math. Thousands of people. Drugs. Booze. Music. No security.

It was almost as if that in itself decided it for him rather than any legal, licensing, or noise questions. Athos couldn't help feeling that if they'd had a gang of skinheads in black bomber jackets, he might have taken a different line. To a policeman's logic, if there was no "official" controlling force, the inevitable result would be carnage. Athos could see him having visions of murders, rapes, stabbings, muggings, and a swift defrocking of himself as senior officer after being crucified in the tabloids.

It goes to so many questions in philosophy and psychology. Is the human instinctively "good" or "bad" if left to his own devices? What came first: crime or law? In the months he'd spent at the heart of the Syndicate, Athos had learned the kind of lesson that made the TAZ so much more than a hedonistic revel. Amongst those thousands, you'll have bad boys, drug dealers, gangsters, the whole roll call of darkness whipped into a heaving mass of loved-up humanity. And almost never, ever any trouble. And yet you go to a three-hundred-person capacity club with a moody security firm on the door and you'll have a stabbing, three bottlings, a load of shit drugs sold, dealers ripped off, and so on. A mini crime wave, regular as clockwork in towns up and down the country.

Accepted wisdom has us believe that official security acts both as a deterrent to crime and a solution. The same conventions insist that the absence of security can only result in a criminal orgy of Hogarthian caricature, and that an authority vacuum releases the ugliest inevitabilities of the human condition. The evidence Athos had seen proved precisely the contrary – going way back to the trust dynamic at his tutorial college versus the reams of rules instituted at Eton, and his own reaction to each. Attitude begets attitude.

But strip it all down to bare humanity, make everyone responsible for themselves and whoever happens to be next to them, and the results are extraordinary. Any incidents that did crop up were quietly handled by a family of strangers united by their environment. A community. The abrogation of responsibility to an external structure or "force" seemed a counterintuitive social dynamic – and certainly not one that encouraged autonomous communities. Now, the E's definitely helped foster this spirit, and the mindset of the kind of people who were at the TAZ in the first place was certainly a factor, but watching people look after the stranger stood next to them was one of the most inspiring sights any of the TAZ family had ever witnessed.

All lost on the commander, of course.

Well. They lost that argument, despite Leary singing "Danny Boy" in a last-ditch effort to save the day. There were eighty arrests where there would have been none. Vehicles were vandalized, windows were smashed in frustration. Everybody lost.

WHITE HOLES AND BABY UNIVERSES

The police station was bursting at the seams. In their Pavlovian rush to slap the cuffs on, the police hadn't fully weighed the logistical flaws in arresting dozens of people on questionable charges. Where would they put everyone? How would they interview everyone? What crime had actually been committed?

The short answer was none. While the building was undoubtedly private property, a Section 6 notice had been nailed to the door claiming squatters' rights and, without clear proof of breaking and entering, there was very little to go on. No noise issues were in play as they hadn't had the chance to make any, and the commander began to realize that the law didn't explicitly cater for what he considered subversive behavior. Short of rushing "Conspiracy To Have a Good Time" onto the statute books, what were they going to do with all these people?

The cargo had been spread across three police stations, and still they were swamped. Athos found himself processed by the desk sergeant's cynical glance and marched off to a cell, where Hermes was already settling himself in. This alone was unconventional: it was unheard of to put two people in a cell together, not least because it would permit them to get their stories straight. Perhaps this was a tacit admission that there was no story to get straight as there had been no actual crime.

Hermes was displaying an unhealthy excitement at being banged up. His eyes darted around the clinically white cell, and you could see the cogs whirring. He was trying to see if an escape was possible, not because he actually intended to break out, but as an intellectual exercise. He grew visibly less hopeful as the cell's barren austerity took hold, sighed, and turned to acknowledge Athos's entry.

"Cunts," he opined gracefully. "One day this will all be virtual," he added.

Athos wasn't really in the mood for cryptic flights of fancy, focused as he was on his incarceration. He gave a noncommittal grunt, and wondered how they were going to get any kip with only a single bed on offer.

"You wait," continued Hermes, unfazed by the lack of enthusiasm. "Before long, the physical world will just be another interface. These people have no idea what's coming."

It was all sounding a bit ranty, to be honest, and Athos had a nasty feeling Hermes was planning to talk through their entire sentence. He sighed again, more heavily this time, but still the hint was sidestepped.

"The World Wide Web will liberate us from this jackbooted paradigm. The ultimate TAZ is taking shape. No physical manifestation and no tangible existence – just a quantum leap into hyperspace. Let's see how you arrest that, you wankers," he shouted at the locked door.

Athos was rather unsettled by Hermes's growing volatility.

Surely if they just kept quiet, they'd be out before long. No need to start upping the stakes.

"Even as we're sat here, cyberspace is growing. It'll be another Big Bang, atomizing into forms so complex that no one will be able to control them. From that primeval cluster of data, galaxies will form, stars will rise and fall, meteors will populate new worlds, and a cybernetic wave will revolutionize our definition of reality."

"Eh?" said Athos, warming to Hermes's theme, but still very uncertain what the fuck he was on about.

"Picture this. An alternate dimension of connected computers forming an infinitely complex web of interdependence. Time and distance melt away as the planet shrinks to the head of a pin. Someone sat at a computer in a remote Indian village with the same opportunities and the same access as someone sat at a terminal in New York. That state of consciousness you can attain through psychedelics – we can fucking build that now through computers, not so they can automate our thinking, but so they can channel our potential."

From what Athos had seen of the internet so far, this was a bit of a stretch. It was a useful tool, to be sure, but all this "William Gibson after a few spliffs" stuff was taking it way too far.

"Come off it, you mad cunt," he laughed. "You sound like you've necked the whole jug of Kool Aid."

"I'm not fucking joking. One day people are going to look back at this point in history and realize just how monumental it was. It's the biggest evolutionary shift since we became self-aware on the savannahs. That wasn't just us becoming conscious, it was the universe creating a means to perceive itself."

"Yeah, not arguing there. The observer effect on a massive scale."

"But now we can construct a new universe that's just as real but exists on an abstract plane of data. Because there's no God, it'll evolve according to the algorithms of a truly self-organizing system. As humans and machines generate data, they won't be able to control what happens to it. We're creating a digital sea of nucleotides from which a new DNA will form. Fuck looking at equations for parallel dimensions – we're in the process of building one. The universe is reproducing."

Athos looked at him doubtfully. This was some high-end cosmic bollocks, to be sure, but maybe Hermes should lay off the chemicals and address the stark realities of his Atari ST. It could barely load up a football game, let alone birth a baby universe. Some sort of intervention might be needed, but seeing as they were locked in a cell, he reckoned enabling him a bit further to avoid an argument was probably the soundest move.

"How can you be so sure it can't be controlled though?" he asked indulgently.

"Scale and multi-polarity. The blueprint was designed by scientists rather than politicians and corporations, and, god bless 'em, they've created an incubator for a self-organizing system. So much data will be generated by so many people that trying to track it all will be like drawing a precision diagram of a universe billions of light years across. They may be able to pick out the galaxies, but the stars, planets, and moons will be far too many to map."

"But surely if computational power keeps increasing, that will narrow. Who's to say there won't be a machine that can't process all the data the world produces?"

"Because it's exponential. A million breeds a billion breeds a trillion. By the time processing power has caught up with the amount of data, it will have multiplied another million times. And anyway, the new architecture of connection will make ideas of hierarchy and control seem like the Stone Age."

"So we really are talking about the ultimate Temporary Autonomous Zone?"

"Exactly. Except this one will be temporary, permanent, and infinite all at the same time. Mark my words. It's coming."

Suddenly, with a disapproving rattle, the cell door swung open. Was it a sign?

Maybe, but it was a bloody well-disguised sign if it was. It came in the shape of a moustachioed constable, who mumbled something about dances in his village when he was a kid and drinking Pernod behind the church hall. Athos and Hermes were mystified until it dawned on them that he was trying to be friendly. It seemed he felt his Pernod-soaked village dances gave him a sympathetic insight into what they'd been trying to do in Lewisham. And to be honest, on one level, it did.

With the awkward bonding at an end, he ushered them out, gave them a quick debrief, advised them to stay clear of buildings that didn't belong to them, and sent them on their way. Deposited back in the world at large, Hermes and Athos took stock, purchased a bottle of Pernod in the constable's honor, and drank it on the way back to Athos's place. Their short stint inside had done very little to put them off breaking the law, but it had definitely inspired them to get as shitfaced as they possibly could.

The squat Athos lived in was on Westbourne Park Road, just a few houses up the hill from the notorious Warwick Castle pub and a hundred meters or so away from the even more notorious Elgin. It was a sturdy enough property, with a certain bleak flair, and despite having been part of Peter Rachman's empire, it had undergone a half-hearted revamp before the housing association gave up on it. Rachman had been London's most powerful slumlord, and despite his flagrantly exploitative practices, his willingness to be an equal-opportunity bastard made the Grove a magnet for the Irish and then the immigrant West Indians – people who were refused tenancy by so many other landlords in postwar Britain.

That had in turn shaped the multiracial character of the area, and despite the unloved Rachman popping his clogs in the early '60s, putting the residential pieces back together had been a slow process. Consequently there were an awful lot of empty houses as the decay entrenched, and even the council was saddled with vacant properties they couldn't afford to make legally habitable. There was an irony for you: laws passed to stop rapacious landlords were actively preventing councils from housing people.

Athos had become quite matey with the hookers who shook their ravaged booty by the phone boxes on All Saints Road. The bulletproof glass in the off-license there summed up the area rather succinctly, and the All Saints Road had been a frontline since the late '60s, when civil rights campaigner Frank Crichlow had opened the Mangrove Restaurant. The Mangrove was a hub of community activism, and its folkloric status was cemented not only by the burgeoning sense of black London self, but by international visitors like Jimi Hendrix and Nina Simone.

The police saw the Mangrove as a hotbed of subversive mayhem from the start. Not only had it dared to organize in support of the black community, it stood up against apartheid, and persecution wasn't far behind. The infamous case of the Mangrove Nine saw the intimidation ratchet up into a set of spurious "incitement to riot" charges. In one of those rare cinematic moments when justice did actually win out, all nine defendants were acquitted, but the frictions remained. Crichlow was arrested again in 1988 on drug charges, despite being a well-known anti-drugs campaigner, acquitted again due to the abject lack of any case, and had just received a compensatory payout. Desperate to have the last word, the authorities finally closed the Mangroveas the check was written, and now that crack had arrived in West London, community activism was jostling for oxygen with the upswell of bad boys.

Athos and Hermes swigged the last of their Pernod and settled onto the curb outside the Mangrove's recently boarded frontage for a valedictory sit-in. Just as they had started to wonder what they were going to do about more alcohol, an aging yet dapper-looking chap sat down next to them and whipped out a bottle of rum. He didn't seem in the mood to chat, and yet the silence felt warm and comfortable. They passed the bottle back and forth, and every so often their companion would break into the soft falsetto of "Police and Thieves" – a mournful swansong for a Windrushed past. And then, with the bottle terminated, he stood up, dusted himself off, tipped his hat, and walked off into the fog. They never saw him again, but they never forgot. *Irie.*

KARMIC CASHFLOW

As another summer approached, another series of meetings was taking place in the bunker. There were two vital issues that needed addressing: one geographic and the other economic. Ever since the Lewisham debacle, there had been an increasingly intense police operation dedicated to the suffocation of the movement. It was as if actual contact between the two sides had given the police new confidence and a fresh spring in their step. The Home Office had upped the prioritization of the TAZ, finally realizing that, without concerted action, it would continue to spread unchecked. Even though the Syndicate had managed a longer run in the shadows than one might expect, the lack of advertising had been superseded by the echo chamber of the zeitgeist, and references to the TAZ were surfacing in unexpected places.

Three had been stopped in their tracks before they had even started, something that suggested a successful intelligence operation, and there had been fleeting moments where those at the heart of the TAZ had almost turned accusatorily on one another. Such destructive instincts had mercifully been reined back in before they could do lasting damage to the trust dynamic, but one thing was clear: they needed to reduce their own predictability.

The season offered another option though: the great outdoors. They had never even thought beyond the Greater

London area before now, but as Claire proposed an inaugural TAZ in the countryside, everyone seized on the idea with renewed hope. It would be a return to nature, a connection with the land – pastoral beauty rather than industrial ghosts. And as if that wasn't enough, a different police force would be starting their counteroffensive from scratch. Police forces didn't talk to each other much and there was no national crime organization of any note – no British equivalent of the FBI.

Plans were hatched and teams dispatched. They wanted to stick to a fifty-mile radius of the capital, if only because there were no guarantees of anyone turning up if it was much further. The community was at present very London-centric, and with it being far from clear that an avalanche of attendees awaited them in the Home Counties, they wanted to make the trip from London feasible. Funny – they had never thought about guaranteeing minimum numbers before. It had always been about concept rather than attendance, but once you've gotten used to a heaving mass of thousands, you become strangely allergic to going back to hundreds.

The other problem was economic – a more pervasive quandary with a greater potential to derail if it wasn't handled right. One of the underlying principles of the TAZ was that money should never, ever be an issue. As far as everyone involved was concerned, money was the root of all evil, and any idealistic society worth its salt would either discount it entirely, or at the very least have a plan to prevent it sowing division.

Many of the bunker family were unequivocally on the dole. They viewed social financial support as somewhere between an Arts Council grant and a Robin Hood-like use of the state's resources, so they were at peace with the apparent dissonance of building a money-free existence on state cash. Tax, national insurance contributions, and all the rest were viewed as the tentacles of bloated power, where forced collections were used to buy arms and invade foreign countries. When viewed in those terms, avoiding tax and redistributing state resources to positive ends seemed like public-spiritedness. Other questions around schools, hospitals, infrastructure, and, yes, welfare support were conveniently omitted from this worldview. Most people didn't think about it at all – not through some conscious hypocrisy, but because in their particular bubble, everything already made sense. No need to actively source a contrary viewpoint, eh?

So barring the likes of Trade, who was still keeping his hand in the mercantile game, most of them saw being on the dole as a badge of honor. It meant they weren't materialistic, as they had just what they needed to survive. It meant they weren't chained to a job they didn't want to do, and it meant they were plundering the treasury of a corrupt state before its lucre could be invested in blood and oil. The irony of forging a principled community based on giving while only ever taking from the bigger community we call society was lost somewhere along the line, but then maybe this was exactly the kind of social and creative experiment governments should be funding. Everything added up.

Except the overall accounts. Individual livings aside, Syndicate funding had so far managed on organic contributions or the "whip-round" model. Different people contributed different things – so the lights were usually supplied by Fat Ron, who had an event-lighting company. He was almost never in the bunker as he had a business to run, but that business allowed him to throw whatever lights weren't already on a job into the TAZ on any given weekend. Sound equipment was usually pooled from a few different sources, which didn't do wonders for audio quality, but that hadn't really mattered because the spirit was so strong. Music equipment was supplied by the DJs themselves, artists were self-reliant for materials, poets worked on inspiration alone, and ancillary costs were low – nothing that couldn't be solved by passing an internal hat. The one thing everyone was clear on was that charging an entrance fee was an unbreakable taboo. The slightest sniff of commerce and the spell would be broken.

The only problem was that the TAZ was in fact a hotbed of commerce, mostly in the form of a mood market. Which is another way of saying a drug market, but the phrase "drug dealer" is so painfully pejorative. The reality of drug dealers in the TAZ was that most of them were community-spirited people who prided themselves on accessing top-quality supply lines, selling excellent substances at reasonable prices, and having the satisfaction of knowing the vibe would be right because everyone was on pure, unadulterated highs. The added benefit was that the sales they made also paid for their weekend out, but there were no kingpins here, just people who believed in the experiences they were offering. And yet the fundamental laws of economics did operate. Drugs were bought and sold like any other commodity in any other context. The only thing that was actually free was the TAZ itself.

But as the AGMs played out, many of the crew came to the conclusion that they needed an investment tranche. That way, they could buy a sound system, some lights, some musical equipment, some new computers, and some new mobile phones. It made sense to centralize the community assets and not have to rely on the goodwill of individuals every time. Steve was a lone voice arguing that the decentralized model they currently had was critical to the anarchic nature of the TAZ, but with Fat Ron having been stuck on a job recently and a whole weekend plunged into darkness, most felt that having a communal equipment store was a great idea. As long as it was everyone's and no one's, they'd be fine. That way, anyone could operate it, and no one person was essential – and that surely was more egalitarian than relying on specific people for specific equipment. No one could ever use equipment as leverage either – not that anybody had tried, but in a hypothetical case of someone using the materials they provided as a means to a different end, the TAZ would be vulnerable to the power play. Not if they had a central hardware bank though.

The theory was ironed out pretty swiftly. All that was left was the small matter of acquiring about fifty grand in a morally upstanding fashion without doing any work. It was a head-scratcher, for sure. And then Havoc had a brainwave.

The hottest new psychedelic on the scene was something called ketamine. It had come onto the radar when someone brought in a book by Dr. John Lilly. Lilly was a physician, psychoanalyst, and expert on dolphin communication with "reputable" written all over him. His roving brief was to investigate the nature of consciousness, and part of that involved experimenting with the sensory deprivation of flotation tanks and injections of ketamine, something he saw as having extraordinary properties. Combining ketamine with the flotation tanks, he noted a series of out-of-body experiences and became fascinated with what the state it induced could tell us about consciousness.

Several of the TAZ community had managed to get hold of ketamine, which was used as a gentle anesthetic for children, the elderly, and animals, but it was extremely difficult to source. Currently, the only available form was in five-gram bottles smuggled out of laboratories, and that made access to its wisdom rather hit-and-miss. But Havoc had been reliably informed that over in India, you could get ketamine in most pharmacies. Over the counter too. What if they were to nip to Goa and bring back a bulk shipment? They would be doing a whole generation a massive cosmic favor.

Might this be another LSD moment, where a chemical locked away in research facilities suddenly became widely available? There were endless cautionary tales about the spread of LSD in the '60s from both sides of the divide. Timothy Leary's well-meaning evangelism turned LSD into a political football while stripping caution from the tangerine sky. Everyone needs LSD in their lives, he thought. Except psychedelics didn't work like that – they were an access code to your own consciousness, not a guaranteed spiritual breakthrough. They might shower some with insight and connectedness, but for others, LSD was a nightmare, unlocking buried memories or hidden insecurities, and the damage wrought by people tuning in unprepared was grave.

More reckless still was the behavior of government agencies who lurched between seeing it as a weaponized truth serum and an elixir of social unrest. The clandestine research that followed saw unsuspecting test subjects dosed and water supplies contaminated, and the subsequent spate of suicides informed LSD's mythology for a generation. I might jump out of a window too if I didn't know I'd taken it. How fucking irresponsible can a government be?

Ketamine, however, couldn't really be administered without the subject noticing, denaturalizing as it did in the stomach. You couldn't turn it into an odorless gas, so the options left were injection or snorting – the accepted method of ingestion within the TAZ. Injections were taking things a bit far and had a gravity to them that the playful roll of a ten-pound note managed to swerve. So they were pretty confident the state wouldn't be able spike thousands of unwitting people with the stuff, and as long as they didn't put on a toga and implore the masses to get involved, it was probably a pretty safe bet.

Ketamine was changing hands for about fifty or sixty pounds a gram at the time – and that was when it was available. Restrictions on how much each person could buy were often applied, and so having a quarter gram to go on a deep-space voyage was something of a holy grail. Apparently, it was about a pound a gram in India, so if they brought back a couple of kilos, they could sell it for twenty, democratize its availability, not be greedy, and still make all the money they needed for new equipment.

The motion passed with loud acclaim, and volunteers were needed to take one for the team. The ketamine came in liquid form before a cooking process turned it to powder, and it wasn't even illegal, as governments had barely heard of it, so there was no risk, no crime, and no apparent downside. Havoc and Chris stood up to be counted, and as the TAZ set its sights on the countryside, it also made a bid for an Indian outpost, the astral plane that ketamine opened doors to, and perhaps a new psychedelic dawn. The future was so bright, it was fucking dazzling.

EXPANSION

The first couple of countryside festivals proved a touch underwhelming in terms of numbers. Six months ago, everyone would have been more than happy with the events themselves, but the creeping notion that attendance was a reflection of the movement's validity had taken hold. Meanwhile, reports of TAZs springing up in Bristol and Manchester had filtered back to the Syndicate, throwing them into a dilemma. On the one hand, the replication and dissemination of the concept was testament to its organic growth. They hadn't got into this to have a monopoly on liberated zones, and yet there were concerns. What if they weren't being done right in all these other places? What if they were a front for some enterprising promoter? What if they didn't clean up properly after themselves?

They were in danger of being given a bad name by others who perhaps didn't adhere to the same kind of ideological purity, and as a sprawling meeting took place to discuss the matter, there were two very clear points of view. One maintained that they should stick to their guns. Who cares what anyone else did? The movement was spreading, you can't franchise chaos, and to worry about any regional blowback from other TAZs was to imply ownership of the idea. What were they going to do: draw up the Marquess of Queensbury rules for an anarchic vortex?

The other camp wanted to find some way to differentiate between TAZ collectives, if they couldn't actually influence the others. Much navel-gazing and urgent debate ensued, and everyone agreed that an attempt to establish what did and didn't qualify as "the right kind of TAZ" would be a step down a very slippery slope. Still though – what if they were the wrong kind of TAZ?

It was Michael Templemann who proposed the most tempting solution.

"Look, I know we've wanted to keep any kind of iconography out of the equation, partly because of the attention it might attract and partly because of concerns about branding, but shouldn't we maybe have another think? After all, the police are onto us anyway, and as a way of clarifying what our Temporary Autonomous Zones are about, maybe a symbol – not a logo, a symbol – would be a good idea at this point."

"Isn't that just semantics though?" argued Jayden. "What actually is the difference between a symbol and a logo?"

"The power and meaning you ascribe to it," replied Michael convincingly.

He had a point. After all, what was wrong with identity anyway? They all trusted one another to ensure it would be generated from the most authentic possible place, and maybe it was time their TAZ had a visual touchstone. With all these new organizations in the mix, surely they needed to protect the sanctity of their mission, just in case the other TAZs did turn out to be rogue outliers.

Steve had been sketching as they spoke and, with mild

apprehension, he held up the piece of paper for all to see. On it was something that looked like a cross between a hieroglyph and a Chinese character. It had the pictorial sense of a rising sun behind two intertwined forms – be they DNA helixes or dancing dervishes – and yet it harnessed calligraphy's abstract elegance. It was, in short, fucking perfect. He blushed with a tentative pride.

Who knows what might have happened if Steve hadn't nailed it then and there. There would have been weeks of indecision, both over the whole idea and its graphic execution, but the synchronicity settled it. It was meant to be.

So now that they had a symbol – not a logo, mind – what the fuck were they actually going to do with it? Jayden suggested that a couple of graffiti artists might be deployed to cryptically paint it throughout London and the surrounding counties. No words, just the symbol, and that way it would penetrate without actually advertising or pushing anything. It would be a sort of shibboleth for those that knew, and a magnetic source of intrigue for those that didn't. It was heralded as a blinding plan, and he sped off to set it in motion.

But hang on, thought Michael. Here they were struggling to get the countryside TAZs off the ground at the very same moment that a new rune was being born. Perhaps the universe was dropping a subtle hint. Maybe some sort of flyer might be in order? Things were on a roll by this stage, and the idea that some cosmic nudgery was afoot seemed plausible. Why not give it a try? Nothing corporate, obviously – just the symbol, white on black. Or maybe the phoneline number too? Yes, that seemed sensible: they'd go with just symbol and phone number. These countryside types may not be quite as sophisticated as the London crowd when it came to digging up hidden forums in cyberspace, and the word-of-mouth thing relied on urban-style clusters. There was nothing wrong with switching up a tactical approach, just as long as all their core principles were still intact. And the unanimous verdict was that they should go for it. Flyers it would be, from Southampton to Oxford. A bolt of excitement shot through the bunker. It was game on.

Havoc and Chris meanwhile had returned from India laden with lashings of ketamine. The customs officer at Heathrow had pulled them immediately, and, finding three T-shirts, three pairs of pants, a pair of flip-flops, and sixty liters of "Ganges Holy Water," decided their admirable attachment to Indian spiritual traditions required further scrutiny. The two voyagers were escorted into a strip-lit white room and the peculiarly British interrogation technique of heavy sarcasm was applied for the next few hours.

They stuck resolutely to their story, and Chris had been sensible enough to memorize the Hindu pantheon for just such an occasion, so after some fairly borderline babbling about Vishnu, they stood at an impasse. Customs knew they were dodgy. Chris and Havoc knew they were on solid legal ground, and neither side was prepared to blink.

Finally, the customs officer played his last card. Six bottles were taken out of the bag and subjected to a series of reactive color tests. The thing about drug testing in the field is that without a gas chromatograph, all anyone can do is test for a specific substance with a specific liquid that will turn a specific color if it comes into contact with a specific chemical. Out came the tests for cocaine, heroin, MDMA, amphetamines – the whole illicit spectrum, but, of course, none of them triggered the alarm. The customs officer just knew this wasn't the full story, and the smug grins that wreathed both Chris and Havoc's faces didn't do much for his sense of humor. Powerless, he took a parting shot.

"OK, gentlemen, you're free to go." He turned to Havoc. "And remember to get yourself a new passport, Cuthbert – this one is about to expire."

"Cuthbert!" howled Chris. "Cuthbert."

"Fuck off," said Havoc. "And if you tell anyone, I'll kill you."

"Oh, mate – your reputation is so fucked. Cuthbert. Ha ha ha ha."

The customs officer allowed himself a wry smile. As apples of discord went, it wasn't much, but it was something.

THE ROLLING STONES

Stonehenge. They couldn't. Could they?

Michael reckoned they could, and he ought to know. He had been at the last solstice gathering there before celebrations were banned, and he thought they could make it work. There were a few red flags to the whole project though. One was the huge military base right next door on Salisbury Plain, another was the proximity and sightline from the main road, and the third was the tabloid explosion it would undoubtedly provoke.

In any other situation, this would be considered an aberration of a venue, a siren call to suicide. Some of the more cautious heads counseled against it from the outset, seeing the whole project as self-aggrandizing folly. But this was Stonehenge, for fuck's sake – the ultimate incarnation of tribal ritual and the ultimate statement of spiritual unity in a cutthroat material world.

There didn't even seem to have been a point at which everyone agreed to the idea; it just sort of became the primary mission. Flyers were printed and distributed, Claire advised on the effect of bass on the ancient stones, military-style plans were drawn up for the taking of the henge, and everything was in full swing.

Tony in particular was wildly enthusiastic about the idea and focused his attentions on the nearby military compound.

He purported to have seen evidence that Stonehenge was a UFO landing site and insisted that the adjacent base was a top-secret alien research facility passing itself off as a firing range. Others had their doubts about any of this, not least the notion that Neolithic civilization was entirely geared to worshipping visitors from another planet, but interests had aligned. Motivation was secondary to the action itself, and whether people wanted to occupy an alien monument or connect with Albion's primal rites, they were agreed on holding the TAZ there. Dissenting voices were drowned out in all the excitement, and as the summer solstice drew near, the Stonehenge TAZ entered the final planning stages.

There was no way they'd be able to take the site in advance of everyone arriving – the lights and vehicles would attract far too much attention. Everyone would have to assemble at the meeting point, a Tesco's carpark just outside Salisbury, and take the site together. People would just have to be patient while the sound and light teams snapped into action and set up. But anyway – a bit of silent reflection would do no one any harm, and as long as the TAZ was fully formed and pulsating with energy by the time the sun rose, it would be a triumph.

There was a rarified buzz in the final few days before the big push. The grapevine crackled with excitement and as June 21 finally landed, the anticipation was almost too much to bear. Friends and relatives as far afield as Glasgow had heard about the impending move, and the sensation that this might actually be a national phenomenon was palpable.

With Havoc and Chris having orchestrated the sale of the ketamine and the new equipment now delivered, this would also be the debut of the centralized asset model. They had managed to avoid getting too high on their own supply, despite Chris's best efforts to play hoover, and gleaming new speaker boxes and shiny new amplifiers now sat stacked in the back of Leary's truck. At 6 p.m. a rather bedraggled convoy struck west from Waterloo and headed down the A303 towards the mythic stones. Or the Tesco's carpark, to be precise.

The first inkling of sunset began to seep across the tarmac. Packed sixteen ways to sideways, the place looked like a cross between a car boot sale, a CND protest, and the first brawls of an untidy revolution. Stereos were locked in mortal combat, hordes of people had spilled out of cars, and someone had even started to build what looked like a shelter despite it not raining and this being a temporary pit stop. Commerce of one sort or another seemed brisk, as the entrepreneurs amongst them ticked up and down the tangled web of cars flogging god knows what. It was as if a lively village had sprung up in less than an hour, and every ingredient of civic life bar authority was evolving at a similarly rapid pace. Shouts and whistles bounced in every direction and the orderly white lines of the parking bays seemed a fitting metaphor for the failed imposition of control.

Critical mass was reached in record time and began doubling. If they held out here any longer, there would be trouble, so signals were shouted and the convoy lumbered off toward the stones. Excitement mounted as the cars in the convoy guessed the destination, and as the henge hove into view, it was engulfed from every side.

Emptying the back of the truck, Leary, Havoc, Jayden, and Athos humped the first few speakers to the center of the stones and legged it back for the next installment. As they returned with the next batch though, they suddenly noticed that their small pile of speakers had grown. And not only had it grown, but some of the speakers were now green instead of black. Hang on.

As they stared at one another in puzzlement, four silhouettes carved an unsteady path through the outer stones and began approaching them. They were carrying speakers.

"Hi, guys," said one of the four newcomers cheerfully and let the speaker he was carrying drop to the ground.

"Hello," said Leary doubtfully. Who on earth were these people?

"Alright, mate," came the response. There was an unmistakable West Country lilt to the greeting. "Do you want to set up together, or shall we do a separate arena?"

Athos felt a sense of outrage swelling at this bloke's casual insouciance. This was *their* thing. Swanning in with his green speakers and regional accent – who the fuck did he think he was? He was just about to say something he'd regret when the angel on his shoulder put the devil in a headlock.

"Shall we keep it separate? That way everyone gets to play and there's no arguments between our two crews."

"Gert lush," smiled the bloke and started sketching out a space for the Bristol sound system. "Brilliant to finally meet the London family."

Eh? London family? The implication was that they were merely a regional branch of the TAZ. They were the fucking originators, for fuck's sake. The devil was back in the game.

Steve came charging in and gave the guy a massive hug. "Great to meet you guys. I'm Steve, and this is Leary and Athos. Great to be possed up together."

Athos calmed down and saw reason. He smiled and went in for the hug too, slightly ashamed of his internal reaction.

"We're the Freedom Collective from Bristol. I'm Jimmy, and these legends are Tom, Lisa, and Shakedown. Let's do it."

A whirlwind of technological construction swept across the circle as fires were lit, stories were swapped, old friends caught up, and new bonds were forged. As the sound system stacks stood mirroring the stones, they burst into life and a rousing cheer went up. The first beats rang out across the countryside and pulled the gathered thousands onto the same twin grooves. The Bristol guys were playing some pretty tidy tunes and there was a real symbiosis between the two semi-circles of sound, each facing away from the other so as not to clash. The atmosphere began to escalate, and as wavelengths converged onto a single frequency, a huge spike of energy resonated through the throng. Dancers spun through the megaliths, leylines were tapped, and time stood still.

The sky turned midnight blue as the first hint of the earth's curve glided over the horizon. The crescendo continued to accelerate. The first rays of sunshine diffused through the morning mists and still the crescendo grew. And then, as peak rhythm took hold, a ray of radiation shot over the heelstone and cast the circle in light. The portal was open. Across the hillside, a rainbow tapestry poured out in every direction, held by the rhythm and surrendered to a tribal unity. It's a curious paradox, finding one's self by relinquishing individualism to communal experience. It's fucking powerful, and everyone should have the opportunity to give it a go.

With dawn bathing the verdant hills, the only discordant note was the relentless chugging of the police helicopter that had materialized overhead. That, and the furious druid who was shouting at the DJ and pointing to a scroll he was thrusting toward the decks. Athos noticed this chap's clear objection to something or other, and hurried over to try to make peace. He pulled the druid away from the music and, in the respite, flashed him his most understanding grin.

Despite today's druids not having a direct line of descent from Stonehenge's original tenants, they had devoted their lives to spirituality, and while their outfits might look a bit Morris dancer, there was no reason not to respect them. The druid made his feelings known in no uncertain terms, and, for a moment, there was a certain comedy in seeing an advocate of natural harmony fulminating in quite such a rage. As far as he was concerned, a bunch of marauding urbanites had descended on the stones with no respect for tradition. And would they turn that fucking racket off.

Athos tried explaining that they had every respect, and that the music was simply a contemporary interpretation of folk, but the gulf was too wide. The druid stormed off, complaining bitterly that the cause of having the stones open every solstice had been set back a generation. You could see his point; they'd been patiently lobbying for years and promising that this sort of thing would never happen.

And now that whole rationale had been bulldozed by one night of urban colonialism. To him, there was a right way and a wrong way to celebrate the solstice – and his way of reconstructing the past was more valid than their new attempt to harness the future.

Athos finally accepted there would be no reconciliation and went for a meandering walk. Weaving in and out of the concentric circles, he ducked under the weathered lintels and strolled past the bluestones' craggy faces. He heard snatches of conversation, tributes to the civilization that left such a legacy, breathless testaments to the magic people were feeling, flourishing meditations on astronomy, and a heartwarming innocence wherever he roamed. And then, just as his optimism was at its peak and he felt he could tell any druid that their gathering was just as valid, he came across a hushed semi-circle of hundreds listening to what can only be described as a haranguing lecture.

"Look Beyond," implored Tony, like a televangelist raising money for miracles. He was actually giving a tour of the henge and explaining where the aliens had landed, how they had refueled, and the exact meaning of the configuration in alien culture. His audience was rapt, though they unleashed their loudest roars against the army for keeping secrets from the public and using alien technology as mind control.

Athos left them to it with a vague sense of foreboding. No one involved in the TAZ ever told anyone else what to do, but Tony was starting to behave more and more like a cult leader. If they weren't careful, he would divert the whole movement into an aggressive jumble of paranoid conspiracy. This wasn't about the Masons or the Templars or the mainstream media, and the moment it was, the TAZ would lose its power and its broad appeal.

Over on the other side of the stones, in a small dip, Michael Templemann too was baptizing neophytes, but in an altogether softer and more educational way. This was much more of an interactive forum, with Michael fielding questions and encouraging debate. If there was a concern to be had, it was that he'd built up a bit of a following himself, something that didn't entirely gel with the multi-polarity of the TAZ, but at least he was using his influence positively.

As mid-afternoon approached, a second police helicopter appeared overhead, and the two choppers had something of a waltz. A few of the crew got together and discussed an exit strategy – how would they get the equipment out without being nabbed? They decided to wait for the cover of darkness and turned the music off at midnight, packed down by halogen, litter-picked furiously until all signs of their presence had been eradicated, and sent the trucks off as part of a wider convoy, hoping for safety in numbers.

Roadblocks had been set up on every possible route, and as Leary slowed the truck to receive a face at the window, he braced himself for arrest. To his surprise, he was merely asked for ID and the truck papers, and while the officer noted down the details assiduously, he waved him through as soon as he had finished. Well, that was easy. Too easy, perhaps?

The drive back to London was excruciating, as tiredness started to bite. The road seemed to go on forever and the service stations that punctuated the journey offered neon gloom rather than abundant caravanserais. Finally breaking the back of it, they entered a very different circle, the M25, and ploughed on through West London until they reached home in Westbourne Park Road. Spent, happy, and covered in glory, they collapsed into a long, dreamless sleep.

LABELS

It was a shitstorm of epic proportions. Maybe it was a slow news day, maybe there hadn't been a good moral panic for a while, but whatever the reasons, the press had gone fucking mental. The first sign of trouble was the Home Secretary promising new legislation on the *Today* program, and if that was happening, then god only knew what the tabloids were saying. Athos legged it down the shop and grabbed a selection of the morning papers. It was a bloodbath.

Drugged up Satanists Storm Stonehenge, screeched the *Sun.*

Reports of Human Sacrifice at Stonehenge, flailed the *Mirror.*

Out of Control Youths Destroy National Monument, barked the *Telegraph.*

Government Considers Curfew, tutted The Times.

Christianity Under Attack, shrieked the *Daily Mail.*

New Mass Movement Sets Sights on Tories, proclaimed the Guardian.

I Shagged a Druid and He Turned Me Into a Squirrel, letched the Sport.

Jesus. This wasn't good at all. So much for "under the radar." This had always been a risk, but no one had expected front-page news on all outlets. The TV was rammed full of unsubstantiated accusations and pundits without a clue; the story was being written entirely by others, and there wasn't a single voice who understood or even cared what had really gone on. Most bizarre of all, live reports from the scene seemed to be set in a sea of rubbish, which made no sense as they had left the area spotless. The rubbish was the clearest visual indicator of the tawdry lack of respect shown by the marauding "Satanists," and because of this one image, the moral high ground was lost. But how had it happened? OK, they'd done the litter-pick in the dark with halogens, but still. They may have missed a scrap or two, but nothing like the landfill being dumped in the nation's front rooms.

There was no time to weigh the implications because over on ITV, some guy they'd never seen before was informing an open-mouthed reporter that this was the first action in the coming revolution. Materialists would be smashed, the capitalist order decapitated, and a new political system instituted. What????? It had never, ever been about smashing the system – it had been about leaving the system to it and cracking on with something new. There was a major fucking difference.

It got worse. The BBC had a wild-eyed "ufologist" calling on the military to release the aliens they were imprisoning and "be honest with the British people." He went on to demarcate the landing site at Stonehenge as established by Tony and the reporter just let him keep talking, knowing he had gold on his hands.

Panic began to set in, and Athos woke Leary and Hermes. Disconcertingly, Hermes seemed to be coding in his sleep, but the polymorphic paradise dissolved as he grasped the matter in hand.

Before long, they realized that they had remarkably few options beyond hoping the caravans moved onto the next salacious story. All three of them were nervous about going anywhere near the bunker in case it was under surveillance, so they whiled away a couple of days in hiding until they could bear it no longer. On the third day, they resurrected themselves and headed off toward the South Bank. The crisis was in session.

Michael Templemann was chairing the meeting. Which was unusual because no one had ever chaired one before. Still, he was speaking sense and encouraging calm. There was no such thing as bad publicity, he insisted, and despite the abject hijack of their message, the best response was through their actions. At this stage of press groupthink, words would be twisted, interviews edited and fuel piled onto the fire, so microphones were best avoided. There was only one thing for it: keep going as if nothing had happened, but with extreme vigilance bolted on.

So they did. A TAZ went off near Brighton and came through unscathed despite the paroxysms of the inexplicably named local newspaper, The Argus. Then two more in Hampshire passed without undue incident. There were now so many people loosely affiliated with the Syndicate that fresh energy was never far away. Who all these people actually were and whether any of them might be a police informant did occasionally generate paranoid moments, but the trust held, and as a result, the movement did too.

Athos had grown increasingly close to Hermes, despite the latter's rather limited set of social skills. They had spent more and more time of late at the radio station, and Hermes was determined to start actually making music rather than just playing it. Punk had democratized attitudes to musicianship by making a virtue of playing three chords badly as long as you had enough balls to play them loudly. Punk was an attitude where permission was seized, and the electronic revolution incorporated that ethos into its emerging identity.

Dance music was in many ways the bastard child of the guitar industry. The Roland drum machines that created all those signature sounds were originally designed to give practicing guitarists a beat to work with so they didn't have to find a drummer. Then Roland decided a practicing guitarist might also want a bassline to work with so they came up with the 303, which as a bass guitar imitation was frankly abysmal. But as the crucible of an unearthly new sound, it was as close to a prophet as musical hardware had ever had. Its squelch, roll, pierce, and resonant frequency was like nothing the world had heard before, managing to be both hauntingly dark and upliftingly euphoric in the same sonic flow.

So you could make cutting-edge techno from rejected guitar toys – and there was something about that which summed up the essence of dance music. It was about metamorphosis: taking one thing and turning it into another. It was about creative recycling, and the use of technology in ways that were never intended – and the advent of the sampler reinforced these core principles. Suddenly you could take a musical phrase from anywhere and transform it into something totally different. A Gregorian chant could become a bassline and some bin lids clanging could be a hi-hat if pitched up far enough. It was a magpie world that allowed musicians to borrow from any existing style without actually having to learn to play it. It was the cut-and-paste paradigm of the future, underpinned by a gleaming rhythmic pulse.

Hermes had been quietly acquiring the best part of a bedroom studio, and without telling anyone, had managed to record a couple of pretty solid tracks. This whole democratized creativity thing was proving effective, and when he finally played them to Athos, the feedback he received was so unexpectedly positive that they put their heads together to see if they could release them. Neither of them knew the first thing about pressing a track to vinyl, or for that matter how to distribute a record once it actually existed, but the spirit of the times was gloriously DIY. The reality was that most other underground record labels had started out without a clue too – it was common sense and determination that would win the day, not A&R men waving contracts.

They didn't actually have any money, and having looked up pressing plants in the Yellow Pages, they determined that they would need about a grand to lay their hands on five hundred records. This didn't seem to discourage Hermes, who had a minor fraud scheme going on the side, something that he kept intensely private and only wheeled out at moments of personal need. And if there was one thing both of them had learned from their experiences on LSD and the explosion of the TAZ, it was that you can manifest the living shit out of most situations as long as you put enough energy behind them.

Now, that may sound like hippy bollocks, but it really fucking isn't. Athos had first noticed the phenomenon when he encountered a very grumpy train worker sat in a ticket office. Being totally in the zone, he had flashed a beaming smile and the bloke turned into a fountain of human munificence. From a smile. Testing had then been ramped up and the positivity principle was applied to more substantive spheres with a pretty damn decent success rate. It wasn't a guarantee, but it certainly shortened the odds. The motivational industry was still in its infancy, Tony Robbins's quarterback jaw was still to achieve international prominence, and we were only just being taught to problem solve by cuddling ourselves, so the thinking was a fuck sight more underground than it sounded.

So with Hermes chalking up the requisite grand through murky methods known only to himself, they cut the vinyl, and three weeks later took delivery of five hundred records. Now what? Well Rough Trade Records was just around the corner from the Portobello squat, so that seemed like a sensible place to start. The weary-looking ponytail in the Ned's Atomic Dustbin T-shirt slapped their track on the turntable, scowled a bit, and then agreed to take twenty copies on sale or return. Which was something.

They spent the next three days visiting independent record shops from Reading to Romford, and while not a single one gave them any cash up front, the vast majority agreed to sale or return. By the end of the third day, all five hundred were in the field, and when they did a second pass two weeks later, they had sold all but thirty-seven copies. And just like that, they had an independent record label. They even made a tidy profit out of the experiment, more than doubling Hermes's ill-gotten float. They decided to call the label Syndicate Records – no prizes for guessing why.

They began to divide their time differently between the bunker and the Portobello gaff that Hermes had now moved into, complete with computers and useless bits of circuit board. Athos had wondered how those computers in the bunker had been paid for, and when he discovered Hermes had even more terminals at home, the plot thickened, but his sideline did explain a lot. They would head to the bunker every other day so as to allow themselves time to work on whatever tunes they could cook up. Athos didn't have the faintest idea how to operate the studio, so he would sit next to Hermes and make squawking noises to intimate how he thought the synths should sound. Athos also became something of a crate digger, raiding the second-hand record shops on Notting Hill Gate for obscure old tunes to sample and classic breakbeats to chop.

The label started to get traction, and the next three releases were surprisingly well received. No shop was prepared to pay them up front yet, but places like Black Market in Soho began taking wedges of fifty at a time, and before long Hermes and Athos were looking at fifteen hundred record runs. Having the radio station definitely helped get the word out, and before long, they had a small but influential group of DJs supporting them.

Hermes began wondering if there might be any mileage in a web presence for the label and even began thinking about the possibility of an online shop. After all, as they stood, their distribution network consisted of Greater London and a few orbital towns. The internet could offer them the world. It wasn't at all clear how an online business might work though – this would be more like placing a global classified ad and seeing what came of it. If some guy in LA wanted a couple of tracks, he could mail an international money order and they could send him the records once it had been cashed. It wasn't quite the lightning efficiency of a fax machine, but it was something. So Hermes set about building an extremely rudimentary website that introduced their label to the world with a drop-shadowed smorgasbord of clip art and low-res images. The future had officially arrived.

HOUSTON – WE HAVE A PROBLEM

So, er… the ketamine. Slight issue there. Despite steadfast early denial, after a few months there was no avoiding it. It had been a miscalculation on an epic scale.

The arrival of the Indian cargo had led to a sudden glut. It had all begun appropriately enough with tentative experiments, but the cheapness and the availability soon began to encourage more extensive use. Athos noticed the first sign that something might be amiss at a West London TAZ when he found Chris licking a wall. Wondering if something might be wrong, he prized the big fella away from his new amour and looked him in the eyes to see if he could help. Chris's pupils lolled back at him with a glassy hue, and a seductive stream of dribble began pouring from the corner of his mouth. Then he lunged at Athos, though it wasn't clear if the impulse was love or violence. Probably the latter, knowing Chris, but still, the fact that his body was behaving like an electrocuted slab of beef was worrying.

Chris came round twenty minutes later with no memory of their encounter, but even the most cursory scan revealed an awful lot of people in a similarly anesthetized condition. Scattered amidst the lagoon of smiles were lobotomized islands of loneliness, transfixed for all the world on a vacant void.

"Have you seen the state of some of these people?" Athos asked Steve.

Steve nodded thoughtfully and rubbed his chin. "Yeah. Not good is it? I dunno – do you reckon it's the K?"

"It has to be, doesn't it?" replied Athos.

"Aye," ruminated Steve. "Let's face it though, it never seemed like the kind of thing you take at a party. Lying in bed with the music on, maybe, but it never occurred to me people might take it on a night out."

And taking it they were. Somehow, the ketamine had gone from an astral portal to a nihilistic cosh. Those who had been mining the stuff with their nostrils stood out a mile: the blank facial expressions, the unsteady legs, the fumbling, the stumbling – if they were indeed having a valid experience, it was internalized to the point of alienation. And they were sitting ducks in case of an emergency. Fire, a police raid – you name it, they'd be hopelessly unable to cope. Plus, it looked awful – to the point that it would start putting people off from coming at all.

The TAZ had never felt "druggie," and if it had done, it would have limited itself to a much smaller cross-section of society. Yes, chemicals were taken, but always to enhance the overall experience rather than to have a private one. Looking around, it was difficult not to conclude that scores of people were so locked into their own bubble that they could have been anywhere. And by being there, muddling through their insular world, they were disrupting the formation of a whole.

Havoc and Chris were naturally very defensive. They had been enjoying hero status since their return, and every time they caught a glance of the new equipment, they felt a spark of pride. But now questions were being asked about the wisdom of importing kilos of ketamine, and while no one was blaming them, they couldn't help but take it personally.

"Look, it's not the bloody ketamine," insisted Havoc. "It's the way people are taking it."

"Yeah, but if it wasn't available, they wouldn't be in this state," riposted Jayden.

"If people abuse it, that's hardly our fault, is it?" shot back Havoc.

"He's got a point," ventured Trade. "You can't blame something we've all had a good experience with for the way people misuse it."

"Says the businessman," piped up Hermes. "That's like saying guns don't kill people, people do."

"Well, they do," said Trade, who had owned a few guns in his time.

"Fucking hell," sighed Claire. "Either way, we can't bring any more in. Not if it's having this effect."

"Agreed," said Steve, and there was a general nod of support.

"But hang on – what the fuck are we going to do for money if we don't?" asked Chris.

"Easy now, Chris," said Jayden. "If it's having a bad effect, money shouldn't come into it."

"Fuck off, preachy," snapped Chris. "I didn't say we should carry on, did I?"

"Twat," said Jayden.

"Is there any K left?" asked Michael.

"I'd murder a line," said Chris antagonistically.

Michael repeated the question with a paternal weariness.

"No," replied Havoc. "Well, maybe, but not in our hands."

"OK, well then, let's have a proper meeting in the week to discuss our funding. Are we all agreed that our involvement with ketamine stops here?"

"Aye," went up the shout as a bassline thundered behind them.

As the morning arrived, more evidence was on display. Someone had nearly drowned in the canal, piles of bodies lay strewn on the floor, and the air of dissolute skank was overpowering. Most people left earlier than usual, and the pernicious effect the ketamine was having crystallized further. It wasn't even as if people were coming out of the K-hole gushing about the magical experience they'd just had; no, this was starting to look like a tabloid version of drug abuse. The road to hell was indeed paved with good intentions.

The funding meeting was pushed back a week and then another, as there were still residual funds left from their Faustian pact. The bunker was getting a bit of a facelift as Steve's symbol was painted onto the walls, and the kitchen was finally getting an upgrade after descending into something Withnail would be proud of. Tony had installed himself behind a desk and was engrossed in the weekly production of his *Look Beyond* magazine. He must have found some funding of his own too, as it was now being printed in full color. The cover story that week featured an in-depth examination of sportscaster David Icke's Damascene conversion, and was accompanied by drawings of what the Queen might look like off camera when she turned into a lizard.

Jayden had started doing a degree in History at Birkbeck, the mature student college of the University of London, and while he still turned up at the bunker regular as clockwork, he was usually to be found by Hermes's computer bank poring over the details of the East India Company and Britain's role in the slave trade.

Trade was particularly drawn by Jayden's focus on mercantilism as the primary shaper of Britishness. From what they could both work out, the imperial land grab had been launched to protect trade rather than the other way round, and despite all the warmongering and pocket genocides, the expansion from trading empire to physical empire had been far more cock up than conspiracy.

Try telling that to its victims, but the more Jayden read into British as well as Dutch history, the more it looked like corporations had ruled the world for a lot bloody longer than he'd thought. Funnily enough, corporate power had come hand in hand with liberalism, and one of the hallmarks of the merchant empires was their political dynamism. Holland in the seventeenth century, Venice in the Middle Ages – these countries had three things in common: they didn't have absolute monarchies, their military focus was almost exclusively naval, and they protected their corporate interests before anything else. And, with that trinity, they punched way above their weight.

Liberal political systems, globalization, and corporations pillaging resources for shareholder profit. Sounds familiar.

The lessons of history as well as the present all pointed to the critical role of economics in any functional system. It couldn't be ignored, and it wouldn't go away if you took enough acid, so the only adult approach was to own it and make it work in the fairest possible way.

Jayden and Trade had a good few fireside chats about this, but they kept circling back to the same position. They hesitated over articulating anything quite yet, at least until they could gift wrap their heresy, but when the funding meeting finally was called to order by Michael, they were ready to float the unthinkable.

Michael opened the meeting with a proposed new system of debate. Seeing as how there were about forty people there, he suggested something he had picked up in his Marxist days. It was a framework for discussion that involved different hand signals for agreement, rejection, question, and addition, and administrating the meeting would be a "facilitator." Not a chairperson, you understand – a facilitator.

It all sounded a bit hippy management consultant, to be honest, but what it did bring was a very distinct structure to meetings that had always been a bit of an unruly free-for-all. Votes had never been taken, organized turns at speaking had never been a thing, and yet somehow it had always worked without any disagreement or trouble. Michael insisted that the sheer numbers meant that they would need a format like this or some people would be excluded and the loudest voices would always win the day. Which made total sense. Reluctantly, Michael offered himself as the "facilitator," and his first action was to ask everyone to not take any steps that affected the group without raising them and having them approved in a meeting.

With that, the meeting began and Jayden spoke up.

"Look, I know an entry fee has always been a massive no-no, but I can't help but wonder if the TAZ being free is as healthy as we think. All these people have jobs or incomes, and yet the TAZ is free. People do business in the TAZ… and yet it's free. We all know that it's about contribution in whatever form, but all this lot off their tits on K – what are they giving? People selling acid – yes, they're bringing quality LSD, which adds to the vibe, but they're also making money without contributing financially to the upkeep of the TAZ. Wouldn't a proper anarchic model in a world where money does exist involve a financial contribution as well?"

There was uproar as Jayden was shouted down. Michael didn't have a gavel, so he banged a hand drill on the table to restore order and reminded them of the meeting "guidelines." Not rules, mind – guidelines. When the howling settled, Trade took up the baton.

"We can't pretend money doesn't exist, guys. We won't last long term if we do. Not saying there's an entry fee and fuck off if you can't afford it – that really would be the end. But how about a donations bucket? Give as much or as little as you want – or as you can."

Michael pointed to Claire, who had her hand up.

"I think that makes sense," she said. "It does take money to run these things, and it has to come from somewhere. Look how badly we fucked up with the ketamine. Wouldn't the best thing be for the community to self-sustain rather than bring money in from outside?"

There was a ripple of nods, and then Michael pointed to Tony.

"Anyone who wants to bring money in any form into the TAZ is a traitor," he said.

Michael pointed at Steve.

"Come off it, Tony – we're talking about voluntary donations here, not pricing up the experience."

"How do we know *they* haven't got to you?" asked Tony ominously.

"It wasn't your turn to speak," Michael reminded him with a gentle rebuke. "Yes, Havoc, you've had your hand up for a while."

"I think it's a good shout," Havoc said thoughtfully. "If we aren't self-supporting, then we'll always be reliant on someone from the outside or a small group of us. If me and Chris were different people and the ketamine thing had actually worked out, we might have ended up pulling more strings than would be right."

After another twenty minutes or so, the motion was put to a vote. Michael insisted that a show of hands might intimidate some people into not voting with their conscience, so he had introduced a system of secret ballots where everyone wrote their vote anonymously on a scrap of paper and put it into a bowl. It was a bit long-winded, but Michael did have a point.

It was a close-run affair, but those who voted in favor of a donations bucket eventually won the day. Tony looked disgusted and straight up called Jayden "Judas," while those closest to Tony jeered the "sellout." It all got a bit edgy there for a while, and in the end, Jayden took himself home, sick of defending himself to a kangaroo court. It could have been the sensitivity of the matter being debated, but Athos couldn't help noticing that no meeting had ever been so organized, and no meeting had ever ended more rancorously. Fucking money.

LEGISLATION ... AND MORE LEGISLATION

The backlash came on multiple fronts. Turned out that when the Home Secretary had promised anti-TAZ legislation on Radio 4 that morning, he actually meant it. Most of the Syndicate, if not the country, were unfamiliar with the notion of a politician keeping their promise, but then this one was cheap and had the advantage of looking tough. Politicians rarely pass up the chance to look tough, especially if they are insecure in their post, behind in the polls, or just wired that way. There's an awful lot of very decent constituency MPs out there, and occasionally even a few in government, but it takes a very special sort of person to keep track of their moral compass at the highest level.

The Home Secretary had a fearsome array of chips on his shoulder and an unfortunate countenance that made him look like an amateur-dramatic Dracula. In one of the most absurd bills ever submitted to Parliament, he set about trying to criminalize a type of music with the casual officiousness of a cultural vandal. Perhaps realizing that just making unlicensed gatherings illegal might result in cabinet colleagues getting nicked at weddings, funerals, and, yes, barn dances, he had to find a way to specify. And he did. It was those bloody repetitive beats wot done it, and in an extraordinary day for democracy, the bill passed into law with any unlicensed event playing music "characterized by the emission of a succession of repetitive beats" made illegal. This included private parties.

It was unenforceable, of course, but in the finest traditions of statecraft, the government cast the widest possible net onto the statute books and then worked out how it would choose to apply it. It's much easier to make law than to repeal it, and politicians love new legislation as it looks like they're actually doing something. Getting anything overturned, however, usually requires a strong swell of public opinion, and this is another reason minorities and "the other" suffer so unduly – public opinion doesn't give all that much of a shit.

He was on solid ground with this one though. The Tory base lapped it up and the media had softened up middle England with tales of drug-addled Satanists, so it was three cheers all round as Mozart turned in his grave.

The immediate impact of the bill's passage through Parliament was a succession of massive protests in the center of London. This wasn't just about the Syndicate or anyone who frequented a TAZ – this was about anyone who'd ever been to a club, had a private party the local stuffed shirt frowned on, listened to a repetitive beat, or just cared about the extraordinary abuse of power playing out. It wasn't so much that the state wanted an end to Temporary Autonomous Zones – that much was understandable – it was the precedent set by discriminating against a certain kind of music.

The TAZ movement had never been against anything or wanted to smash the state in any way, but confrontation had now come knocking. There was a reluctant politicization, knowing that the language and actions of opposition would change the nature of the TAZ. But they couldn't just bend over either, and they joined the patchwork of protesters in Trafalgar Square to march against the government.

Predictably, it changed nothing, and predictably, a few complete wankers gifted the tabloids their front page. Tens of thousands marched peacefully, and yet five or six people couldn't resist putting bandanas across their faces and smashing up a few shop windows in Oxford Street. Take *that*, society.

Sure enough, the cameras were on hand and the next morning it was all "Reign of Terror in West End" and "Violent Thugs Destroy Businesses." The implication was that they were dangerously high on repetitive beats, and the sooner they were banned, the better. Like so many protests before and after, it was betrayed by an imbecile few and the salient points were terminally sabotaged. It's not a media conspiracy either, as some would believe – the bottom line is that violence in Central London sells papers and measured discussions about a parliamentary bill don't. Athos had been nowhere near where it had kicked off, but the news filtered back pretty quickly that Tony and his mob had been the ones responsible. Seriously – did he have anything in common with Tony? What were they doing on the same team?

It was difficult to judge the exact impact of the new laws over the next year. Plenty of TAZs were stopped in their tracks, but then plenty others went ahead as planned. More of a concern had been the reaction toward the donations bucket, which had gone down like a lead balloon. Requests for donations were met with blank stares, critiques of greed, lectures on materialism, and every now and again, an actual contribution. It was extraordinary when you thought about it – none of these people would have done a day's work for free in their own field, and the disconnect between workable anarchism and the day-to-day realities of the TAZ was growing. The Syndicate had expected some initial resistance, but getting people to understand the logic proved nigh on impossible. Try as they might to explain the notion of a self-sustaining, self-reliant community, they kept running up against a knowing look that seemed to say, "Yeah, justify it all you like, we know you're selling out."

Frustration built on both sides, and suddenly there were sides. The steadfast refusal to understand that there were costs and someone had to meet them seemed beyond belief, and the notion that small contributions on a voluntary basis were the only way they'd be able to protect the integrity of the TAZ was lost in the crossfire. The vast majority of attendees simply weren't prepared to pay, and somewhere along the line, the association between the two meanings of the word "free" had gotten hopelessly entangled. For something to be liberated, it didn't have to cost nothing, and being free of charge potentially endangered its ability to stay free of pervasive influence.

As if to rub it in, ketamine was flooding the pathways. That first large-scale haul that Havoc and Chris had brought back had been the cracking of Pandora's Box. They may have shut down the operation after seeing the consequences, but others had taken up the mantle, and the trail of incapacitated zombies only grew. Tony was lobbying hard for the imports to resume, arguing that it was happening anyway and they may as well be the beneficiaries, especially as the donations bucket had proved such a miserable failure. The glee Tony exhibited at the implosion of the contribution model was barely concealed, and the reaction had prompted several others to rethink their attitude toward financing too.

Syndicate meetings were growing increasingly tedious. Bless Michael and everything, but the endless hand signals, agenda tabling, motions, committees, subcommittees, and all the fucking rest of it was wearing Athos down. Perhaps the loudest voices had been silenced, but now power began resting in the hands of those who best adapted to the Byzantine meeting format. Athos and Hermes had actually been formally censured at a recent meeting for not having put their decision to start a record label to the floor. Maybe they shouldn't have called it Syndicate Records without consulting everyone, but they had meant well, and it was open to anyone in the bunker to release music on. Shit, they had even donated all their profits to the Syndicate when the donations bucket plan proved so spectacularly ineffective. Being called out in what amounted to a show trial had been bruising for them both, and the net result was that they spent less and less time at the bunker.

Abuses had started to appear on the fringes of the TAZ: there had been a couple of muggings, and a batch of contaminated ecstasy had yielded terrifying results at one East London gathering. There were no deaths, but something had been far from right, and at least fifty people had undergone an intensely traumatic few hours. Maybe all these things had a lifespan? Maybe legislation was the least of their problems?

Athos wasn't ready to give up yet though – far from it. Hermes, on the other hand, was growing frustrated and had the restless air of someone searching for a new mission. That unease didn't extend to the record label though, and the two threw their energies fully behind its expansion. Being censured for it actually felt like a free hand, and they cared less and less about what the rest of the Syndicate might say about the music they were making or the business model they were nurturing. They would never understand why making a living from creativity was wrong, while selling ketamine wasn't.

Sure enough, the ketamine imports resumed with Tony at the helm. It was difficult to understand how Tony and Michael managed to coexist, as they were so radically different. Athos started to wonder if they needed each other, somehow – whether having the biggest loudmouth in the group conform to the governance structures validated Michael, and whether having his motions formally passed validated Tony. There was definitely a hint of mutual dependence, and as people like Steve, Tank, and Claire began to peel away, both Michael and Tony's positions consolidated.

Tony had been further empowered by the increased politicization wrought by the new laws. Suddenly the state was a clear enemy and not just something to be ignored. It fed every tangent of his worldview, and his assessment of the new legislation as an Illuminati plot to silence its enemies had the merit of both polarizing tension further and characterizing the TAZ as something so powerful it needed silencing. Which again was something Tony was able to make capital from. Now it was a struggle – it was us against them. It was a fight to the death and everyone had to pick a side. Tony was in his element.

Steve had been shruggingly frank. The Syndicate, and indeed the TAZ in its current form, wasn't what he'd signed up for, and Claire began to think about the career in physics she'd put on hold. Trade had moved to Argentina to broker lithium deals with some dodgy Aryans a couple of months back, and Jayden was devoting more and more time to his degree.

Tank was furious about the ketamine episodes, and seeing the donation bucket pushed away week after week had made him question everything. The utter refusal to engage in a fair economic dialogue, combined with the changing behavioral tide, suddenly looked like hedonism – even consumerism dressed up as philosophical purism. Consumerism. Jesus – had they come full circle? Was the TAZ actually a form of consumerism? Regrettably, it was starting to look that way.

When people cherish an experience, but refuse to contribute toward its survival, that's even more extreme than your garden-variety consumerism. At least when you buy new trainers or a new stereo, it's a straight transaction that no one has any illusions about. The TAZ had tried to establish itself outside that dynamic, but if something can't be sustainably free, then surely a system of voluntary donation was the only non-transactional option. Buying fucking ketamine was back to a transaction again, and no one seemed to begrudge that, so at some point you had to wonder if anything made sense.

Therein lay the rub. People would walk into a TAZ with a hundred quid in their pocket – buy booze, buy drugs, get a cab home – and all those transactions seemed entirely reasonable. So why was chucking a fiver, or even a couple of quid, into a bucket such an outrageous imposition? The layers of hypocrisy seemed so manifold to Tank that he couldn't bear to be involved anymore and he took the hardest exit, heading to an ashram in India with a devastating abruptness.

Tank's departure sealed it for Steve and Claire, who had been close to him since way before the Syndicate days. That was the movement fractured for them, and as Claire took up a position at Imperial College, Steve decided to try his hand at painting, buoyed by the success of his symbol. The rest of them all stayed nominally within the fold, but with increasingly heavy hearts, and you got the sense that if Leary, Havoc, Hermes, or Athos had known what to do with themselves instead, they would have sacked off the whole thing.

A holding pattern then developed, and the Syndicate came ever further under the control of Michael, Tony, and their respective factions. Michael was still the "facilitator," while Tony never actually had any kind of formal position – he would have lost his authority had he taken one on. "Manifesters" were voted in to oversee the execution of any "suggestion" the Syndicate forum had approved, and, to be honest, the whole thing was looking increasingly like a cross between *Animal Farm* and the New Age Civil Service.

Meanwhile, Rome was burning, and as the Syndicate debated whether or not to write a constitution, the TAZs grew more and more ragged. The appeal had narrowed, and all those bright-eyed positive sparks from a thousand walks of life were gradually superseded by a procession of munted crusties. There were barely any black people left, and the strong gay contingent had thrown over the TAZ for an altogether more glamorous basement scene in Soho.

So much power had come from diversity, and that now looked like a distant memory. It was difficult not to conclude that the central pillars of the TAZ movement were crumbling, though as the 11th Congress was opened by Michael, you'd be forgiven for thinking they were talking about a completely different place. The more "suggested guidelines" they passed, the more the realities on the ground seemed like a cruel joke.

Hermes had started talking about going to America. He had grown close to a group of computer engineers in San Francisco through one of his numerous online forums, and they had invited him over for a couple of months. Realistically, there didn't seem to be much worth staying in London for beyond the record label, and they were all still young enough to pivot – young enough to have a crack at a second dream. Athos was desperate for Hermes not to go, as he hadn't the faintest idea of what to do with himself – it was all well and good Hermes having a new calling, but what about him? He'd joined the Syndicate at sixteen, and now, at the age of twenty-one, he didn't have a clue how to start again.

Reluctantly, he began thinking about a job of some sort, if only to fill his days. This was treason of the highest order for the old Athos, and all that "brainwashed cogs in the capitalist machine" stuff was coming home to roost. But this wasn't a U-turn on that scale – no, he wasn't so skin-deep in his convictions that he'd do any old shit for a wage. The job hunting wasn't a sudden acceptance of the prevailing paradigm; it was an admission that he didn't have a direction, and so wanted to see if anyone else had any ideas. What he was really looking for was something with the same depth of purpose as the TAZ, the same creative fulfillment as music production, and the same kind of people as the early Syndicate at the helm. Thing was, there weren't too many options that ticked those rather demanding boxes.

After much deliberation, he finally decided to try his hand at the film business. London was no Hollywood, but it did have a solid little industry of its own, albeit more for TV and independents than major blockbusters. He had answered an ad placed by Pegasus Films in Dean Street. Pegasus were looking for a general intern, but their ad did promise opportunities and a steep learning curve. They had released a couple of excellent documentaries in the last year, and Athos began picturing life as a documentary filmmaker. He was sure that if he found himself on a worthwhile project, legwork wouldn't be an issue. Making the tea, doing research, liaising with agencies – he was right up for it all if he believed in the subject and tone of the film being made.

Qualifications were somewhat moot – he didn't have any, and they didn't need any as long as he knocked the interview out of the park. Ultimately, five years with the Syndicate had given him a degree of maturity and competence far beyond someone leaving university with a Media Studies degree, and luckily, Juliette Moran, who was interviewing him, picked up on it straightaway.

It would be a few days until he received an answer, but he pounded down the stairs of the Pegasus building and shot out into the street with a renewed spring in his step. Hanging a right, he strolled over to Berwick Street to check out the record shops and bought a few bits at the market before wandering down to Piccadilly Circus and on towards Haymarket. Suddenly, out of the corner of his eye, he caught a glimpse of Tony.

Tony was about the last person Athos wanted to bump into, and he ducked into a doorway before he was seen. Edging his neck back out millimeter by millimeter, he surveyed the terrain, and, seeing Tony again, he recoiled rapidly. Tony was chatting to someone, but Athos couldn't for the life of him see who it was. He waited in the doorway for another few minutes and then slowly extended a periscopal eye. Tony was still there, but he was obviously saying goodbye – Athos could tell from the body language. After a final handshake, Tony set off in the direction of Trafalgar Square, and his companion began walking back toward Athos.

He was wearing a suit, which raised an immediate question. What the fuck was establishment scourge and anarchist renegade Tony doing talking to some bloke in a suit? Maybe it was his lawyer, but Athos immediately felt butterflies flutter through his stomach. He had a really weird feeling about this. The besuited mystery man had started whistling and was now only a few feet from Athos's dug-in redoubt. He knew that face. He fucking knew that face. Jesus Christ… It was Henry Rutherford.

In a flash, he was back at school with Henry marching him to the headmaster. This made no sense at all though. What would an Old Etonian in a suit be doing talking to fucking Tony? And more to the point, what was Tony doing talking to him? Surely Henry represented everything Tony loathed, and it was beyond him what strange quirk in the fabric of space-time could possibly have brought such unlikely bedfellows together. Just then, Henry displayed a tasty bit of footwork, spun round, hailed a cab, and jumped in. Before Athos knew what he was doing, he'd flagged a second taxi down, bundled himself aboard, and actually said the words, "Follow that cab."

They sped down Whitehall, chugged past the Houses of Parliament, and rounded onto Millbank. Just as Athos was starting to relax into the journey, Henry's taxi unexpectedly swung up Horseferry Road, took the first left into Thorney Street, drew to a halt, and Le Rutherford tottered out. He paid the taxi as Athos watched carefully, and then proceeded to cross the road. He met a lady on the other side, and as they shook hands in a businesslike fashion, Athos, to his absolute astonishment, recognized her too. It was Mrs. Bourne, his old friend Jason's mother.

It took him a moment to put the pieces together, if only because the conclusion was so outrageous. He paid his own cab from the limited funds he had to his name, retraced the route onto Horseferry Road and walked back to Millbank to see if they really were where he thought they were. They were.

The taxi had stopped outside the back entrance to Thames House, which by any other name was MI5 headquarters. He knew for a fact that Mrs. Bourne worked for the security services, and from what Athos could see, she clearly worked with Henry. And Henry seemed remarkably cosy with Tony. There was only one explanation. Tony was an MI5 agent.

SHOWDOWN

But it didn't make any sense. Tony was the strongest critic of the state, the ultimate rebel. How could he possibly be an undercover agent? Surely if the security services had planted someone, it would be a fringe participant reporting back on movements, plans, locations, and all the rest. How on earth did it serve any purpose to have an agent dedicated to making the movement more extreme and more hostile to the state? It beggared belief.

It didn't beggar Hermes's belief though. Athos was expecting the same stunned reaction he'd had, but Hermes nodded sagely and said, "Yup. Makes sense."

Athos demanded to know how Hermes could remain so calm. And for that matter what he meant by "makes sense." It didn't make any fucking sense to him.

Hermes seemed to pass into a Zen-like state of beatitude. Maybe this was how Jesus had managed to take the whole crucifixion thing so infuriatingly well. Which reminded Athos: that grassing cunt had actually called Jayden a Judas.

Hermes nodded some more and stroked his chin. Athos nearly smacked him.

"Think about it," said Hermes. "If you're clever – and to be honest, I never gave MI5 this much credit – you'd realize that repression is a totally outdated control mechanism. No point battering people if you can chuck an apple of discord in and let your enemies self-destruct. The TAZ was dangerous because it didn't fit into any manageable category. So they made it manageable."

"Doesn't explain why MI5 wanted us to believe in aliens and ridiculous conspiracies."

"But it does. We weren't rebelling, and we weren't flogging an ideology; we were quietly pulling thousands of people out of mainstream thinking and giving them a blank slate. We would discuss ideas sensibly, and there was always doubt to everything. That was far too grown up and undercover a revolution. But if people saw the TAZ associated with lunatic conspiracies and tin-foil hattery, then it would remain on the fringe forever."

"So are we saying that the whole thing was a way to discredit the movement?"

"Not only that; the more adamant he encouraged people to be and the less doubt anyone had, the more the movement would corrupt from within. Look at how we ended up, for fuck's sake. It was genius."

"And all that 'Look Beyond' shit. My god, the irony."

"Yup. And sowing paranoia. If you start to buy into a conspiracy, paranoia becomes par for the course. Paranoid people are easy to manipulate. Just look at any dictator. They were all protecting the motherland from some conspiracy or other. Anyone crossed them – bang, they were a secret conspirator. Trust no one but your leader. Makes perfect sense."

Athos reflected on this. He couldn't help but begrudgingly admire the masterstroke MI5 had pulled off. And they probably had such a laugh doing it too. Fair enough to plot this from a wingbacked chair in Whitehall – all's fair in love and war – but Tony… what a twenty-four-carat cunt. He'd lived amongst them for years, and all the while he'd been selling them down the river. And had he really got all those tattoos for this?

Athos marched toward the front door.

"Where do you think you're going?" asked Hermes.

"I'm going to fucking tell everyone – what do you think I'm doing?"

"You haven't got any proof, and he's got a following. Honestly, you're not thinking straight."

"We can't just leave it. We'd be as bad as him."

"Well, steady on, but I know what you mean. Still, don't you want to wait until the next one of Michael's Politburo meetings?"

"What, and just sit on it? Fuck that."

"The 12th Congress, or whatever Chairman Mike is calling it, is on Saturday. I still think it's a bad idea – anyone who believes the Queen's a reptile and Stonehenge is an alien landing site isn't going to believe Tony's an MI5 agent, just because you saw him talking to some bloke you were at Eton with."

"I don't give a shit – we're trying."

It didn't go well. Tony hadn't managed to survive undercover all those years by caving as soon as it came on top. Backed into a corner, he had one avenue out and he shot down it like an RPG. The tables were instantly turned, and the whole episode was dismissed out of hand: Athos was an

Illuminati stooge trying to sow division in the Syndicate, and they should have all known years ago, because what else would a posh boy be doing in their midst? In those dark days before camera phones, Athos had not a shred of proof, and it seemed so ridiculous to everyone at the Congress that he was laughed out of the room and then formally expelled from the Syndicate – something that took about three hours and five rounds of voting.

To be fair, he didn't have the strongest case. He'd seen Tony talking to someone in the street and then admitted to knowing not one but *two* MI5 agents himself. Tony neither looked nor sounded like an establishment operative, whereas people might be persuaded that Athos could be. No one bothered asking themselves why Athos would out himself in such amateurish fashion if he was a plant, because, well, things had moved past the critical-thinking stage. Belief had become an accepted form of truth, and further analysis just seemed like weakness.

EXIT – PURSUED BY
A MONKEY

Athos began work at Pegasus the next week. Juliette had been impressed at the interview and he hit the ground running, quickly making himself indispensable and mastering tasks like package delivery, spreadsheet operation, and taxi booking. There were a few episodes of more substantive research, but by the time two months had passed, it was all wearing a bit thin. Gratification was far from instant, and despite the fact that most ambitious young producers would have relished the opportunity, he was struggling.

The bottom line was that he'd never had any self-discipline whatsoever. He'd fucked around right the way through his checkered academic career, and his time with the Syndicate had been one long adrenaline rush. Nothing had prepared him for putting in years at the coalface, and without Pegasus asking him to direct their next documentary after three weeks as an intern, he began casting a wider net for thrills.

He was living a lonelier life these days. Hermes had gone to San Francisco swearing blind he'd be back in two months, but two months had passed and Athos had received a sheepish call to say he wouldn't be back just yet. He still kept up with Steve, Leary, and Jayden, though he didn't see much of Havoc and Claire – not because of any rift, but just because life. One person he had kept in touch with since his Gloucester Road days was Ben Abrahams, and despite them not having met up more than once or twice a year during the TAZ years, they still had a close bond. Left to his own devices, and without an all-consuming passion, Athos needed to plug the hole with some kind of kick, and it wasn't long before he found what he was looking for in the shape of a white rock.

Crack definitely has its upsides. It's a blinding rush, it's basically distilled cocaine, and when smoked in a glass pipe, it's conveniently portable. It also has a few significant downsides: bankruptcy, isolation, and an intensely sketchy edge that after a while needs medicating itself. Valium was a short-term solution, but pretty soon, Athos found himself on the well-trodden path to heroin use. Up and down, white and brown, yin and yang – speedballing it was the only way to maintain a long-term relationship with either drug.

The Yardies he was scoring off up in Kensal Rise had long recognized this fact, and every last one of them made sure they sold both. There had been a lot of hysterical press about crack-dealing Yardies, but from what Athos could make out, they were just a bunch of really sound Jamaican guys trying to make ends meet. He had money, so he never reeked of desperation, and before long, he'd grown pretty tight with a core crew of his dealers. He even went to one of their weddings.

Things escalated quickly and he was smoking both white and brown in the Pegasus toilets within a couple of months, and a parting of the ways started to look inevitable. Sure enough, the same eye that had recognized Athos's potential now saw it being squandered, and with the greatest diplomacy, he was invited to find a new calling.

Lurid tales of drug addiction have been told in endless other tomes, so there's no point in wasting much time on a sorry period. Needless to say, the money ran out, and after a few high-end hustles, he found himself penniless and in debt, and even his closest Yardie mate had to cut off supplies until he paid his tab. Next thing he knew, he was shoplifting meat – something he didn't even know was a saleable commodity – and waking up every day soaked in tremulous sweats. Turned out he was fucking rubbish at shoplifting, and despite wandering through the aisles in the only suit he hadn't pawned, he got nicked on a ridiculously regular basis.

This descent into the black hollow of his soul was playing out against a background of almost mesmerizing optimism. Cool Britannia was in full swing, and the stomach-churningly PR name said it all. The whole era felt like a marketing campaign.

The merchandising of cool had been around since the late '60s, but now the line between manufactured and spontaneous all but disappeared. Blur and Oasis battled for chart position and the textures of youth identity, the Young British Artists exploded onto the scene to pioneer the hype economy, and sweatshops started churning out celebrity. Style hosed down substance, and in the moment that marked both apogee and implosion, middle England's grinning Joker, Tony Blair, swept to power on a wave of hope. The moribund Tories were out, fresh blood was in, and the fact that you wouldn't buy double glazing off the new prime minister seemed but a minor detail. There was a glorious wind of possibility that hadn't been seen since Kennedy promised to land a man on the moon. The future beckoned in neon lipstick.

Athos had started to notice changes around Portobello too. It almost seemed like everything had changed in a single weekend, when a flood of arrests saw his old mates, the phone-box hookers of All Saints Road, vanish into the dragnet. Around the neighborhood, the more obvious bad boys seemed to have been surgically removed, a couple of boutiques selling overpriced candles had sprung up, and two ultra-slick coffee shops had mysteriously appeared. He hadn't even noticed any renovation work, and yet here they were, caffeinating a brave new world.

The changes were a double-edged sword. Romanticizing the past as we do, we forget the grease-soaked shitholes, the miserable throwbacks to bully beef, and the grimy pallor of 1970s' mediocrity. Swish new whites and bold new fonts definitely weren't as depressing, but then character had been engraved into every gutter over the years. These new places traded on having "character," and yet if you scratched the surface, they bled beige.

Thatcher's bid to turn the working class into middle-class stakeholders saw initial success as a new generation of homeowners boarded the ladder. Problem was, even as the Tories flogged thousands of council houses, they were so entranced by neoliberal promise that they didn't bother building any new ones. The economic turbines spun and, before long, former council houses were being flipped, black families were on a steady exodus, and shades of Chelsea began popping up in the Grove. The film *Notting Hill* was a fatal bullet, managing to turn the Saturday market into a tourist shrine and painting Hugh Grant as the face of a newly bourgeois sensibility.

Commercialization is a far more pernicious tool than repression, and whether this was stumbled into or deliberately implemented, everything changed. Instead of relying on the stick, society produced a huge sack of carrots, inhabiting the areas that most threatened it. Rather than running round the country raiding TAZs, the government changed tack, doling out all-night licenses like a drunken lottery winner. Taking the illicit thrill out of nightlife, they incubated a brash new scene, and the superclubs came preening into the mix. No longer were DJs hidden behind a wall of speakers to swerve hierarchy; now they stood atop towers, preaching to a moneyed congregation. DJs became superstars, losing their edge, their danger, and some of their soul in the process.

The alcohol industry reinvented itself after the panic of the early '90s, when people ditched beer for E's and water. After years spent lobbying the government to "bloody well do something," they got proactive and the alcopop was born. Marketed directly to "yoof" with a cynical flourish, they blew the cobwebs from booze's image and before you could say "WKD," the tills were ringing with readies. Club culture was sanitized and monetized in one fell swoop, and with consumerism now talking a more streetwise language, very little emerged to push back against it. With repression, there's an identifiable entity to push back against. With commercialization, the surrender was voluntary, unwitting, and apparently permanent.

Athos finally came to something resembling his senses in mid-2001. Five and a half years were missing in action, and for the life of him he couldn't believe how time had slipped so silkily through his fingers. Poking his head out of smack's womb, he realized that this couldn't possibly continue, and he knew his only hope was getting out of London. There were too many psychological triggers; he'd called a dealer from every phonebox, smoked rocks in every stairwell, and walked every pavement with loosened bowels in search of a tenner. No amount of holding hands in a circle was going to break that spell, and he racked his brains for options.

Athos had kept vaguely in touch with Hermes over the past five years. He had stayed out in San Francisco, immersed himself in a hacker collective, and bottom-fed on the fringes of the dot-com bubble. Email had proved a real blessing, as there was no way they'd have kept in touch otherwise, and now that Athos had taken the decision to sort his shit out, he put out his message in a Hotmail bottle. The response was semi-encouraging.

Problem was, Athos had sworn he was getting clean a few times – you can't call yourself a proper junkie until you've had at least ten false dawns. Most of his friends had reached the point where there was nothing to be done but leave him to it. Nothing they could say or do would make a difference, so they walked that uncomfortable tightrope between feeling guilty and cutting off ties. The subtext had always been, "we're here when you're ready," and Athos was now ready to cash that chip. The question was: would they believe him?

Hermes had a precariously balanced life in San Francisco and didn't need a fucked-up Athos to come clodhopping into the middle of it. He had mates, a non-imaginary girlfriend, a creative and economic ecosystem that probably couldn't survive the introduction of a new species, and a huge slab of doubt marinating on the counter. But at the same time, he did feel slightly responsible, always wondering if his leaving and consequent abandonment of the record label had stripped Athos of his last positive mission. And he did love the cunt too. He just didn't know whether the relationship could be rekindled after nearly six years. We've all been there: that one-time brother or sister who took the other fork along the way – forever remembered, but forever lost.

The aspect that worried Hermes most was the same thing that gave him hope. Athos had periodically sworn to reform, but beyond a load of self-involved misery, he hadn't taken any steps to stop himself backsliding. Now he was asking if he could come and stay with Hermes as a stepping stone to a new life in California, and that sounded like progress. Hermes took a week to reply as he weighed the pitfalls, and then sent Athos a warm but stern email back, outlining the conditions he would have to meet. He'd need to do his cluck before arriving so that first impressions on Chiara, Hermes's girlfriend, weren't fatal. He'd need a couple of grand to get himself started. And he'd need to know that continued supping at the narcotic teat would render the arrangement null and void. If Athos could manage the first two, then the third had a shot.

Athos spent a month gouging over Hermes's email before resolving to give it everything he had. He booked himself into a two-week residential rehab and phoned his parents for the first time in years to see if they could help financially. Phillip and Leila had heard this sort of thing before and were extremely skeptical, but he was their only child and they had nothing left but forlorn hope. They too were encouraged by the California plan and told Athos that if he made it through the fortnight and came directly to them without accidentally scoring en route, they would provide a plane ticket and a couple of grand. They couldn't write him off without a final Hail Mary.

It took three months on the waiting list before a rehab slot finally opened up. It was no luxury sanitarium – no yoga, no hydrotherapy, and no expensive sympathy – that much was for damn sure. No, the Max Glatt Unit was bleakness incarnate. It performed its Hippocratic duties from the former asylum wing of Ealing Hospital, behind walls Wormwood Scrubs would be proud of and with bars on every window. It was a gruesome rogues' gallery, with alcoholics dribbling in corners, Valium addicts spasming on the floors, and bullying nurses wishing they were anywhere else; a toxic desperation seeped through the linoleum corridors.

Despite *Trainspotting* painting heroin withdrawal as a surrealist concerto, the reality was brutally mundane. No toilets were violated, no walls melted, no babies appeared; he just felt unbelievably shit for a week. It was like a really dire flu transformed into torture by the knowledge that a split second on the foil would bring the sun back out. We accept our lot with flu because there's nothing we can do about it, but with heroin, knowing the solution was a bus ride away piled on the psychological angst. Sleep was snatched on a minute-by-minute basis if he was lucky, and, most excruciating of all, every minute felt like a week, as time's relativity twisted into a cruel smirk.

There was fuck all to do bar swap war stories with the other inmates, smoke like his life depended on it, and watch TV in the common room. The choice of channel could have been grounds for war, but everyone was in such a state that content really didn't matter; it all played out the same banal way. As Athos pulled into the home straight of the second week, he began paying a bit more attention, and as he tuned blearily into BBC London news, he suddenly shot out of his seat.

He was looking at the Waterloo roundabout – the same abandoned office building that housed the bunker in its loins and that had become a dank symbol of the holes punched in progress. Somehow, the building which should've been prime real estate had made it through the '90s without attracting a single suitor. But her long stint on the shelf was finally over, and such was the rejoicing that the betrothal made the news.

Athos stared at the television and wondered what had happened to the bunker. Had it finally been discovered, had Tony shopped the lot of them, was there a 372nd Congress, and was Michael teaching the developers how to facilitate inertia? And then he caught sight of something that made him spit out his tea. The property magnate behind the multimillion pound regeneration was none other than Nick Wilkinson, erstwhile Shoreditch dairy owner and patron of the arts.

Time had been kind to Nick, and he retained all the vivacious optimism that had dazzled Athos, Trade, and Jayden all those years ago. He really was the cheeriest fucker ever to find trespassers on his land, and his enthusiasm for arty squatters hadn't lost any of its baffle. Now here he was, taking over the bunker in all its grimy glory. Athos couldn't resist shouting out that he knew him, and while his alignment with millionaire property developers drew a frosty glare from most of his fellow inmates, one by the name of Peter nodded knowingly.

"Yeah, that cunt. Bought up half my manor. Colonized the fucking gaff, and now it's all trendy – he's minting it."

Athos nodded in acknowledgment. Shoreditch and Hoxton were the poster boys for regeneration in London, that much was common knowledge, but he had never considered that the fresh-faced Arthur Daley they met that day could be connected to its rise. Somehow, an absolute dive of an area had become associated with the avant garde – with art, with music, with Cool Bloody Britannia, and now the ad executives were moving in.

Artists will go wherever it's cheap and lively, and it occurred to Athos that if Nick's offer hadn't been an isolated incident, there might be a pattern here. Shoreditch certainly hadn't been lively, but if Nick had found takers for his squatting offer, the liveliness may have become a self-fulfilling prophecy. If he remembered that day right, he had more than just the dairy too. What if Nick had been a strategic fucking genius? What if Nick had been playing the long game, bringing in the artists, making the area trendy, luring in the professional classes with the promise of cultural relevance, and then flogging them loft conversions as the market soared? A proper cunt.

But was he? Surely everyone had been a winner. Artists, musicians, and hipster collectives had been able to nourish nearly a decade of unrestrained creativity rent free, the area was thriving, and he'd made a bloody fortune. Athos was far from sure that Nick had done anything wrong. Yes, he'd exploited trendifcation and guided it toward gentrification, but then a whole generation of creatives had exploited his buildings. It was a symbiotic relationship, and while the future looked sterile, no area ever retains its chops for long anyway. As long as there was another inner-London area to take its place, that was just the urban organism evolving. And Hackney would never be gentrified. There was no way.

His sojourn complete, Athos called a cab from reception and bid the driver toward Barons Court, where his parents lived. It was touch and go on the journey – he was fighting back a tsunami of temptation, but knowing his parents had booked his plane for the morning and that the slightest sniff of skag would set him back to square one, he held it down until he'd pulled up outside his parents' house. They welcomed him in with a hope they hadn't felt in years, and that evening was a long overdue moment of redemption.

They chatted honestly about the past, shared hopes for the future, and told playful jokes for the first time in years. Phillip wheeled out all the old puns that had so appalled Athos as a child, their sheer resilience gilded by history. They laughed, they cried, they drank, they hugged, they kissed, and when they finally fell asleep in the living room, they were a family once more. It didn't matter that the prodigal son was buggering off again the next morning – he was moving toward the light and that was more than enough.

ZEPHYRUS

The flight had been a struggle. Finding himself in the middle seat, Athos's claustrophobia triggered before takeoff and the next eleven hours were one long twitch. Finally landing just as he started to hyperventilate, he steeled himself for his next ordeal: passport control. 9/11 had torn America's sense of security to shreds, and with the Bush administration lashing out wildly at anyone who might be an enemy, borders had tightened dramatically. He'd managed to get a visa despite his rather lengthy record, and while he hadn't actually done any time or clocked up any charges beyond petty theft, he was shitting himself. The rest of his life would be in tatters if he had to go back to London with two grand and no plan, but his primary fear was being deposited back on another fucking plane.

He needn't have worried. The immigration officer waved him through after the most cursory of interrogations. He collected his bag, took a deep breath, and pounded on through arrivals, where Hermes nervously awaited him. The reunion was reminiscent of two cats sniffing each other – Hermes was looking for signs of liability, Athos was looking for signs of doubt, but as they hugged, the years melted away and they were brothers once more. Hermes was high on relief – he'd expected far worse, and while Athos was about ten kilos thinner than he remembered, the years of caning it didn't seem to have done any lasting damage.

Hermes was so chuffed that he took Athos home via the scenic route. The Golden Gate Bridge was just as impressive as the brochures promised, though Athos had never realized it was quite so bloody long. What he hadn't been prepared for was the giant tide of fog that rolled across it, shrouding the bay in opaque mystery and sending a shiver down his spine. They pressed on toward the few skyscrapers San Francisco had signed up for, swept past Presidio, turned toward downtown, and, after the best part of an hour, they drew to a halt on Geary Street.

Athos hadn't been sure what to expect, but having the San Fran mission as a beacon of hope for the last few months had inevitably romanticized it. Reality's handbrake arrested his wilder flights of fancy. Where were the cable cars, the quaint wharves, the rustic houses, the ubiquitous hippies, and the urbane sophistication? This – well, this was a little bit shit.

There wasn't time to fully assess the neighborhood as his primary test awaited: meeting Hermes's girlfriend, Chiara. Hermes had made such a big deal of this moment that Athos was expecting a domineering socialite who didn't suffer strays gladly, but she turned out to be a five-foot whirlwind of warmth, generosity, and razor-sharp intelligence.

She was half-Chinese, which didn't explain the name, and a Stanford graduate, who oversaw IT systems for several large firms in the Transamerica building. This meant she would be out a lot, and while Athos didn't doubt the sincerity of her welcome, he was switched on enough to know that the key would be to keep her sweet, make himself useful, and keep as low a profile as possible. Her being out all day would help strike that balance.

They settled into a welcome lunch, and having regained a little of his natural flair, Athos ingratiated himself, demonstrating a comprehensive knowledge of Chinese history and even cracking the one Mandarin joke he knew. That was the thing about heroin addiction: there had been plenty of time to catch up on his reading. He sprang into action as soon as lunch was finished, clearing the table, washing up, offering to cook dinner, and making all the right noises. Chiara was sold, and Hermes was grinning ear to ear, ecstatic that Athos hadn't turned up a gibbering mess.

The deal was that he'd be independent within six weeks, so after politely excusing himself at around nine o'clock to give the couple some time, he awoke the next day raring to find a job. Chiara had already left for work, so Athos made Hermes a coffee and settled in for an orientation chat.

Things hadn't been smooth of late. The Wild West days of slapping the letter "e" in front of absolutely anything, then launching an IPO a week later were finally over. The capacity of the human mind to relentlessly repeat the lessons of history while convincing itself that "it's different this time" never ceases to astonish. Investors were queuing up to fling money at the flimsiest of start-ups, and having wrapped their heads round the internet pretty late in the game, Wall Street made up for it with all the zealotry of a new convert. In a data version of manifest destiny, it was about grabbing as much virtual land as possible, and only then checking to see if the homestead thrown up on it would last the winter. As for the native Cyberians who clung to open-source idealism – fuck 'em.

Any pretense of investment being linked to potential earnings went flying out the window as the rush to outbid competitors heated up. Ideas were seeded before they were fully formed, businesses were funded before anyone checked they could keep their promises, legal structures were flippant at best, and the trade in hot air was rampant. Market share was superseded by mind share – having a head start, throwing cash at brand awareness, and associating company names with emergent sectors in the consumer mind. Amazon was the best example of this done right. By the end of the '90s, they *were* the online bookstore, and by pumping money back into development, they managed to build in brick while others flailed about under canvas.

Most weren't as successful though, and while many of the ideas that foundered did re-emerge in a different form and become successful businesses, such was the clamor to get in on the ground floor that due diligence was abandoned and sober thinking went on the piss. Even major players like AOL choked on their own hubris, so by the time Clinton left office, the party was over and people were wondering where their trousers were. Still, the dot-com bubble represented the best and the worst of capitalism: funding innovation and accelerating progress, while chasing a golden mirage.

Hermes had thrown himself headlong into a project called Visuatron after meeting a hypnotic young entrepreneur called Larry Baker. Larry regaled him with tales of open-source spaceship building, lifting African countries out of poverty, artificial intelligence, and the schematics for high-functioning robots before inviting Hermes aboard the good ship Visuatron. Larry had raised a fortune in funding and was the toast of Silicon Valley. Hermes couldn't believe he'd landed so spectacularly on his feet.

Larry offered him a whole department, and the hacking collective Hermes was a part of was drafted in to design interfaces for the launch. The company's golden egg was high-quality video streaming, and while pretenders like Microsoft had skin in the game, no serious analyst expected anyone to challenge the Visuatron supremacy. A futurist titan was being born before their very eyes.

Hermes felt that his talents were being wasted, and he was desperate to get into the research incubator that had built the compression algorithms. Larry, however, kept insisting that he was doing far too important a job and his engineers had everything under control. A launch was planned, and what with Larry's flair for theatre, a beta test was out of the question. No, it was Vegas or bust, and fight night would be their triumph. The heavyweight championship was set for the MGM Grand, and it was all hands on deck to transmit live and direct to the world. Hermes and his crew, "Offshore Signal," had built a stunning website, and despite their concerns over whether they had the server capacity to handle huge amounts of traffic, Larry brimmed with confidence.

Well, the night arrived, and Hermes was glued to his computer with a case of champagne. His website now had a video player embedded into it, no doubt by the boffins who'd crafted the software, but it stayed resolutely blank. Concerns began to grow, and tests on other laptops also came up blank. Fear's icy hand grabbed Hermes by the balls, and he started frantically phoning people to see if they had a signal. They didn't. Chat rooms were already jeering furiously and the Titanic was sinking fast. Hermes legged it out of the apartment, jumped into his car, and sped off to Larry's offices, where he found no sign of life beyond the words "Sorry guys – it's been a blast" scrawled on the whiteboard.

Turned out that Larry had fucked off to Rio with nineteen million dollars of investors' money. The whole thing had been a massive con; there was no software, there was no incubator, there were no boffins – it had all been an illusion. And a shoddy one at that. Hermes couldn't understand how no one had demanded proof that this video software even existed, let alone had the potential to set new industry standards. He puzzled over the unnecessary pageantry of a big Vegas launch too until he realized it had been an ostentatious diversion. Larry's flight took off ten minutes before the streaming was due to start. He even sent Hermes a postcard.

Being associated with the highest-profile fraud in internet history did Hermes's prospects no favors at all. Chastened and fuming, he resumed some light hacking, but his stock within the Offshore Signal collective had also taken a pounding as the promised equity in Visuatron vaporized. So here he was, just about getting by, and filling Athos in on the gory details.

Athos drank in this cautionary tale and the two headed off for a chaser. They popped round the corner to a bar called Kentucky Renegade to down some artisanal bourbon and chart a course for the coming weeks. There was a "Help Wanted" sign behind the bar, and with a few whiskeys inside him, Athos pounced. With a job sewn up, a celebration was called for, and he inquired as to whether Hermes had a decent weed supplier. Hermes looked at him doubtfully, wondering if a joint might not set Athos back on the road to ruin, but after a half-hour lecture on why all substances except smack and crack were still totally fine, he relented and agreed to take Athos to see Terra Baba.

He said the name as if it might mean something to Athos, but as they drove into the Frisco night, it was obvious that he didn't have a clue what Hermes was on about. Born Frank Gershowitz, Terra Baba had studied at Berkeley in the early '60s before partnering up with Owsley Stanley to build sound systems for the Grateful Dead. After going their separate ways in 1966, Gershowitz set up the most advanced illegal laboratory in California and proceeded to knock out a stream of experimental psychedelics.

In 1969, as momentum reached its peak, he suddenly announced his retirement from the chemistry game and set up a radical commune down the road from Esalen. Built on principles of ecological harmony and vigorous sexual experimentation, it attracted everyone from John Lennon to Timothy Leary, but after a couple of karmically resplendent years, his enthusiasm waned and he grew tired of nubile neophytes seeking tantric wisdom. Devoting himself to celibacy, he moved to a mountaintop in India for the next decade, meditating the years away and growing the kind of beard that could sustain a whole ecosystem. He'd finally returned to the States in the mid-'80s, complete with a grand new name, and moved back to Haight-Ashbury, which had lost much of its innocence in the intervening years. Today, he taught transcendental meditation, powered his third-floor ashram with homemade solar panels, and dabbled in quality weed supply.

Athos was immediately taken with the old guru and the two struck up a bond. Over the next couple of weeks, they returned daily – Athos's shift at Kentucky Renegade didn't start until 5 p.m. and Hermes was at a loose end, so they spent a good deal of their free time hanging with the Baba. Athos did some half-hearted house hunting, but figured he had another week or two of "acclimatization" before things started to get dicey with Chiara. Terra Baba was a fount of countercultural tales, breathing life into all those books Athos had read through his teens. Hermes had already told Terra Baba about the TAZ movement in the UK, and the story of its unraveling was a familiar one – apparently, his randy commune had ended in not dissimilar fashion. They compared notes and swapped fixes for the next big push; though in his late 50s, Terra seemed far keener to try another idealistic experiment than either Athos or Hermes, who were still smarting from the Syndicate.

A month passed, and Athos proved as good as his word. He moved into a vacant apartment two floors down from Hermes and Chiara, and while both of them had envisaged his independence being at least a couple of blocks away, it worked, and the three of them became a tight little unit. Chiara even tried setting Athos up with a couple of her friends, but after some disappointing one-night stands, both called a halt to the matchmaking before Chiara started hemorrhaging mates. Life tending bar at the Renegade was fun, if short term, and as Athos began to get a firmer grip on the "hood," he realized he was in very familiar territory.

They were living in the Tenderloin, which was an edgy mix of pimps, dealers, artists, hobos, hookers, junkies, and revolving kingpins. In some ways, it had echoes of Portobello: it was a short walk from downtown and rubbed up against much more affluent districts; walk a few blocks and it was a different world. The Tenderloin had a terrible reputation and was a sea of liquor stores, pawn shops, and the occasional church offering alternatives to chemical escapism. Athos knew that crack could almost certainly be obtained about three feet from his front door, and yet somehow he didn't want to go looking. His new life was progressing nicely, and he just didn't feel that magnetic pull to fuck it up quite yet. Nope, he was his old self again and loving every minute of it. Being in the seediest part of town only added to the vibrancy, and made him feel like he was really under the city's skin – the only concern he had was the American penchant for deadly firearms. Back in London, if you got shot, there was almost always a reason: gang wars, grasses, disputes over huge sums of money – if it happened, you usually knew why. But here, any old muppet could get a gun and people got shot over ten bucks or crossing the street in a "provocative manner."

Staying out of the drug game but making friends with the local bangers proved a sensible strategy. Being an outsider had been difficult initially, but it ended up working in his favor, as he wasn't implicated in any of the local gang politics, which, to be honest, were a fucking mess. None of it made much sense – people declared apartment buildings as territory, dealers robbed other dealers, Asians fought other Asians, Hispanics fought other Hispanics, blacks fought other blacks, they all fought each other, and even Metternich would have despaired at the complexity. The human turnover rates were high too – not so much from deaths but incarceration.

The War on Drugs was like nothing Athos had ever seen in the UK – addicts getting twenty years for possession and tin-pot dealers doing life for half an ounce. The edge was way fucking harder in the States: the game was sandwiched between death and life inside – and that made the stakes obscenely high. Still, even with the poor being fed relentlessly into a privatized prison system for corporate profit, somehow most of the bangers were pretty sound if you knew how to chat to them: no fear, but no threat – and being an outsider fucking helped. As for the police – well, Athos was white, so he hadn't met any.

Two months or so into his new life, Athos was weighing a quick trip to Canada to get his visa renewed when Terra Baba called, waxing lyrical about a special surprise. Athos and Hermes were both intrigued as Terra B never knowingly undersold, and as they sped over, they wondered what kind of bud he'd laid his hands on. Well, it wasn't weed. Nope, the old genie had managed to get hold of some DMT.

For those unfamiliar with those initials, DMT is the active ingredient of ayahuasca and portal to the shaman's spirit world. It stood for Dimethyltryptamine, which is naturally produced by the pineal gland, and scientists have suggested that elevated production of the tryptamine may account for the transcendental nature of near-death experiences. So here was a naturally occurring chemical that the brain kept a lid on for reasons best known to itself, but one theory was that our current evolutionary level wasn't ready to cope with its lens. Others dismissed that as hippy bollocks, but bollocks or not, it was produced naturally and it did have extraordinary effects.

Neither Athos nor Hermes had ever come across DMT, though they had both been dying to try it since their teens. It was the holy grail of exploratory consciousness, and the marriage of spirituality and consumerism found a way to take the stuff without needing an Amazonian shaman and a couple of spare weeks. DMT can be smoked to induce a fifteen-minute trip rather than the full ayahuascan odyssey, and there was a reason for that. The ayahuasca brew also contained an MAO inhibitor which stopped the brain naturally mopping the DMT back up. Fucking weird how the brain works; it's almost always about stopping the clean-up rather than introducing something new. Cocaine, for example, stops your brain soaking up dopamine instead of producing more, so in many ways, drugs were about inhibiting reaction rather than instigating action.

Terra Baba unwrapped a rather leaky-looking leaf to reveal the psychic treasure. It was orange, sticky, and reeked of mothballs, a scent which immediately filled the room. He had a couple of pipes, some ash, and a long speech prepared to bless the voyagers, though to be honest, they could have done without the speech. And with the magus finally winding down, Hermes and Athos were ceremonially presented with a pipe each. They looked at one other with a nervous glint in their eyes, rolled their fingers around their lighters, sparked them up, and put flame to pipe.

The doors of perception came flying off the hinges.

VERSION 2.0

The streetlights flashed past. And still there was silence.

Athos and Hermes had barely exchanged a word since they left Terra Baba's place. Awestruck by what they had just encountered, they jumped a cab home, as neither was in any condition to drive. Athos was about ready for the post-match analysis, but Hermes was lost in a web of neurons, concentrating with almost religious intensity on a small stain atop the window.

They arrived back at their building, hugged, made sure the other was OK to be left alone, and headed their separate ways for the night. Athos had a fitful, dreamless sleep pierced by the snapshots he'd managed to pull back from the ride. That was the thing about smoking DMT: it compresses a twelve-volume epic into a light-speed trailer. He'd managed to come back clutching a few fragments, but it had been breakneck. Processing would take a while yet.

All of a sudden, he heard an insistent knock at the door. Fumbling for his phone, he checked the time. It was 5:23 a.m.

Hermes had a wild look about him. His hair was even more vertical than usual and his nose seemed ready to drill through the wall if admittance wasn't forthcoming. Athos beckoned him in bleary-eyed, and pointed at the kitchen as if to say, "You're making fucking coffee." Hermes obliged, and minutes later, he clattered two steaming cups down on the living room table.

"To what do I owe this dubious pleasure?" chided Athos.

"OK – I wanted to wait last night until I had a better handle on it, but I think I've got an idea."

"Better fill me in then."

"You remember when we were sat in that cell after Lewisham? I was banging on about the future of the internet, and you thought I was talking out of my arse."

"Well, you were a bit. Not totally, I'll give you that, but events haven't exactly lived up to their billing."

"Anyway, for some reason I was back in that cell last night on the DMT. Don't worry, not in a bad way – in a fucking amazing way."

"Ooookay," said Athos, worried that psychological damage may have been done.

"I saw this huge network of connection – a glimpse into an idea."

Athos wasn't in the mood for teasers. Not at 5:30 a.m. "What idea?"

"A website that fundamentally changes the architecture of connection. You know that Friendster thing that just launched?"

Athos nodded.

"Extrapolate from there to a platform where all media, all news, all music, all video – every single atom of online content can be embedded into a network. Every day, you can see the best videos, the best articles, and the best art – all curated by friends and people who share your interests.

It would be like a clearing house for ideas, creativity, information – you fucking name it. And the constant stream of input would maintain perpetual motion."

"Interesting point about self-curation. So I see a couple of things online that I think are important or funny or whatever, and put them onto this network. If everyone does the same, then I have a kind of highlights reel filtered through people I trust or respect."

"It's the ultimate self-organizing system. Every single person inputs and exports information, and content on the network is naturally selected by individuals in a kind of digital Darwinism. The network itself produces no content, plays no role, has no editorial policy; it just – sorry to use the word – facilitates the tits off information sharing. And by information, I mean literally anything."

"What happens if people spam it though? You need some kind of editor."

"Well, this is it. Where did it all go wrong with the Syndicate?"

"Human nature."

Hermes looked at Athos intently and put his fingertips together.

"Exactly. So we're going to take human beings out of the equation and run the entire network on algorithms. They'll be a bitch to code, but once we've got them right, it'll be like the algorithms of nature. Then the nurture part will play out in a textbook model of a complex system as millions of individuals channel data through it. The feedback loops will self-determine what's 'good' or 'bad' content by the amount of activity each piece of data generates."

Athos was awake now. "And with millions of people around the world tweaking the parameters by either introducing more data or interacting with something already on the network – you've got a full-blown chaotic system. With no guiding hand," he trumpeted.

"YES! Bang on. And the network will store every single mouse click from every single person to build an ecosystem where algorithms learn. So each person's individuality reinforces itself and shapes the network in their own image. It's the ultimate cortex for global society. The ultimate community and the ultimate individualism."

More coffees were made, mind maps were sketched, and inspiration ricocheted around Athos's small apartment. As soon as the clock hit seven, Hermes dashed upstairs to get Chiara and fill her in. By noon, the two members of Offshore Signal who were still talking to Hermes after the Visuatron fiasco had also set up camp in Athos's front room. Which was ironic because he didn't even have a computer.

The months rolled on and prototypes were built, shot down, torn up, and rebuilt from scratch. They were on a shoestring, which made server capacity difficult to come by and meant other commitments were needed to keep everyone fed. After about five months, a glitching first draft flickered into life, but the problems were legion. Hope and frustration danced together, taking turns to lead, and almost eight months to the day since the Eureka moment, the five of them couldn't avoid the elephant in the room any longer. They needed cash.

No one wanted to go shopping round the usual VC suspects, terrified that such an idealistic vision would crumble in the face of financial reality. They insisted to one another that they didn't want some money man corrupting their anarchic model, but at the back of everyone's mind was the fear that it would be unworkable otherwise. Why would anyone invest if there was no money to be made? Silly season was over, the bubble had burst, and financiers would be a lot more circumspect. It was an intractable problem, but they didn't break stride. Chiara took out a loan that bought them another couple of months and a few more servers, but they couldn't even launch to a network of thousands as they stood, let alone millions.

And then something happened that sent everything juddering back into perspective. Hermes's phone rang at about 4 a.m. one October night, and as he answered it with a volley of swearing, he sat bolt upright in bed. It was Claire ringing from London and it wasn't a social call. Choking back the tears, she broke the news. Steve had died in a car crash.

Hermes and Athos were shell-shocked. They could see his face beside them as clear as day – kindness radiating from every smile, life flooding from every glance. Neither of them had ever met someone who was quite so completely kind, someone whose inexhaustible empathy made others want to better themselves. For Athos, Steve had been his first friend in a new life, a protector, a guide, and a fucking diamond. For Hermes, Steve was the conscience he never really had himself, a twinkling reminder of all that was good in the world.

Broke they may be, but there was no question of missing the funeral. The others understood, and Chiara admitted that she'd never seen Hermes cry before. They booked themselves return tickets, and with nowhere to stay, Athos phoned Ben Abrahams, who had turned into a bit of a property magnate, to see if they could crash at one of his flats. He didn't have anywhere empty, but was in the process of renovating a place in Swiss Cottage where they were welcome to stay if they didn't mind it being a building site.

The funeral was a strange blur of collision. Both Athos and Hermes realized that after all those years in the trenches together, they didn't know Steve's last name. It had been the most normal thing in the world – the TAZ community didn't really work like that, but now that they stood at his graveside with the priest committing Steve Nicholson to the ground, it suddenly reinforced the distance death had forced between them.

The religiosity of the funeral was weird too – Steve had been a straight-up atheist, but then his parents had lost him to the Syndicate early on, so maybe this was a way to bring their son home. His mother seemed a crumpled soul and his father was a study in normality, which felt just as alienating – they just didn't add up as Steve's parents, so maybe they hadn't known him as well as they thought. But would anyone recognize their parents in the same situation?

Funerals need to be celebrations of life rather than a solemn requiem, or we'll all go mad. And after the purgatory of the Christian burial, the old Syndicate crew went down to the nearby riverbank to toast their fallen brother. There was no Tony or Michael, of course – Tony had disappeared off-radar a few years back and Michael was teaching. No, this was the real Syndicate: Leary, Jayden, Claire, Tank, Athos, Hermes, Havoc, and Chris, and even Trade flew in from Argentina. Chris had softened over time too, and he wept openly. They skimmed stones and drank red wine, leaving old wounds to heal and concentrating on the magic they had once known together. Youth fluttered in a golden haze, snatched away but forever free as they kissed the void.

They promised to meet up more regularly and it was heartfelt. Life may have spun them down different lanes, but the love ran deep. Hermes and Athos had another few days in London, so they visited every member of the family in their new worlds, meeting their partners, in some cases their children, and in others their tally of empty bottles.

Ben had proved a cracking host – the kitchen was a pile of rubble, but there were beds in the bedrooms and everything. His sharp, cheeky verve had shades of his father, who had died himself a couple of years back, and one night, as Ben ushered out his builders with a round of backslaps, Athos ran their website idea past him to see if he might have any funding suggestions.

Ben furrowed his brow to chisel away at the problem. They could trace his thought patterns by his facial expressions, but the way he kept mouthing "no" and shaking his head every few seconds was unsettling. Suddenly his face lit up. He smiled broadly before his eyes narrowed into a wry tickle.

"I think I've got just the man."

"Brilliant!" yelled Hermes.

"Hang on," said Athos. "You sure, Ben? We need a silent investor – with emphasis on the word silent. Someone who won't have unrealistic expectations. Or any expectations at all, to be honest."

"Mmm, yeah, still think I've got it."

"Between the three of us – he may not see his money again. We're on a wing and a prayer here," added Hermes in a rare pang of self-defeating honesty.

"Yeah, I pretty much worked that out for myself, thanks," winked Ben.

"So who is it?" persisted Athos.

Ben tapped his nose in infuriating style. "You'll see. Eight tonight. Let's meet at Osterio Basilico, and I'll bring him along." Something was up. He was practically shaking with unspent mirth.

Osterio Basilico was in the Grove, which immediately set Athos's temptation sensors flaring. He still had about six dial-a-rock numbers etched into his brain, but he held fast and they nestled into a table. Eight came and went, and as a quarter ticked by, Hermes began shifting doubtfully in his seat. They needn't have worried. At twenty past, Ben opened the door with a triumphant grin and bid his companion over the threshold. There, in a shiny green Versace suit with black chintz swirls, stood the last person Athos had ever expected to see.

"Errol the King," proclaimed Ben, and the two arrivals shook helplessly with laughter.

"Jesus fucking Christ," spluttered Athos. "I don't believe it." Hermes looked suitably baffled, but kept his counsel.

"How… I mean, what… How the hell are you, Errol? God, it's been years."

"Ya bumbaclaat," boomed Errol with a massive smile plastered across his face. "The king is in the building."

Athos still wasn't totally convinced that they weren't having him on. The green suit alone was a study in slapstick. Well, it turned out that, against all odds, Errol hadn't been trying to scam them all those years ago. What they didn't know was that he'd been selling hash since the early '80s and his proximity to Kensington Market, an alternative labyrinth where Freddie Mercury once ran a stall, had ensured a roaring trade. Fast-forward to the mid-'90s, about three years after Athos saw him last, and the ten pound notes he'd been methodically saving finally hit 150 grand. He'd spread his bets, and while a couple of positions had drained to nothing, he'd struck gold with the others.

He had ridden the dot-com bubble for all it was worth, diving in and out of the market with an agility that defied his enormous frame. No one manages to save 150 grand off ten-pound hash deals unless they have an almost superhuman self-discipline, and he applied that rigor to his investments, never staying in long enough for the emperor's clothes to fray. Here he sat, roaring with glee, a master of the universe, who in his 50s had played the technological bubble like a fucking piano. And somewhere along the line, he'd swapped his tracksuit and stained white T-shirt for some seriously jazzy threads.

Nope, Athos still couldn't believe it – but there it was, and Ben was reveling in his incredulity. Hermes stepped in with the pitch as Athos did a goldfish impression and Errol got it straightaway. He offered them five hundred thousand, which was beyond their wildest expectations, and then further cemented his position as Santa by saying he would be staying in London so would only need an update every quarter.

He wanted 30 percent of the business though, and after much wrangling, they settled on twenty. Which was academic because they currently had neither a business nor a business plan – just a very unstable beta version. Errol didn't seem to mind too much though – he had connected with the concept instantly and saw its game-changing potential. This was the mind-share phase, and if they could pull off what Hermes was showing him on his laptop, then they had more than enough to dominate. They drank a round of grappa to toast and Athos hugged Errol as if to say, "Sorry I ever doubted you." Errol read the hug and held Athos by the shoulders. "S'alright... But don't fuck me now, bwoy."

They stumbled back out into the street, and Errol bid them farewell, his suit glowing in the lamplight. Ben coughed. Nothing. He coughed louder. Still nothing. So he stopped hinting and laid it out. "So, what's my cut?"

"Cut?" goggled Athos. "He's just as much my mate as yours."

"Is he fuck. I brought him in, didn't I?"

Athos suddenly had a realization. "Hang on – how come you're still in touch with him? Did you actually invest back then?"

"I certainly did," smiled Ben smugly. "All the rest of you thought it was a total blag, so I knew if I said anything, you'd grief me up. But, yeah, I chucked in two grand. And the big fella more than delivered, so here we are. What's my cut?"

Five percent it was, but on condition that Ben became their business advisor. He may not know an algorithm from an alkaline, but he was fucking sharp, and maybe they did need a wideboy. Hermes practically insisted on it – he had been very impressed by what he'd seen, and knowing full well that the rest of them had all the business acumen of a wooden plank, he saw meeting Ben as part of the same synchronicity that brought them their investor. It was meant to be. Ben promised at least some time in San Francisco over the coming months, but he also had a UK property portfolio to manage.

"Oh yeah," said Ben as they hugged goodbye. "Forgot to ask – what's it called? The website, I mean."

Athos was just about to reply that they hadn't got that far when Hermes, quick as a flash, blurted out, "The Syndicate."

"Nice," said Ben as Athos nearly fainted. "Laters then, lads – I'll be over in a few weeks."

With Ben gone, Athos rounded on Hermes. "You fucking what?"

"It literally just came to me. But think about it."

"I am thinking about it. It's a terrible idea. Jesus, the last thing we want to do is raise that fucking specter."

"Look, we both believed in the Syndicate, didn't we?"

"Yes, and I still haven't recovered from what happened to it."

"Exactly. So let's take it back. I dunno if it's Steve dying or seeing everyone again or what, but this whole vision is basically an evolution of the TAZ and the Syndicate. We owe it to ourselves. Fuck Tony, fuck Michael, fuck what happened – the idea itself was always pure. And now we have version 2.0 with algorithms protecting us from ourselves – let's give it another try."

Athos wasn't convinced. "But apart from anything, isn't it a weird name for a global network? We know it came from anarcho-syndicalism, but to a lot of people it'll sound like a crime syndicate. That worked as a double meaning when we were doing illegal gatherings, but now?"

"Mate, where's your psychological radar? People love an edge. Trust me, it'll work. And the whole thing is subversive as fuck anyway. It's got the potential to revolutionize how we interact – taking communication power away from media corporations and democratizing the living shit out of it. It's the ultimate heist."

Athos smiled and nodded. He had a point.

THE SYNDICATE – PART 2

Athos's apartment was proving woefully inadequate, and they turned to the landlord, an elderly Vietnamese gentleman called Quang, to strike a deal on a nearby basement. Signing a year's lease, they decamped into the new space and things began to accelerate. No one had stopped to think about company shares until 20 percent went to Errol, but suddenly things felt very real. A discussion needed to be had, and they decided that the only decent thing to do was a straight split. Athos, Hermes, Chiara, Friction, and Atalanta divided the remaining 75 percent and agreed that whatever pieces were given away in the future, they'd all take an equal hit.

Atalanta and Friction were the two hackers from Offshore Signal who'd kept the faith with Hermes after the Visuatron collapse and they'd been a key part of the new Syndicate's inception. Atalanta grew up in New York, and unlike the thousands who head east to seek their fortune, she'd bailed in search of adventure. A skip or two ahead of outstanding warrants, she reinvented herself in the Bay Area and floated through a hodgepodge of start-ups while designing a search engine for the net's underbelly. Having launched it, she realized that some really dark shit was going on, but before she could ask herself who the fuck she thought was going to use it, she was elbowed out by a consortium of Russian gangsters. Finding a home at Offshore Signal, she had risen to become their most dashing coder; her signature style was respected up and down the Valley and her "Don't Fuck With Me" smile became a thing of legend amongst her failed suitors.

Friction was the world's most miserable bastard. He ticked every dysfunctional box of a prickly high achiever: his lanky, pallid exterior, his OCD, his utter lack of any social grace, his diet of dried noodles, his obsession with solitude, his disdain for anyone he considered "incompetent," and his mesmerizing tic collection which ran from eyebrow to foot. All was forgiven though because he was a fucking genius, and while Atalanta hacked like a skate champion, Friction had an uncanny ability to plug his brain directly into the matrix. It was like he had a neurological interface with his hardware that precluded the mechanics of thought and execution – shit just manifested. Even he was struggling here though – there were so many variables to get right.

Chiara ditched her job in late 2003 to go full time, and she started to look ahead to the test phase. They needed a network of at least a few thousand to iron out the kinks and get a feel for how the engine ran, so she wondered whether her old professor at Stanford might be able to help. Stanford would be an ideal test bed – it was nearby, it was crammed with computer geniuses, and it had the numbers to serve as an excellent closed model. The only downside would be the reams of smart-arses who had spotted a flaw or thought they could write more elegant code.

It was a fantastic idea, scuppered only by the discovery that Stanford was totally mafia'd up. Not by your run-of-the-mill Cosa Nostra, you understand, but a tense hierarchy of students and researchers who jostled for position on pan-university rollouts. Simply having been a student there wasn't going to cut it, so they'd have to find another solution. She took an optimistic stab at Berkeley, but was knocked back with even shorter shrift. Fair enough really – why would a university help incubate an external project, especially when they have a financial stake in their own student start-ups?

They needed an alternative though, and they needed it soon. Not only was a circle of thousands needed to test the network, they also needed to start seeding the outside world. Even if they risked not testing it, which would be heavy-handed and irresponsible, how were they going to find any users? Virality relied on an initial cluster, and if they couldn't find one, their launch would be a hollow whisper.

Atalanta was as close to a star as the hacking community had, and while her offbeat sexuality played some part in that, the bottom line was respect for her prodigious talent. With a mainstream approach foundering on the campus fence, she made a few calls back east, a few calls down south, and finally a few calls down the road. The beauty of calling it The Syndicate was the implication that it was secret, underground, and a little bit naughty. With some lateral thinking, she realized this was their greatest advantage, and she pinpointed ravers, festival goers, and hackers as the perfect primary sphere. Looking at the philosophy around Burning Man and its local offshoots, it seemed the perfect synergy, and if they could tap into that, they could be onto a winner.

Cajoling friends and contacts into signing up and spreading the word, she opened direct lines of communication with party organizers, skaters, set designers, sculptors, musicians, DJs, graphic designers, painters, techno pagans, tattoo artists, dancers, circus performers, bar owners, club owners, festival forums, and hackers. Leading with a conceptual edge rather than "hey, will you help test our new business?" she single-handedly created a stir around The Syndicate – all by sticking to its roots. Had they gone down the university path, the initial cluster would have been far more conventional, but here they were, providing a community tool for the community they all hailed from.

Uptake was remarkably swift, and "Syndicate" was whispered through the scene. Atalanta had very sensibly told everyone that it was a secret and that the invitation was only for their closest friends. This promptly poured kerosene on the fire, as the one sure way to get people to talk about anything is to implore them to keep it undercover. Codes were distributed that allowed people to join the beta site, and they rapidly became gold dust. Anything as anodyne as a start-up launch would have been met with groans, and joining the site would have felt like a favor. But this had the lure of danger.

A social network is only as relevant as its prevalence in the outside world – who wants to join if no one they know is on it? But if The Syndicate didn't have the benefit of ubiquity, it did have a subculture to draw on. Now that subculture had a cutting-edge digital platform, and every single person who joined felt a sense of ownership, a "by the people, for the people" authenticity, and the exhilarating caress of secrecy. This was their thing.

It had started as a closed loop in the Bay Area, but with Atalanta helming the rollout, New York was the next to come on stream. Chicago followed, with Denver hot on its heels, and then Seattle, Los Angeles, and Houston. In each city, an established subcultural network was the artery in, and as more cities received their codes, the "entities" function of The Syndicate came into its own. People could of course create personal profiles and connect with other individuals, but bands, festivals, artists, clubs, and events could also have standalone pages that looked and behaved like personal ones. People from coast to coast were drawn into shared orbits.

Debate and, critically, banter had been incorporated into the design. The Syndicate wouldn't last five minutes if it was just a load of static pages where people airbrushed themselves. That would put it somewhere between a dating site and a total waste of time. Communities thrived on connection, on discussion, on argument, and on comedy. Open the doors to all of those and you might get somewhere. So interactive comment threads were vital, and, sure enough, new relationships were built.

A band might post a new track, and underneath a forum would coalesce. Everyone could see everyone else's comments and, before long, connection requests based on the cut of a stranger's jib were firing across the continent. Ongoing jokes would develop and groups began to form. The comment threads almost invariably proved more entertaining than the original posts and somehow it never felt as ploddingly linear as a normal web board. Shards of open-source gold spiked through the network.

It was the cross-fertilization of conversation that really gave it life. Grumpy fucker he might be, but Friction had infused the interface with a fluidity that was alchemical in effect. If you sat a user down and asked them why the Syndicate felt like a real-time community and why Friendster didn't, they wouldn't have been able to specify. That was the thing about genius design: the magic is intangible. The coding may yield some algorithmic insight, but just as the greatest science is art and the greatest mathematics is poetry, so too it is with computers. When something electric happens, there's no rationalizing it – it just instinctively, naturally is. And that's something no university can teach, no money can buy, and no company can guarantee.

As The Syndicate grew, the basement began to attract more bodies. In much the same way as a record studio fills out with concentric circles of involvement, coders, original invitees, and a patchwork of creatives somehow found their way to the nerve centre. Being based in the Tenderloin had its disadvantages, and now that they actually had something worth protecting, the founding five started to worry about being robbed.

Athos felt this was an area he had some expertise in, and he brokered a series of summit meetings with the local gang leaders. They were just on the borders of Little Saigon, which meant the S Town Dragons held the most sway. Striking a protection deal with gang boss Lo Chi, Athos intelligently decided to cover his political bases and spread the love to Carlos, Mexican chief of the Suicide Squad, and the six-foot wide Fridge, who ran the 7th Street Souljaz. Which didn't fully add up, as there wasn't a 7th Street anywhere in the hood. With bilateral agreements inked, they were still exposed to unaffiliated crews and shotgun-wielding junkies, but at least they had eyes on, and guaranteed reprisals discouraged troublemakers.

Ben came over for a visit around Easter. Errol's lawyer had proved far more exacting than Errol himself and the kind of reports being received from SF weren't meeting his standards. Ben was in a strange position: he had 5 percent of the company, but he was also Errol's middleman and felt loyalty to both camps. He had ostensibly come to help them expand, but also to make sure Errol's investment wasn't being pissed against the wall. While he recognized that tapping into the alternative scene was a great way to build early momentum, he was keenly aware that it was finite and fiendishly difficult to monetize. He also disapproved thoroughly of the Tenderloin HQ, despairing that their ghetto offices would never be taken seriously at the highest levels. Every time he pushed for a move to the heartland of Silicon Valley though, he was met with contemptuous stares. This was no ordinary start-up, and the fact that it was born in the hood and drew on subculture for its lifeblood made its identity deeply individual, finely calibrated, and a dangerous thing to fuck with.

Terra Baba had been appointed spiritual advisor to the Syndicate – an honorific for weed supplier and muse.

He levitated with excitement early on, and as he saw the organism evolve, he thanked his current deity of choice for the chance to live another revolution. He understood nothing of coding's technical intricacy, but he knew beauty when he saw it, and as the molecular structure of the ecosystem grew with every new user, he started a series of paintings that depicted the emergent multiverse. As if to nail his colors unequivocally to the mast, he orchestrated a ceremony of great pomp to declare that henceforth he would be known as Terra Byte, though the Baba would remain available for meditation lessons. No one could possibly begrudge him a share of the company as he brought such sparkle, and it was agreed that he should be given 5 percent, with even Ben admitting that he helped vibe it.

Disagreements had been limited, but they resolved to learn the structural lessons of the first, doomed Syndicate. For starters: fuck all this governance by committee shit. Yes, they would always try and reach consensus, but with five of them, a vote would be conclusive if it came to it. They didn't have time for hand-holding. Second: the open-door policy was slammed shut. It wasn't even about protecting share percentages – the chaos wrought by having a "yeah, come aboard" outlook would be fatal. And by chaos, they meant the wrong kind. Anyone who was taken on would have to be agreed on, either informally or by a short, sharp vote. They needed to bring something unique to the table and standards were high; just being shit hot wasn't enough, and being a total legend wasn't either. People had to be outstanding in their field and totally fit the groove – not because of some masturbatory sense of self image, but because at core this was a group of friends on an adventure. You didn't even have to be a particularly nice person – look at Friction. It just had to click, and there was no template for that.

With network numbers nearing the hundred thousand mark, word reached the crew that a *Wired* journalist wanted to come and spend some time with them. Opinions divided over the wisdom: some felt it would be the end of the online underground, while others felt that was precisely the point. This was a global project, not another self-referential movement. A lot had hardened since they last ran something from a basement, and while the idealism was even more ambitious, the manner in which it would be administered was pointedly different. No endless fluff and no fucking factions.

They had been expecting a twenty-something gamer type, but when the journalist arrived, he was in his forties, looked like he'd once vomited with Nirvana, and announced that Terra Byte once fucked his mother. He didn't hold a grudge though, and after that first, tense silence, he settled right in. His first investigative act was to locate the weed stash and biff up a whopper, and by the next day, it struck them how important it was that he'd come for a week instead of a couple of hours. If whatever he ended up writing was based on a quick interview, it might well have been OK, but by living the Syndicate for a week, they were sure he'd get it. Everything was thrown open for debate, from piracy to public launch to expansion plans, and they had a real rapport going. With the week up, he politely asked if he could keep visiting even after the article was published, and they were more than happy to smile an open invitation.

The article finally came out in July 2004 under the headline "Is This the World's Coolest Website?" They were ready for it and launched fully public that same morning. Everything went fucking nuts.

IGNITION

Being labeled cool almost invariably heralds the bursting of the bubble, but the concept held as numbers doubled and then doubled again. The network was building itself, and they had no control over its evolution.

There were no rules, no limitations, no incentives, no cheesy interactions from HQ – just a medium in a hall of mirrors. The content on the site was still heavily skewed to the alternative scene, which was only to be expected. *Wired* was the first major organization to commandeer a page on the site and its presence started to increase steadily as it began posting links to its own articles. Growth rates rocketed, stalled, and then started to inch up again as the rumor mill turned.

Slowly but surely, friends of friends of friends who didn't give a shit about festivals started to pile aboard, and the gradual dilution began reflecting a more rounded version of society. The amount of content was relatively limited, and so anything published by an individual's network would come up in their chronological feeds. In the first few weeks following the public launch, they still had a vague handle on how membership was diffusing – there were usually a couple of identifiable degrees of separation, but before long, they gave up trying to map the pattern. The most promising statistic was the average daily time spent, and Chiara had been watching this like a hawk, knowing that if the median wasn't rising, alarm bells should be ringing. The online cemetery was full of sites people eagerly signed up for, used twice, and then abandoned, so the amount of time existing members stayed was as vital as the proliferation of new ones.

The graphs were never steady as growth ebbed and flowed; some weeks would stay near static while others broke records. This could be explained to some degree by press articles or someone famous name-checking the Syndicate, but not entirely. It really did feel like planting a seed, watering it a little, and then watching it burst into a rainforest.

A gaping oversight surfaced early on and for a moment looked like it might sink them. How they had got this far on a project that had anything whatsoever to do with the internet and not factored in porn was a shocking lapse in realism. It wasn't long before some seriously fringe wrongness started piling up in the feeds, and Athos realized that if they didn't act quickly, they'd be analed out of existence. Hermes put up a fight, insisting that they couldn't interfere in the system, but after seeing a donkey get fucked on his own feed the next day, he came back to the table in a more conciliatory mood.

Determined that no human being should be able to censor content, he proposed a porn filter that would identify nudity or sexual acts and send back an error message to the uploader. He wasn't happy about it – it smacked of meddling, but having seen what happened to the internet at large, he realized that they'd be saturated in tits and plumbers if they didn't build an early-warning system. So Friction designed the filter, and while it wasn't foolproof to begin with, it was continually updated and grew increasingly calibrated. With porn out of the equation, that just left violence as the last visual taboo even they didn't want to break, but there was no sign of it as yet. They'd cross that bridge when they came to it, as it wasn't remotely as easy to design a filter to catch the infinite ways humans have invented to kill each other. Porn was relatively easy, and Hermes took solace in the fact that it was just a system parameter, not interference.

They took on another couple of people, as much for analysis as for tinkering, and pretty soon, they needed another fifty servers. Errol's investment was still breathing, but as they raided the piggy bank again and again, they realized it was the tip of the iceberg. They were going to need more money – maybe not right this second, but soon.

Having naively written a contact section into the site, the phone soon started ringing off the hook. They hired Atalanta's younger brother, Jody, to handle comms, and despite his most tolerant phone manner, he was on his knees within a fortnight.

A good 70 percent of the calls consisted of questions that had already been comprehensively answered on the FAQ page. Another 10 percent had problems so nonsensical that assistance was nigh on impossible. The next tranche of 5 percent were cold-calling venture capitalists, if you can even call them that – Athos would lay money half of them were scammers. A further 5 percent consisted of companies who wanted an inside advantage if they joined the site. And the last 10 percent was the motherlode: complete and utter lunacy dressed up as casual inquiry.

"Can pets have pages? Are you a government agency in disguise? Can you call the police because my friend's cat is missing? Send a photographer round to take my photo. Can I speak to Bono? Can you delete my girlfriend's profile? Your website tried to eat me. How do I check my child's messages? What's the point of this game anyway ..."

The list went on, and Friction started keeping a bloopers reel. After a while, the joke wore painfully thin, and despite wanting to maintain personal relationships, reality soon intruded and they took the number off entirely. And so the emails started flooding in. Shit – they needed more people.

Ben hadn't sat on his laurels since bringing Errol to the table, and patrolled the Valley in search of fresh investment. He saw himself as the arch realist, and while idealism was all well and good, benefactors in shiny green suits were in short supply, so at some point they'd have to swim with sharks. His role would be to find the most palatable set of gnashers, but if he just went on a tour of VC offices, he'd diminish his own position. The investors would see another begging bowl and his crew would think he was selling them out. It was a lonely place.

He knew perfectly well that they'd be a footnote without investment, but the level of knowledge he was dealing with was terrifyingly low. All five of them had at one point argued for an IPO, apparently believing that it would lead to millions of users part-owning the company. When he pointed out that a few major funds would inevitably end up owning the lot while they cashed in for pennies, the begrudging "well maybe you're right but I dunno" was intensely frustrating. He didn't tell them how to code, for fuck's sake.

Funds were dangerously low and caution needed binning. He had one major lead, but it would need to be handled just right. Raymond Armstrong was far and away the most eccentric investor in Silicon Valley. He went skydiving every morning because "running is for cunts," he drove a converted Cessna light aircraft that had been adapted for the road, he had a notorious habit of throwing his desk out of the window when piqued, and he married someone from a new country every year, describing his bedroom as "the embassy." He was so gloriously bonkers that Ben was pretty sure he could bring the others onboard. They had a horror of predators in gray suits – well, this one was wearing a silk dressing gown.

Problem was, Armstrong was famously dismissive of new projects and would only invest very rarely. He had made his fortune in microchips and providing systems to the Pentagon before falling out with them over the invasion of Iraq. This alone made him perfect: a man who put principle over profit; Ben could definitely sell this. But he was a wily fucker too and wasn't about to start singing "Imagine" anytime soon. Mercurial, feisty, probably certifiable – he was the prize catch.

Ben decided to take up skydiving as a means to get closer to him. He fucking hated heights, which was a problem, but his dedication saw him through. After a few near misses at the airfield, he brought Atalanta along with him, wondering if good old-fashioned sex might sell. She was way too confident in her own skin to take offense at playing honeytrap, and decided that if she was to be bait, she may as well have some fun. Turning up in a Lara Croft-style outfit, some steampunk goggles, a top hat, and an Eastern European accent, she pulled off in two days what Ben had been trying for three weeks. Before Armstrong knew what hit him, he was inviting her to Paris for the weekend.

Others may have faltered at this turn of events, but Atalanta wasn't others.

She cocked her top hat, raised her goggles, and said, "I'm not going to Paris with you. I'm not going to fuck you. I have the single greatest idea on the internet and I want you to back it. If you don't, you're a fool, and if you do, I'm still not going to fuck you, though I might teach you a thing or two about skydiving."

Ben almost fell over. He knew that sassy was on the menu, but even he hadn't been expecting anything that brazen. He could hardly look. There was no gray area here – it was either going to work or blow up this bridge entirely.

Raymond smiled like a child who's just been given a tank for Christmas. He nodded. And then nodded some more. Then a bit more. The nodding was getting awkward. Was he having a stroke?

"Ten a.m. My office. Tomorrow. Bring anyone who matters."

It went down better than Ben had feared. Maybe he had underestimated the steely edge that Athos and Hermes were starting to show, but they were thrilled by the news, and hugged both him and Atalanta for having played it so stylishly. Ben admitted that he'd been worried about their reaction, but Hermes laughed it away.

"Look," he said. "This isn't a drum circle. We need cash. Legit cash too. The ideals are the parameters of the network itself. That pretty much can't be fucked with. So where we get our money isn't going to keep me up at night. As long as they aren't corporate pricks who miss the point, I got no problem with it. And if nothing else, sounds like tomorrow is going to be an experience."

It certainly was. The first thing they noticed was a roped-off exclusion zone at the side of the building. Athos politely asked the lady who was walking them from the gate if they were renovating, but it turned out that Raymond's office was directly above and flying desks were a hazard. They stifled a smile and followed her up some stairs into a long corridor lined with eighteenth-century-style portraits of his wives. Do billionaires think, *Right, I've made the money, now I need a "thing"*, or do borderline personalities achieve disproportionate success per capita? The frosted glass double doors opened and the six were beckoned in.

Athos, Hermes, Ben, Chiara, Atalanta, and Friction took their places at an unexpectedly small conference table. It was more of a desk really, and they struggled to fit around it.

"The Treaty of Versailles was signed on that table," said Raymond, appearing from behind a bookshelf. "I keep it to remind me what a stupid fucking deal looks like. Comfortable? No? Excellent."

As icebreakers went, it was novel. Friction forced an unconvincing smile and started to mumble something about a PowerPoint presentation, but Raymond cut him down with an imperious hand.

"Please, spare me. I don't do boredom. Give it to me in thirty seconds."

There was a tense silence, until Athos thought, *Fuck it*, and went on instinct.

"It's a microcosm of the internet. You can use it socially, but fundamentally it's a medium. Content you see is posted by pages you choose to interact with, and the site logs every interaction to help it learn. The data collected is used to shape user interaction. It curates experience through a detailed number crunch of everything a person ever does on the site – rudimentary AI. We're nearly at a million users, we're going global, we need money to expand, and this is the opportunity of a lifetime."

Raymond nodded. "Potential," he said.

Was it a question or a statement though? The inflection gave nothing away.

"I'll give you ten million," he said. Quite the follow-up line. "If you can tell me how I ever see it again," he continued. "And don't give me that mind-share crap."

They had been prepared for this. Advertising is a weird one. Its use in public space is an egregious incursion on liberty, where walking down the street is a corporate psy-ops attack. Seriously – who sold off our field of vision?

But it was part of the deal when it came to free content and no one could reasonably argue there's anything wrong with that. If you want to watch TV and not pay a subscription, then ads are the trade-off. Equally, if you buy a subscription, you don't expect ads. Even when you have both, like in a newspaper, the ads are subsidizing the cover price. Yes, of course they all make profits, but profits would be factored in anyway. Ads turned direct financial pressure into indirect financial pressure, and you could always opt out by not taking the free content. No opting out of public space though.

"Advertising," said Hermes. "But not for another year. It's the kind of thing our core membership will see as 'selling out,' so we need to continue diversifying our demographics first. Also, we set the parameters. No neon shit. There's going to be a straight format that blends it into the site design, and if people don't like it, they can fuck off. They'll be understated, camouflaged even, but we'll fuck the integrity of the whole thing if it's blatant. And that's not us being precious – that's just good business. How many companies fell apart because they changed the feel of their product? Well, this isn't even a product – it's an interface for people's lives. Dangerous thing to fuck with."

Raymond roared with laughter. "I like you guys. You've got a deal. Judging by your projected growth – my projections, not yours – you should be at ten million users next year. If it continues growing at that rate, the advertising model has potential. The answer is yes. But make it twenty million structured over two years – ten now, ten when the advertising starts. And I want 20 percent. Don't even try to negotiate that."

They didn't. The trick of going a bit dominatrix on an alpha male had so far paid off handsomely, with Atalanta doing some preliminary whipping and Hermes applying the nipple clamps. Clearly not many people spoke to Raymond like that, but pushing it would be a mistake. They vacated his office, and began the tortuous contract process with his legal division. Raymond kept dozens of lawyers on salary, so they had no incentive to drag things out, and yet still they worked in months rather than days.

All in all, it had been a solid day at the office. And then the phone rang – Chiara's mobile to be precise. It was the *New York Times*.

THAT BRUSH OF SILK

The *Times* wanted to do an in-depth feature on the Syndicate and, in even better news, they wanted to set up a page on the site as well. There had been extensive board-level discussions about whether the "Gray Lady" should be seen anywhere near something called The Syndicate, but with circulation falling and every consultant saying they needed digital real estate, they were ready to take the plunge. And once the *Times* was on board, the rest would follow.

It was the best possible example of Athos's phrase "microcosm of the internet." Here you had the world's best-known newspaper using the Syndicate to post links for content they'd already published on their site. Which made the Syndicate a distributor.

Currently, they relied on readers going to their site and flicking through the articles. What the Syndicate gave them was a newsstand on every corner. If people followed their page, then they would see the articles the *Times* chose to post – not in some *NYT* part of cyberspace, but tucked between a new track from your favorite band and a photo of someone naked up a tree on their stag night. That was a whole new kind of distribution. And best of all, it was fucking free.

They had wondered whether businesses should be charged for using the site, but it was one of those "who decides where the line is?" issues, so they sacked it. Through all the new financial deals, with all this mainstream engagement, the fundamental principle of a self-organizing system was rock solid. They could afford to make compromises in other areas, as none of them affected the evolution of the organism itself. Getting businesses to pay would have been fatal. Everyone was equal, whether the *New York Times* or Joe Bloggs. Each had the same opportunity and each accessed it on the same terms.

Speaking of compromises, they began to accept that Tenderloin HQ had run its course. Their inner cyberpunk loved dealing with all these highfalutin organizations from a gang-defended basement in the ghetto, but they had to grow up a bit. There came a point where it wasn't edgy anymore, it was just counterproductive. If they needed geography for an edge, something was seriously wrong. They were being so subversive on such a grand scale that jeopardizing that for a primal scream was tantamount to criminal. It was like turning up to con a corporation in a pair of ripped jeans rather than a Savile Row suit. Appearances count, and if you want to pirate the establishment rather than play small-time rebel, then learn to co-opt the symbolism of power. Yes, it may corrupt you, but not if you corrupt it first.

Part of their resistance was the total lack of inspiration they found in Silicon Valley. Athos had always pictured the crucible of a techno future looking a lot more like *Blade Runner* and a lot less suburban soccer mom. For a start, there were no skyscrapers – just huge, sprawling campuses. To be fair, they were probably more effective working environments, but they felt like gated estates and created no sense of a coherent whole. You might be stopped by security if you tried entering a Wall Street skyscraper, but seeing them towering above Manhattan made them feel part of the community, whether you approved of their practices or not. Silicon Valley was a disjointed convention of Camelots, each with their own particular fiefdom.

Reluctantly, they moved their offices into a fair-sized warehouse on San Jose's Hamilton Avenue. Manicured it may be, but San Jose is an auto sprawl – one of the least attractive aspects of American town planning. San Francisco was a bit like New York and London, in that people actually walked, there was human traffic, shops and cafes wove together, and there was a direct connection to other human beings. Here, people looked at you funny if you walked, everything had a parking lot, distances were unnecessarily long, and retail bubbles from malls to three-store laybys stripped civic life to its most functional form. People loved it though – it was apple pie and picket fences dripping in technological money.

They all found small houses – bungalows really – and started to take a bit more of a salary. No one quite knew what they should be paying themselves, especially as they didn't have any turnover, just a pot of investor's money. They decided on fifty grand a year each, and while that didn't go far in San Jose – like *really* not far – it was about all they felt comfortable with. Anyway, who cared if home was a dump? They were at the office twenty hours a day. Within a month, they installed five mattresses in the warehouse for when they couldn't be fucked to go home, or cracked a few midnight whiskeys.

HQ expanded to around thirty people, not to mention an accountancy firm and a legal team on retainer. Pressure to censor had risen in line with their user base, and all manner of special-interest groups, from anti-porn to anti-blasphemy, had tried to leverage their worldview. So far, the First Amendment had proved sturdy enough, but only after a good deal of money had been wasted on defending various actions in court.

One of the first major lawsuits they had to deal with was a dispute over the name, and the plaintiff was none other than Michael Templemann, who had unbelievably trademarked "The Syndicate" – something they had signally failed to do. Athos and Hermes boiled with indignation at both the opportunism and the pomposity; the very fact that he'd filed for ownership summed up everything that had gone wrong with the original Syndicate. They didn't have much of a legal defense, so in the end, they had to pay him off – something Athos and Hermes couldn't even be in the room for.

One morning in early 2007, two gentlemen appeared unannounced at Hamilton Avenue and were shown into a conference room still dripping with fresh paint. They were from the FBI, and it was one of those "social calls" the federal government occasionally embarks on when they're feeling neighborly. The first ten minutes of coffee and cake were wrapped in euphemism, but before long they were warming to a national-security theme. After a further half hour pecking away at the perils of terrorism and the glow of patriotism, they straight up asked for a back door into the network so they could keep an eye on "troublemakers."

Clinging onto his cool, Athos replied that they would unfortunately not be able to comply, and immediately called their lawyers to reinforce the position. The Feds weren't surprised – it had been a long shot after all – but as if to mark their territory, they left a FISA warrant behind and the carousel began. The Syndicate fought it, of course, but to no avail; the warrant had been rubber-stamped, and the standard entreaties about privacy, trade secrets, damage to company trust, etc. fell on a deaf gavel.

This was very surreal territory. Their medium was being used to extract information about what someone had said. Nothing about the Bush administration or governments in general inspired the slightest confidence that the warrant stood on solid ground, but there wasn't a thing they could do about it. It was just one name, so pretending it was an isolated incident proved seductive, but the second soon followed, and then the third.

Maybe they really were saving the country from imminent attack, but it felt dangerously grubby, and it took a bottle of whiskey to wash away the shudder. But what can you say when a court order is presented and the stakes are death?

2008 arrived on a wave of hope. The cronyism of the Bush years was over, and the election of Barack Obama raised the phoenix from the ashes. For the first time in years, there was a heartfelt belief that what the United States claimed to represent might finally transcend rhetoric, stop sounding like cheap satire, and actually anchor in progress. Channeling idealism over ideology, Obama pulled off the unthinkable by managing to convince even the most skeptical liberals that hope might not be a mug's game after all.

Maybe politics could deliver, maybe we were all on the same side, maybe we really could change the world through existing institutions. His race was redemption in itself, not just for those who'd borne the yoke of oppression, but for the oppressors too – even as they railed against it.

He walked the line masterfully: post-racial on the one hand, but downright fly on the other – no Uncle Tom he. If you think a white politician is trapped between a rock and a hard place when discussing race, just try being a black politician. The crushing legacy of slavery, Jim Crow, and today's polished prejudice weighed hard, while the suspicion and perceived powerlessness of reactionary whites stood ready to raise the Confederate flag. Black kids were being gunned down in the streets; they needed their president, and their community needed his voice. But Obama was wise enough to understand the archetypal white fear of blackness unleashed. It wasn't about validating that fear – it was that nothing would heal until it had been assuaged.

He was too black for some whites, too white for some blacks, but for a huge swathe of the country, he negotiated America's fundamental fault line skillfully and with great empathy. Original sin had looked in the mirror and it didn't shatter on sight. That was more than many had expected. None of the Syndicate six ever forgot the tears that streamed down their faces as a man who might once have been a slave sang the American Dream like a gospel hymn.

The FISA warrants continued apace though. The financial system was in meltdown and he had healthcare reform to pursue, so maybe he hadn't got round to the surveillance state quite yet. Give him time.

User numbers broke twenty million and the first advertisements began appearing on the site. That very same day, an article was published in *The Wall Street Journal* that valued the company at three billion dollars. Three billion fucking dollars.

Ever wondered how being catapulted into Croesus-style wealth might feel? Well, you ain't missing much, because it doesn't feel real in the slightest. Very little changed on the ground beyond a tenfold increase in people, organizations, and companies who wanted a sit down. They still hadn't made a fucking penny and were still on a fifty-grand salary, despite paying their employees far, far more. Top whack for top people, but that was the cost of doing business. Without a dime earned though, it was a stretch to hike your own wages without feeling like a hypocrite. Every last person from coders to cleaners took the valuation with a gigantic pinch of salt. The dot-com bubble wasn't long in the rearview mirror and nothing about Hamilton Avenue felt like a billion-dollar operation.

The modern economic system is a synthesis of physical and abstract. Goods are manufactured, commodities are consumed, land is farmed, products are purchased – all these represent the physical economy. Then you have the semi-abstract economy, which is comprised largely of the service sector – companies whose activities provide value to their customers, but no actual physical exchange of "things" takes place. So far, so good. But then you have the fully abstract economy, which oscillates between the heights of human ingenuity and the depths of human folly. New commodities were spun from thin air as parasitic financial instruments grafted phantom layers of profit onto physical transactions.

Take mortgages: there's a loan and a property. Fine. But then the loan is repackaged, bundled in with other loans, and sold on multiple times. Each transaction abstracts the package further from the initial exchange, and after a few iterations, it becomes a spectral chip in a global casino.

Now factor in credit default swaps. A lender can take out insurance against a debtor defaulting on their loan. Sensible. But so can anyone else. In fact, ten different people can take out insurance on the same loan, even though nine of them didn't actually lend any money. So if the loan does default, the payout is ten times the size of the fucking loan because all ten policyholders get paid. Go capitalism.

This is the kind of abject fuckery that alienates Main Street and erodes faith in elites. A six-year-old could spot the holes, and throwing tax dollars at the resulting landslide is no way to nurture the social contract.

Their valuation felt the same. Yes, they had a market share that showed little sign of slowing. But they had a total revenue of zero, with a baggy business model based solely on advertising. Tens of millions maybe – but three fucking billion? They couldn't take it seriously.

Just as well too, because there was a spanner in the advertising works. Their new "business department" had been studying the uptake and, well, it was laughably low. After a month of intensive analysis and endlessly rerun computer simulations, they arrived at the bleeding obvious. Why the fuck would anyone pay to look like an advert when they could look like a post?

It wasn't quite as schoolboy an oversight as it sounds. Posts by businesses would only be seen by the converted in their network. The hope was that companies would advertise beyond that to try to reach new people. It made sense on paper, but in practice, not so much, and the income stream was paltry. There was another problem too.

Critical mass had mutated to bite them in the ass. There was now so much content being rammed through the network that the average person was drowning in data.

Hermes urged calm. This had been the whole fucking point. At some point, the algorithms were always going to start filtering content. All those servers bulging with stored behavior that could be used to sculpt the system in earnest. If someone's content elicited your engagement, you'd see more of their posts. If you ignored it a few times in a row, you'd see less of it. Democracy, plain and simple.

It saved you the trouble of actually voting too – how fucking efficient is that? A skeptic might have enquired how the collection of this much data was any different from a FISA warrant, but such churlish cynicism was waved away. The government was using it for opaque means. The Syndicate was using it to help people be themselves. The combination of data collection and algorithms meant that the site kept learning and responding in real time. Every single node on the network was different, personalized by the person looking in. It was the ultimate symbiosis of individuality and community.

So the feeds stopped showing everything and cherry-picked based on behavior patterns. The timing was unfortunate though, coming around the same time as they launched the advertising business. Companies were outraged at the loss of visibility, claiming the algorithms were rigged to strong-arm them into paid advertising. That genuinely hadn't been the case, though few believed Ben when he tried to smooth ruffled feathers.

What they failed to accept was that the playing field was still level; only the rules had changed. If you smear out mindless corporate drivel, people stop seeing your shit. If you find creative ways to be relevant, then you'll be democratically rewarded by visibility. The algorithms actively encouraged better content without any kind of centralized control. If that isn't progressive evolution hardwired in, then what the fuck is?

Success bred complaint: it's like an addiction, blah blah blah. Was it fuck – this wasn't some imaginary simulation, this was as interesting or as boring as you and the people you knew made it. There were no avatars here; this was basically a global pub with all your mates sat round a massive table and all your favorite interests popping over for a chat. People said it stopped them living real life, but what was "real life"? A much smaller spectrum of geographically close friends?

If there was one trend that bore scrutiny, it was the growing addiction to documenting rather than experiencing events.

The smartphone was on the rise and suddenly everyone was a photographer. The Syndicate had a mobile version of course, but looking around concerts, lighters in the air had morphed into phones, and an awful lot of people prioritized photographing the band over losing themselves in the music. Athos in particular worried about this, possibly because he was the most computer illiterate of the crew and so didn't see every technological advance as necessarily "good."

But one night at a Jay Z concert, he had a disconcerting sense of déjà vu. All those phones in the air – thousands living life through an LCD filter… It had shades of a ketamine dancefloor – a sea of individual bubbles rather than a union of visceral experience. The comparison might be a stretch, but it was there nonetheless. But technological evolution is necessarily disruptive – all these add-ons to consciousness would settle in time.

UNDERGROUND OVERGROUND

"'Hey, how are ya?"

"Pleasure to meet you, Mr. President," beamed Athos. And d'you know what? It was.

The West Wing was hosting the tech sector's brightest sparks, and invites had been extended to the Syndicate. It was one of those milestones where you check yourself and think, *how the fuck did I end up here?* Obama had a languid charm, and while Atalanta had prepared extensive admonishments about the uptick in FISA warrants and the growth of the surveillance state, somehow it never cropped up in conversation.

The guy was a fucking dude: unashamedly cerebral with a playful smile and some serious flavor. Laughing together with the man himself made the whole question of state intrusion feel like it was playing out in a different dimension. Who, *this* guy? But he's one of us ... And there it was again: that primal tension between individual and institution that Athos had felt outside the headmaster's office at Eton.

What they saw in Obama bore no relation to the activities of government agencies, and while his magnetic personality spoke their language, the same could be said of a personable oil exec. He may be a hoot with plans for green investment, but his organization was plundering the planet's resources and converting them to greenhouse gasses. It added up, but then it really didn't. Such is the paradox.

The bigger they got, the more problems they battled. They were so consumed by detail that they never stopped to think just how surreal the scale was. The Chinese had banned The Syndicate altogether after being refused data on Chinese citizens, and it dawned on them that they were trying to apply their economic model to the internet. State capitalism was the "pro-cake and pro-eating it" version of a market economy – taking a share of the capitalist bounty while amputating the liberalism that came holding its hand.

It was working too – somehow a communist bureaucracy was managing an economy that looked pretty damn capitalist. Could they do the same with the internet? Could you reap all connectivity's benefits while maintaining an iron grip on its intrinsic liberty? They were giving it a bloody good go, employing tens of thousands of monitors, and while closing down online dissent may seem like the most doomed game of Whac-a-Mole ever, they actually seemed to be keeping up.

So much for Hermes's jail theory about exponential growth defying control. Turned out Moore's Law could be mirrored way beyond transistor counts.

They all needed a holiday, but it was like trying to escape existence itself. Neither treehouse nor mountaintop was far enough away, and if Athos spent more than a few hours without Wi-Fi, the panic attacks would inevitably begin. Maybe the Syndicate was addictive after all?

The thing about a global highlights reel is that an embarrassment of riches rapidly transforms into an expectation of excellence.

Not long ago, we were lucky to see one amazing thing a day. Consequently, we really gave it our attention: listening to albums, staring at paintings, marveling at nature. Rarity enhanced deeper experience as we lived for a leisurely while with our fascination. But as feeds filled with myriad moments of wonder, processing each one became inexorably quicker. The question we had to ask ourselves was whether we were experiencing excellence or just recognizing it. The problem with a highlights reel is that you miss the atmosphere, the detail, the hot dog, the smell of the stadium. Were our brains turning into expert processors? Were computers shaping us as much as we shaped them?

Athos brought this up with Hermes as they walked through the streets of the Mission after a pilgrimage to Terra Byte's place. He wasn't blind to it, but he was defensive nonetheless. For him, all that might be true, but evolutionary consciousness was exponential. The more information our brains processed, the more they had to evolve new pathways. This was a shift, for sure, but humans have always clung to the past, even as they chart the future. Time didn't stand still, and it wasn't at all clear that human society could either. We run on algorithms too.

Athos was preparing his counterargument when he heard a fleeting refrain that exhumed the most buried of memories. It was music and it was coming from a basement. As they approached, the sound sharpened, and Athos realized it was the old acid-house tune – that melancholic slice of analogue soul: Annette's "Dream 17."

Gobsmacked that someone was playing it, he scrambled down the stairs, with Hermes in hot pursuit. It looked like a private party, so, mindful of gate-crashing etiquette, they stopped and smiled weakly. A red-headed girl in a black leather jacket waved them over impishly.

"Hey, guys, come on in. Is this your first time?"

Athos shot Hermes a cautious glance and turned his attention back to La Rouge. "First time doing what?" he asked uncertainly.

"First time at a TAZ," she laughed. "Welcome aboard, newbies."

Hermes was about to start spluttering, but Athos touched his arm.

"Yeah," said Athos. "But we've heard of it."

They stepped inside an ultraviolet chamber. Fluro paint spiraled across the walls, and their eyes adjusted to the amethyst light. Several hundred people were jacking to an up-tempo groove, and the atmosphere fizzed with energy. Drinks were swung overhead, couples locked in sinuous sensuality, laughter roared through the juking snares, and symphonic chatter bounced joyously off the walls. Uncertain of what to do with themselves, Hermes and Athos spotted a bar on the far side and, edging through the melee, they ordered a couple of beers. They grinned at each other in disbelief and clinked bottles. A TAZ. Here. In San Francisco. Now.

There was no sign of any ketamine, any committees, or Tony – so maybe these guys had a shot. It was quite the characterfest too – scanning the room, they could see VR headsets, people dressed as stuffed animals, a biker having his beard braided, a collection of lost-looking Tibetan monks, crews of bangers, break-dancers, MCs, gamers, and a couple of CEOs they knew from the conference circuit. Athos toyed with hitting the dancefloor, but he couldn't stop rifling the ramifications long enough to find a rhythm.

It would be an exaggeration to say he felt he was home, but there'd be a kernel of truth to it. Syndicate.com had been a giant intellectual exercise, but this was a return to feeling, to a rowdy hedonism and the casual misplacing of ego, if only for a moment. The word "ego" has come unstuck from its original definition, but as a vehicle for the rational mind, it had been at the forefront of Athos's recent reality. The TAZ had always been where euphoria melted rationalism.

"Molly?" said a bare-chested dude beside him with a huge snake tattooed on his breast.

"Er, no. Athos. Sorry, man."

Jake the Snake gave him a quizzical look, wondering if this was an attempt at humor. The blazer and chinos Athos was still doggedly sporting gave him further pause. Deciding cops didn't have English accents, he elaborated.

'Nah, man. I mean Molly. Like X – you know: MDMA?"

The fog lifted and Athos broke into a fiendish smile. "Oh fuck, yeah!"

It took about twenty minutes to kick in, and while it wasn't the strongest pill he'd ever taken, it was one of the cleanest. He introduced Jake to Hermes, who swiftly followed suit, and they raised their beers aloft once more. The music swung out of acid house into sizzling funk and then thumping tribal techno. Oh yes, oh yes. The dancefloor pulsed and Athos found himself hugging Jake tight until a passing cloud of pheromones whisked him away. Mainlining chemistry, he scanned the swarm for the source. The red-headed girl from the door was a few bodies away, and, catching her elfin glance, their eyes spoke a sensory yes. Athos's body tingled, and before he knew it, they were locked in a serpentine kiss. Then, without so much as a goodbye, she snatched herself away, smiled impudently, pressed her number into Athos's hand, and vanished into the crowd.

Determined to save the number before the night headed south, he pulled out his phone.

"Jesus, is that a Syndicate app?" said a total stranger who had materialized beside him.

Athos turned his head briefly and nodded in an "I'm not feeling chatty" kind of way, hoping his intrusive new companion would fuck off.

"Dude, you need to get rid of that."

"Eh?" grunted Athos.

"They're fucking evil, man," the guy continued.

Intrigued, Athos swiveled to face his new focus group. "What do you mean, evil?"

"I mean evil, dude. Like, as in heinous."

"Yeah, I got that. I'm just wondering why."

"It's a front for the CIA, man."

Athos sighed. They did have a Tony.

"How's that then? I always thought it was pretty cool."

"That's what they want you to think. I know for a fact that behind the facade, it's really a massive data-mining operation. They record everything, like literally everything about you – it's the biggest spy network in the world."

Athos goggled. He was reasonably sure they hadn't become a CIA front, but how on earth did this guy know about their data collection? It was top secret, protected like kryptonite, and the only hint of its existence was a prosaic line buried in their stultifying terms of service. There was no way he could possibly know unless someone from the company had told him.

"What makes you say that?" he probed.

"We've been in their system."

"We?"

"Yeah, found a back door. You should see the shit they've got stored. It's fucking dark, man. I'm Brian, by the way."

Someone in the security department was going to get a stern talking to in the morning. Athos decided that the only responsible thing to do was hang out, cultivate this guy, and pump him for information, though subtly and with plenty of lube. Which, ironically enough, was what he was being accused of anyway.

Brian turned out not to be a Tony at all, and once Athos managed to get past the CIA thing, he found himself really warming to him. Hermes came over a few minutes later, and the three of them had one of those full-spectrum cosmic chats that reminded them of the TAZ heyday.

They covered everything from healthcare to quantum gravity, and the saner Brian sounded, the more seriously

Athos took his comments on the Syndicate. It wasn't so much that they were casually drinking with someone who'd hacked them, but that they'd always imagined people like Brian to be in their corner. As time went on, Athos decided that he could justify floating a "hypothetical" version of why the data was really stored.

Brian shook his head. "Nah, man. Shit, even if that is it and I never got far enough to know for sure, it's still dangerous. Information is power, and power fucking corrupts. No company should have that much data. I've just started working on a project that puts secrets back in public hands. Information needs democratizing and governments need to know someone's watching them. We've got a built-in system to protect ourselves from self-corrupting– we just publish everything. Blind justice, man – put it out there and let people decide."

"What's it called? We'll check it out."

"Wikileaks."

THE CONTENT
PARADOX

"It's not fucking working. I don't care why it's not working. It's not fucking working. Fucking fix it. Fucking get a new plan. Fuck you, fuck your mothers, fuck your grandmothers, and fuck your fucking cousins."

There was a deafening crash. The six of them stared at the desk-shaped hole in the window.

"I haven't got a cousin," piped up Friction like a fentanyl Eeyore.

"Your whole family stopped fucking when they saw what a fucking abortion you were. I will fucking destroy you all if you don't fucking fix it. Now fuck off."

They shuffled out of the headmaster's office wondering how the hell six people on power lists had proved so powerless. Raymond took "activist investor" to a whole new level, and they had no doubt that blowback would be ugly if they didn't pivot.

The advertising model was a bust. Put simply, no one clicked on ads anymore. The brain had evolved a defense mechanism that filtered them out, and if the natural screening process didn't work, there was ad-blocking software everywhere.

People hated advertising, even when it was discreet. The prevailing consensus saw it as a malevolent cancer that only morons fell for – an impulse only aggravated by endless spam. Barely anyone made the connection between the free content they were receiving, the free services they were exploiting, and the ads that appeared alongside. And the problem was way, way bigger than the Syndicate alone.

The organic nature of the early internet precluded the parallel development of a business model. So much focus had been devoted to avoiding materialism's pitfalls that monetization fell somewhere between oversight and heresy. This was an open-source revolution, a cybernetic world of perfect Platonic form.

Viable online businesses tended to involve the exchange of goods and services. Retail architecture had been ingeniously reimagined, but the premise was as old as the hills. The notion of content was new though – especially content as free-floating particles. Traditionally, content came as part of a precommodified package and existed solely within that framework. This film came on this video tape. That album came on that record. All those "content carriers" made sense as economic units.

That idea of content embedded into a "product" was fading. It had gone from being a nucleon to an electron in volatile orbit. Films were now astral. So was music. So was photography. All of them existed in a virtual space that felt more like a communal encyclopedia than an "item." A shared human database.

In the process, content grew increasingly divorced from economic value. Maybe it was the mind-share rush, maybe everyone was breathless with idealism, maybe technological progress outstripped economic development, or maybe it was just the psychology of abstraction.

All those newspaper sites who posted free content were starting to struggle. Napster may have been nixed, but the perception of music's economic value would never be the same again. Torrent sites were everywhere, films were bulldozed through, series wolfed in a voracious gulp, and paying for any of it seemed absurd. But films, TV, and music had fallen victim to the law of unintended consequences. Across the hall, information sites, media sites, service sites – all these sectors opened the bidding at zero from the very start. Now they were frantically bailing water and their infrastructure was cracking.

Perhaps they all bought into the delusion that content was like a free vial of crack. If you could just get people hooked, they'd start paying for it. Maybe they believed advertising was the great white hope. Maybe both. The problem is that once you've set the bar at nothing, it's near impossible to raise it without a monopoly. And it was fiendishly difficult to maintain a monopoly online; Google may have managed it, but most companies still sacrificed profit to stay competitive in a lean, predatory jungle.

Behavioral patterns changed. Newspapers used to be tribal touchstones that could count on loyalty. That translated online to a degree, but with physical circulation plummeting, the surveys pointed to an alarming trend. When asked if they would pay a subscription fee, a disturbing number of people answered that they'd just get their news someplace else.

Cycles tend to self-reinforce. As newspapers fell into financial difficulty, they started wave after wave of layoffs. Those that didn't go to the wall downsized dramatically, and while losing a few correspondents to an AP byline may not seem like a massive deal, the cumulative effect was deadly. With reliance on the news wires growing, different papers started publishing the same Reuters story and output grew more generic. Just as newspapers needed individuality most, they started to read like everyone else. And that perpetuated the notion that you could get your news anywhere as it was all the same anyway.

The spiral deepened. With new players like Buzzfeed in the game, newspapers worried that they weren't relevant enough and took the fateful decision to get down with the kids. First, their overall tenor got more gossipy and then it turned derivative. Celebrity news, novelty surveys, memes, top-fifty lists – you name it. Once-hallowed institutions were sounding like teenagers, which was no surprise as they were hiring interns to find them "quirky" content. Instead of individuality, homogeneity ruled supreme, and news dumbed down well past the point of self-respect.

There were exceptions, there were fightbacks, there were bastions of quality. But the cannibalistic trend continued. Way too many eggs had broken in advertising's basket, and paywalls were only realistic for a very select few. The ones who'd clung on to their standards had a chance. The ones who shredded their identity trying to stay afloat were doomed. The free model had ended up diminishing the standard of content and taking those held accountable by local journalism off the hook. What a fucking surprise.

The Syndicate was staring down the barrel at the same infuriating dilemma as everyone else. People didn't want to pay. But they didn't want ads either. That gloriously anarchic vortex of hope, idealism, and liberty had created a whole generation of spoilt children. It was the fucking donations bucket all over again.

Athos and Hermes couldn't believe that it had come to this. From abandoned London warehouses to a billion-dollar global company, they were still wrestling with the same problem. Athos quipped that it was enough to turn you conservative. At least you knew where you stood.

"So what the fuck do we do?" Atalanta rapped on the desk.

"Monthly fee," said Friction. "It's the only way to keep our identity. Otherwise we'll end up with sponsors and shit."

"Can you imagine the clusterfuck if we announced a subscription fee?" asked Athos. "Petitions, chest beating, the whole nine yards. Even if we got through the howling, we'd lose millions of people."

"And what's the point of a network if it's not growing?" remarked Atalanta.

"Careful, you sound like a banker. Growth isn't everything, you know. Quality, not quantity," replied Hermes.

"Yeah, but in the real world, people will migrate to another network. We stand and fall on being the biggest. The second we're not, someone else will be. And you may as well start measuring the coffin if that happens." Ben was speaking some hard-nosed truth.

Hermes groaned. "I swear I didn't sign up for this shit. Listen to us, we're protecting market share like a fucking corporation."

"I don't know if you've noticed," said Friction drily, "but we are a corporation. So we should probably grow up and stop using it as a pejorative. The question is, what kind of corporation do we want to be?"

"I'm not OK with just being dominant for its own sake."

"None of us are, so spare me the moral outrage. These are real-world choices. We're playing idealism at the highest level, and it's shades of gray up here. If you want black and white, then go become an activist," hissed Atalanta.

"She's right," said Athos. "OK, so subscription won't work. More obvious ads then?"

"I guess so. OK, we change the format of our ads," replied Hermes, brightening from black to charcoal. "Take them off the sidebar and stick them in the feed. People will complain, but fuck 'em. Or we could introduce a subscription option to not have any at all."

"Won't work," said Ben. "It's one or the other. Having two versions is messy. You got Twitter coming up now too; there's market share to worry about."

"But Twitter's an ADHD tagline machine."

"Fucking attention spans."

This was another unexpected side effect. People weren't just processing things faster, they were processing them piecemeal. Average video watch times were well under thirty seconds, and an image of a complex painting would command ten seconds at best. The brain was a quick study, and after a few years dealing in highlights, it had begun generating its own York Notes.

Humans had become so adept at processing data and so impatient for the next hit that the brain started making shorthand assumptions. A synopsis of the salient points was created by analyzing key parameters. Watch the first ten seconds of a three-minute video. Then skip to the middle, then skip to the end. *Et voilà*. Got it.

Twitter wasn't the cause, merely a symptom. And while pithy punch lines might work in 140 characters, fully formed thoughts certainly didn't. Were we turning our whole fucking reality into a highlights reel? Were the dopamine hits of the quickening the most pernicious addiction of all?

"ATHOS!"

He'd been lost in a reverie. "Yes, let's try it."

"OK, ads in the feed – we'll work up an acceptable ratio and give it a go."

They nodded their assent through gritted teeth.

THERMONUCLEAR

Athos stared at the vast cavern of servers. It had a Death Star feel to it: all minimalist blacks and insistent LEDs – the apotheosis of the machine age. A titanic archive of personality, identity, and memory buried in the most impersonal landscape imaginable. It was an extraordinary human achievement – the capture and digitization of essence – and yet there was a silent tension between the emotions they held and the cold circuits they were suspended in.

He was, on paper, not far off being a billionaire, and there was an unexpected undertone of shame. It didn't sit right with him somehow; there was nothing he could directly identify as the dissonance, but there was a strange emptiness, as if he could be revealed naked at any second. They were all paying themselves more these days too, the clutch of "keeping it real" loosened by reality itself. At least he had love in his life – maybe he should focus on not fucking that up and stop indulging his inner neurotic.

He had found solace in the San Francisco TAZs – nothing participatory but an anonymous emancipation. It was part *recherche du temps perdu*, part decompression, and part Trinity, the vivacious redhead he'd so intensely connected with. They had played casually for a couple of months before Athos realized he'd never had a solid relationship in his life and piled pressure on himself to make this one work. It proved cathartic, warm, and gorgeously intimate, so on their six-month anniversary, he invited her to move in. His living arrangements had upgraded too; he now called a huge white villa home, and while it bristled with rooms he never set foot in, he managed to eke out a few cosy corners. Or his interior decorator did anyway. He had a household staff now as well, something that had taken a while to adjust to, but it became pretty addictive, and now he barely noticed when his maids padded the marble corridors.

They had all fluctuated in slightly different directions, freed up by the ever-growing team at Syndicate HQ. A management layer had been drafted in for the day-to-day running, and while the founding five and Ben remained heavily involved, it was very much on their own terms.

Hermes had started a foundation that funded research into Artificial Intelligence. Having grown increasingly messianic about enlightened machines and traveling extensively to preach the gospel, he took to one of those earpiece microphone things like a duck to water. TED talks, Davos – you name it, Hermes was there to fly the futurist flag. He and Chiara had split up in mid-2010, though after some initial bloodletting, a tentative peace was brokered and the ceasefire proved solid enough. The Syndicate was the joker in every decision, the shadow behind every emotion, and none of them green-lit a vendetta without factoring in the dynamics. Hermes had a string of model girlfriends now and spent many a weekend in Los Angeles smoking glamour and popping paparazzi before crawling out of the clubs at dawn. It was measured hedonism, a salty taste for celebrity, and a few white lines of self-indulgence. No stress – he'd fucking earned it.

Ben had finally been made an equal partner. The delay had been an oversight more than anything– they'd have given him the share after he hooked Raymond, but he was too shy to ask, and they forgot to offer, almost thinking he already was. He'd settled in Palo Alto, and his property portfolio back in the UK was a very different-looking proposition now, brimming with stately mansions and grand townhouses. Raymond too had found love, or at least what he convinced himself was love. His current amour was a six-foot Ukrainian bombshell called Tatiana, and while no one begrudged him his happiness, they did wonder what their pillow talk consisted of. Somewhere between "Do you want to fuck?" and "Can you extend the limit on my credit card?" they imagined, but despite avoiding the conversationally challenged Tatiana, they wished him well. And advised him to get a pre-nup.

Chiara plunged into a depression after the break-up with Hermes. Despite having been a founding member of the team, she worried she'd be isolated and slowly squeezed out. No one could fuck with her partnership deal, but after so long inside the bubble, she succumbed to a wave of insecurity. Was she there in her own right or because of her relationship with Hermes? It was entirely self-induced – the others loved her warmth and wisdom, and the fact that she wasn't Hermes, but it took her nearly a year to accept that, and a jagged few months it had proved. Finally, after using the gym as a proxy for self-esteem, she settled down and Atalanta introduced her to one of the key players at Burning Man. With a new beau in the mix and Black Rock City as her summer home, her natural joie de vivre resurfaced.

Friction had surprised them all. He had cheered up. Not by much, but it was noticeable to the edge of concern. His friends wondered if he'd been at the happy pills or become a Scientologist, but the truth, when it finally outed, took them all by surprise. He'd stumbled out of the closet and into a torrid affair with a Salvadorian guy called Javier. When he announced it at a partners' meeting, he'd been somewhat miffed by the fact that they all burst out laughing, but before he could take umbrage, he was swept up in a congratulatory hug. The comedy was mostly rooted in the fact that any self-respecting gay man had actually agreed to date this unkempt bundle of cynicism and dried noodles. As gaydar went, Friction was on the "*Error – Asexuality detected*" end of the spectrum, but Javier had awoken something in him: maybe liberation, maybe love, maybe gymnastic sex – but whatever he and his flex had managed to pull off, the new Friction was a hit.

Atalanta's love life had started to resemble that of Elizabeth I, albeit with a few well-vetted fuck buddies at court. Every power player in America wanted to fuck her, date her, or marry her, and her synthesis of Tank Girl, badass genius, wealth, and signature steampunk made the titans drool. It had gotten to the point where she was described in those terms – a strange sexism where people wouldn't just accept her as Atalanta, they had to describe her through analogy. It was an indirect denial of her individuality, as if such a vibrant woman could only be explained by a flotsam of pop-culture references. They meant well for the most part, but such is the post-feminist reality. So with every master of the universe on her case, she refused them all, knowing they prized her as the ultimate trophy. She held out for the right guy, but with no sign of him, she kept her relationships casual and low profile. The net result was to make her even more desirable, and when she started getting marriage proposals from weird Indonesian billionaires, she doubled her security team. Which didn't do much for her chances of meeting Mr. Right.

Alas, the clouds were gathering. The self-organizing system had weathered every storm. But this …

In the spring of 2010, the *Washington Post* published a major exposé of bullying, harassment, hate speech, homophobia, sexism, and racism on the Syndicate – the whole gamut of human indecency. It was fucking good journalism, annoyingly enough, and as Athos read the harrowing personal accounts, he wept with shame. A shame tinged with panic.

There had been several suicides, people who'd tried blocking their stalkers but found themselves cornered. There was actually a page called "Lynch A Local Nigger," and another that advocated sodomy by sharpened foreign objects. Women seeking abortions had been bombarded with bible verses, teenage girls jeered at for their weight until they slit their wrists, and mass beatings posted on the site to rapturous applause. Wherefore art thou self-organizing system?

The floodgates burst. The day after the *Post* published, hundreds of victims plucked up the courage to speak out. Oprah ran a special on it, Fox News seized on it to savage a liberal bastion, the major networks ran hot with macabre flagellation, and the president himself asked Congress to look into legislation. Capitol Hill frothed with moral outrage, but behind all the headlines, the falling valuations, the hysteria, the lectures, and the frantic calls from Raymond, the six of them were profoundly damaged by their wayward brainchild.

The Syndicate was of course a morally neutral medium and so couldn't take full responsibility. But at the same time, it had acted as a catalyst without offering iron-clad protections, and that needed addressing. Neo-Nazi groups and rope-toting good ol' boys may have murdered a black man anyway, but having a page on the Syndicate pumped petrol onto the burning cross.

It offered legitimacy. Here was a page about lynching that looked like the White House's page. Or a church group page. Or the LA Lakers's page. Existence within the same visual framework had been designed as a leveler, but it leveled moral perception too. If the lynching page was so bad, it would have been banned, and by boasting fifty thousand connections, it looked accredited by both popular acclaim and the site itself.

It got worse. Taking the lynching page as their primary case study, they discovered the micro-community had actively egged itself on. People posted pictures of "the nigger I just schooled," and comment threads cheered them to the rafters. So it wasn't just "freedom of speech"; this was having real-world consequences: breaking families, torturing young men, and rigging up a global noose. How the fuck had they ended up empowering racists?

As the six frantically brainstormed, the pressure snowballed. The White House Chief of Staff called to "express the president's confidence that an urgent resolution would be found," while charities, the ACLU, the NAACP, lobbyists, journalists, politicians, mayors, and grieving mothers filled the airwaves with opprobrium.

"Face it," said Ben. "We're all sitting here pretending we don't know how to fix it, but we fucking do. Let's just get it done already."

Hermes shook his head in absolute disbelief. "I just don't get it."

"Yes, you do," replied Ben. "Yes, you do."

Athos added his voice. "I suppose the Syndicate is now so big that it's stopped being a community of like-minded people and become a straight-up reflection of society."

"And also, we staked way too much on decent people shutting the bigots down," added Atalanta. "That works on a general page – like, if someone puts a racist comment on a CNN thread, they get ripped by other commenters. What we forgot to factor in were like-minded communities where everyone thinks the same. Who polices that? A nonracist wouldn't even know that lynching page exists."

"I hate to point out the fucking obvious," sighed Friction. "But you guys both just used the phrase 'like-minded' to describe two totally different scenarios. That's the problem right there."

"Exactly," said Chiara. "The original Syndicate community was on the same wavelength. They all thought one way about stuff like this, and that seemed normal to us because we do too. But a bunch of bible-bashing homophobes also all think alike, and they have their own self-policing system."

"Yeah," said Athos. "If you started posting pro-gay stuff on their pages, they'd self-police that quick enough. So the self-organizing system is working – just not in the way we hoped."

"I honestly thought we'd get some kind of equilibrium. That the good would balance out the bad. That people would look after the person next to them," mourned Hermes.

"And in a lot of cases they do," reflected Athos. "But there's so many sub-communities that this isn't one big forum anymore. It's got millions of subdivisions. Some are nasty as fuck, and so far removed from anyone who might challenge them that they reinforce their own worst elements. That's the fucking feedback loop. That *is* chaos theory."

"How could we have been so blind? And what do we do?" asked Hermes.

"We bring in human editors," replied Ben. "It really is that simple."

"But how the fuck is that going to work? The whole concept falls apart if humans have any control over the network equations."

"Newsflash. The whole concept is already falling apart."

"Look, Hermes. Just think of it this way. We'll personally interview them all, make sure they're good people. It will all be taken on a case-by-case basis, and we'll draw up really tight guidelines for what should be banned or removed. If there's a gray area, they can refer it to one of us."

"Banned," said Hermes. "Banned. Now we're the fucking police."

Athos cast his mind back to Lewisham and the fundamental question: which came first, crime or law? Looks like they had an answer.

Hermes held out, arguing that all the shit they were seeing was the legacy of law. Lynching was a legacy of slavery, homophobia a legacy of religion. You couldn't separate out what was happening from its historical context. It was academic though. This was the real world, not some philosophical debate. People were dying.

A round of hiring commenced and an editorial team was installed. They were building a new campus further out of town, but it wasn't ready yet, so things got very claustrophobic at Hamilton Avenue. No one had been expecting a sudden influx. On the plus side, it allowed the six of them to monitor the monitors and make sure personal prejudices weren't leaching onto the network. Judging bias through a subjective lens. God, what a fucking mess.

EVOLUTION

Things stabilized. Despite the damning coverage and the horror stories stacking up, the vast majority of people weren't directly affected. So they shook their heads at the watercooler, despaired of humanity in the broadest terms, and carried on exactly as before. Community, it seemed, was relative.

2010 was a turbulent year. Wikileaks released their most high-profile cache of classified documents, throwing Western governments into a paroxysm of rage. The jury was very much out over their methods, which drew on aspects of the Syndicate's philosophy: release the forces of chaos and let them settle where they may. Information was a public right and secrecy an inherently corrupting force. The documents they published did nothing to contradict this position, demonstrating a litany of cock-ups, shoddy conspiracies, and the use of "national security" as a fig leaf. It was a gamble though. The documents hadn't been screened, and while that was a familiar concept to the Syndicate, they kept their counsel.

Meanwhile, autocracies were falling like dominoes. The Arab Spring erupted across North Africa and the Middle East. Tunisia, Egypt, Libya, Yemen, Syria, and Bahrain all tumbled, and as news escaped the net, it became clear that the Syndicate had proved instrumental both to the formation of the protests and their reporting. Operating in real time and encouraging the spontaneous growth of localized as well as international networks, it was the perfect medium for mass mobilization. Meeting points were set, groups sprang up, videos of police brutality were shared, and the uncontrollable wave of information caught authorities fatally on the hop.

The templates for authoritarian control were cumbersome, dated, and utterly unable to cope with connectivity. The vast majority of Arab leaders were of the old school. They'd come up in the '60s and '70s, where a few simple rules applied. Control the army, control the press, purge your enemies, enlist a huge spying network to disappear anyone who whiffed of activism, and send in the troops if all else failed. It had served them remarkably well, but by 2010 it was a typewriter tactic in an iPhone war. Bloated by power and insulated from critical thinking, the Arab autocracies were blindsided by the surge of organization.

On the ropes and reeling, they fell back on the one surefire remedy that had never failed them: violence. It was the biggest mistake they would make.

When leader after leader sent in the thugs to beat insolent youth back into submission, they hadn't factored in the instant capture and distribution of evidence that technology spawned. Miscalculating further, they didn't realize that rather than intimidating the rebels, the footage actually galvanized the struggle. Weighed down by aging generals and golden statues, the tanker couldn't turn in time, and governments just kept doubling down on violence. The further they went, the more they fanned the flames.

Cool Britannia could have taught them a thing or two. Bread and circuses propped up regimes a lot better than blood these days. Cosmetics were the new control and subtlety a virtue. All anyone needed to do to stay in power was play "father of the people," blame a few corrupt ministers, propose a new constitution, and then, once everyone had fucked off home, make a couple of skin-deep changes and quietly murder the loudest voices as they slept. Repression had been superseded by manipulation – but try telling that to an aging strongman.

Even as the Syndicate model was pilloried for enabling bullies, it was lavished with praise over foreign revolutions. And when governments started trying to ban it, or better still tried to turn off the whole internet, the scale of its influence only amplified.

It was the critical mass theory writ large – by the time a government realized a protest had been flash-mobbed, it was too late to shut it down. Wonder what the Lewisham commander would have made of it all?

The Syndicate finally moved into their huge new campus outside Palo Alto. There was a ribbon-cutting ceremony and everything. The whole place felt faintly ludicrous, but the six took a wing that was free of the more gimmicky design flourishes. Apparently the whole "lifestyle" thing was vitally important to "nurture the creative process," and despite Athos feeling that creativity belonged on the edge, it was formalized nevertheless. It occurred to Hermes and Athos that the architect might be a distant cousin of Michael Templemann – the labored insistence on "facilitation" was all too familiar, but getting involved would have meant taking full responsibility, and in truth, they just didn't care enough about the trimmings. The staff were flush with excitement, and when the electric quad bikes were dramatically unveiled, trumping Google's Segway fleet by two wheels and five miles an hour, company pride rocketed. What was next – robot cheerleaders? Still, everyone seemed happy.

The human editors had so far proved a success. In fact, they managed to stave off a potentially fatal crisis when the pornographically violent ISIL started trying to upload execution videos onto the Syndicate. They had never managed to get a fully functional violence filter operational, and despite creating a semi-successful version that caught people on their knees and people in black standing beside them, the automated filter had also managed to delete a surprising amount of innocent scenarios. ISIL knew all about the filters, savvy fuckers that they were, and found increasingly elusive ways to film murder. Incidents had been relatively few and far between, but a barrage of murder porn started assaulting the network. The human editors proved their worth right then and there.

Feedback was gathered from users, and after a lengthy study, it turned out that there had been an 80 percent drop in harassment cases. There had to be a review panel too; just removing stuff without recourse would have faced cure off against disease. Any takedown could be appealed and the case went to a different set of editors. Justice was being preserved to the best of their ability, though the line between free speech and hate speech was nanometers wide.

Not everything was as obvious as incitement to murder, and there was a whole catalogue of cases that could have gone either way.

And then, in 2011, an article by *The Onion* was taken down. The deletion was satire's crowning glory, and *The Onion* was over the moon. Much like banning a book sends sales through the roof, having a huge website censor a satirical article because they believed it turned out to be solid gold. With a week, it was the most-read article anywhere on the internet and the papers had a field day.

The press are a right bunch of fuckers. They were the first to savage the Syndicate for not doing enough, and now they were eviscerating them for doing too much. It was extremely frustrating, but hey, that's what the press are for. Their job isn't to be blameless or even consistent – it's to hold people to account. And the Syndicate returned the favor by providing a rolling forum on the media. They complemented each other, and the healthiest sign of liberty was the press shitting all over the Syndicate while using it as their primary distributor.

The Onion takedown raised a broader question. There was a huge volume of sites peddling absolute bollocks and no one was quite sure what to do about it. If a page insisted that drinking camel piss would cure cancer, was that just freedom of speech or was it dangerous? What if someone stopped treatment, downed liters of the stuff, and then died? Where was the line?

The site was full of tin-pot Tonys too. All over the network, pages scoffed at the mainstream version of events, dismissing centrists as sheep. But if you signed up to their version, suddenly you weren't a sheep anymore – no, you were a warrior for truth. The mainstream media was rife with bias, money, and influence – that much was undeniable. But their leanings stopped short of outright lies. It was far more nuanced than that.

Much of the media's bias was rooted in what they didn't report. Omission was the most effective tool in bending facts to a worldview, and a close relationship with the establishment didn't do fearless investigation much good either. In America especially, political reporters were leveraged by access. Don't report that and we'll give you an hour with the president. Don't report that or we'll pull your credentials. Access was currency, and a lobby reporter would be all but useless to his bosses if he was sidelined from official briefings. The down-to-the-wire race to break a story three minutes before a competitor depended on it.

There were other ways to sculpt a perspective, the pejorative use of vocabulary being the most prominent. One man's terrorist is another man's freedom fighter or lone wolf. The US were sabre-rattling ten thousand miles from home, but the other side was the aggressor. Interviewees too were key. If a TV news channel reported a story and then discussed its ramifications with an "expert analyst," much would depend on the guest they'd chosen. Athos in particular grew frustrated at how Iran was almost invariably discussed by neoconservatives and members of CIA-funded opposition groups. No one really put the other side to many a story, and that in itself was propaganda. But lies?

Institutions like the *New York Times*, the *Washington Post*,

CNN, MSNBC, etc. lived or died on their credibility as fact dealers. When Jayson Blair was exposed for fabrication, the *Times* took a drastic hit, and they couldn't afford a repeat. The editorial layers at any respectable media outlet were tightly structured to avoid reputational suicide – sources needed verifying, facts needed checking, and an army of lawyers were on hand to hold the line between informed reporting and wild conjecture.

But this rigor didn't extend to a vast hinterland of digital media. You could basically chuck up any old shit, and as long as the writing sounded authoritative, there'd be an audience for it. Many of Tony's favorite themes were still going strong – Illuminati plots, Bilderberg machinations, false-flag operations, and central bank cartels – while new gems like chemtrails staked a claim. The false-flag operations were particularly interesting, rooted as they were in a kernel of truth. The intelligence agencies had fabricated a few things in their time, but to hear many of these sites, there wasn't a single real terrorist in the world.

The CIA had to an extent made its own bed; the constant meddling in other countries, the funding of coups, the selling of weapons – all of these were documented. The problem was that crying wolf had engendered skepticism, and most of the evidence only emerged years later. So how did anyone know for sure that this latest development wasn't Langley up to its old tricks again? It was a vicious circle, and the net result was increased credibility for the conspiratorial view.

What should they, could they, or would they do to

address this? For Hermes, the short answer was nothing. He maintained an increasingly evangelical faith in the natural filtration of the self-organizing system, absolutely convinced that this was a fringe fad and sanity would come good. People would figure out the facts in the end, and to interfere would be to diminish truth. Truth doesn't work if you cloak the alternatives – that becomes a spoon-fed worldview. It only works if people choose it over falsehood; any attempt to rig the process undermines the conclusion. They couldn't take down these pages – not just because there would be First Amendment challenges, but because it was Arab-strongman thinking.

In a funny way, all the bullshit actually aided the process. For Hermes anyway. He was much more concerned about the state of the new ad system.

When advertisers realized no one was clicking on their ads, they lobbied furiously to fuse church and state. Newspapers found themselves in such financial straits that they agreed to "native advertising" – ads that blended seamlessly into "real" content. So news websites started publishing pieces that looked like an article, but had been planted there by a business. The Syndicate was doing the same: ads looked like they came from an individual's network.

The consequence was to erode faith in journalistic independence even further. The policy was justified by flagging the content as sponsored, but it was in no one's interest to make the flag flutter, so in a skim-reading paradigm, many missed the small print. It was a brave new world – advertising and news as almost interchangeable concepts.

Hermes was disgusted at their own complicity. The others were too, but grew more sanguine about the compromises needed to keep the digital economy alive. Athos and Hermes nursed an ongoing rift for several months about their respective attitudes – Athos thought Hermes should be more circumspect, and Hermes felt Athos should be less supine. The new campus was so absurdly large that they didn't meet often enough in the corridors to thrash it out properly, so it festered under the surface.

There was another faultline too. All this buying up of other companies – what the fuck was that about? The Business Affairs department had submitted a series of takeover plans for review. Messaging apps were the new Rat Pack in town and despite the six not seeing how any of them concerned the Syndicate, the MBAs were adamant it was a zero-sum game. Put simply, they said any communication medium affected the company. If they didn't own them, they'd be forced to fight them.

It was all a bit King Herod. While they weren't being asked to actually slaughter any babies, they were being asked to adopt them lest they prove a threat in adulthood. Raymond and his team were very insistent that the buy-ups went ahead, and so they did – you couldn't keep doing good work if you were six feet under. You need to have power in order to make people's lives better.

George Orwell may have spotted the flaw in that particular bit of logic, but it was also fucking true. Oppositions don't enact beneficial laws, governments do. They fuck it up almost every time, but there's still no health care reform without office. There's still no minimum wage without office. As Friction said, they were a fucking corporation – what kind did they want to be?

With Hermes appointing himself Purist in Chief, he grew estranged from the others, drowning his sorrows in a bevy of swimsuit models and mountains of cocaine in Miami. As 2011 skidded into 2012, a new election round was complete, Obama was back in the Oval Office, the Tea Party was proving an electoral force, and the country was polarizing in a way none of them had ever seen before. It was like conservatives and liberals lived in parallel universes. Neither could believe that the other could possibly see things the way they did without being either unhinged or criminal. Healthcare was a socialist plot designed to destroy America, as far as conservatives were concerned, and pro-lifers were bigoted patriarchs to liberals. And don't even start with the guns.

As positions entrenched, facts were slaughtered in the crossfire. The explosion of digital media chipped away at a fundamental pillar of political debate: objective truth. And the Syndicate's architecture only expedited the process.

VAMPIRE CALAMARI

The six of them sat around the conference table. Whichever fucking idiot decided to build the walls out of glass needed shooting. It was like being in the most tedious museum exhibit imaginable, and seeing their staff eying them up as they rolled past on their electric quads did their sense of humor no favors at all – not least because their meeting hadn't turned up yet.

They had been called to order by a rather tetchy Raymond. He had "much to discuss," which didn't bode well, and they sat there in tense anticipation. What they weren't expecting was for him to be accompanied – he'd usually fired his assistant on the journey, so when reception radioed through a party of five, they couldn't help but be intrigued.

Raymond swept in with four Italian suits in tow. He introduced them briskly as his advisory team from Goldman Sachs – no names, mind – and as Athos tried to imagine any of them jamming a blood funnel anywhere, they took their seats and the meeting began.

"OK," said Raymond. "Can you give these guys a brief summary of where we're at with the advertising parameters?"

Hermes exhaled sharply as if to register his reluctance on the record.

"All the data we store is used to steer specific ads towards specific demographics. So if your interests include gardening, you'll have gardening ads come up in your feed. If you're into baseball, you'll have an ad for bats come up. The idea is to lessen the sense of spam and not alienate people from using the site, while keeping ourselves financially viable."

One of the suits tidied his papers. And then again. Probably a tic of some sort. Then he spoke.

"And how much have you made this clear to advertisers? The targeting, I mean."

"Well, to be honest, we've tried not to make a song and dance about it. We don't really want to have the data conversation, and while we wouldn't be against the idea of discussing it with an advertiser, we aren't looking to make it common knowledge. People trust us, and even though the targeting is more for users, that's not how it will read. People will think we're monetizing their personal information," said Athos.

"Well, you are," chipped in a second suit.

"I disagree," said Hermes. "The Syndicate learns how to feel the most 'you' possible. Ads are just another part of that. There's no point flooding someone's feed with things they have no chance of connecting with."

"Very noble," smirked the first suit again. "But that's what advertisers are looking for. Relevance. No one wants to pay for a scattergun approach – their campaign has far greater value to them if they are hitting a potential client base instead of a random cross section."

"And that's what we're giving them," said Atalanta with a note of steel in her voice.

"Not if they don't know about it. There's huge untapped revenue in small businesses that wouldn't dream of traditional advertising, but might be persuaded to put a few hundred bucks into something that directly hits their customer base," said suit number two. The other two were just the muscle, it seemed.

The first suit chimed in again. "So how do you know to target ads to specific groups?"

"We use the data stored on their company page and match it with users."

"But if you expanded your advertising interface and let people target specific demographics themselves – age, location, political affiliation, interests, etc. – that would give advertisers tailored control. And that has huge value."

"Fuck that," coughed Hermes. "That's a total shift in feel. That's giving advertisers a weird level of access to people's data."

"Not really," said Raymond. "They don't get the data. They just get to choose the parameters instead of it being automated. It's a client service."

"Our 'clients,' as you put it, are the users, not the advertisers," snapped Friction.

"That ship has sailed," replied Raymond. "They're both your clients. Or this isn't long for this world." He waved a regal arm at the new building.

"And these gentlemen have another few ideas too."

"Yes," said the third suit, finally finding his voice. "We think that the mobile app could be used to record audio and feed the streams into an algorithm that would identify areas that can be commercialized in real time."

"Wait – what?" Hermes shot out of his seat. "Record people's calls?"

"Not just their calls. People talk near their phones. So say someone is having a conversation about a holiday, their Syndicate feed could have hotel and flight ads in it five minutes later."

"That's fucking disgusting!" yelled Hermes. "Tapping people's lives to sell them things? Fuck me. Advertising within site parameters is one thing – you can justify that as opt-in. But tapping people's phones? It's fucking illegal, for one thing."

"It's a gray area. Another few lines in the terms of service and probably no calls as the other party hasn't consented. A lawyer question. But it's still opt-in. Part of using the app. They'll have agreed to it in the terms of service."

"Fuck you and your weaseling rationales!" screamed Hermes, whose forehead veins seemed to be priming for explosion.

"HERMES!" shouted Raymond. "Just you listen here, you motherless fuck. This is the big league. You can take your hippy bullshit and shove it up your ass. Now sit the fuck down."

Hermes sat down stewing. Raymond had presence.

"Listen. We're going to be going public soon."

"No, we're not," answered Athos.

"Yes, we fucking are," replied Raymond. "I'm not putting another red cent in, and turnover isn't high enough to sustain it. We need to go public. And before we do, we're installing a full advertising interface for businesses. I'll compromise on the recordings, but you're going to compromise on this. Period."

With that, he stormed out. It took a second for the suits to realize they should probably leave too, and they shot a parting look of aggressive sheepishness before backpedaling out of the room.

A heated debate broke out in the conference room. Hermes was adamant that Raymond and his jackbooted capitalist storm troopers could fuck off. Ben instantly assumed the counter position, arguing that they probably did need to go public at some point, and if they did it sensibly, they could retain a controlling share. Then they could throw off Raymond's yoke and spread reliance wider. And if the advertising "à la carte" was the price for freedom, then so be it. For fuck's sake, Google had the most heavily monetized data operation in the world and everyone still used them.

Hermes flung a chair across the room in frustration. "It's not about whether they stay or go – it's about what the Syndicate is and what it represents. Maybe they would stay, but the trust is gone."

Athos added an exasperated voice. "Hermes, it's not about us – who cares if people trust us? The Syndicate was never about us."

"Not trusting us – trusting the medium. Jesus – trusting the whole fucking internet, for that matter. It's all going to shit – that frontier freedom is fucking dead. And you're offering us up as pallbearer."

In the end, they voted to pass the advertising measure.

There wasn't much fighting it – they either had to get smart with the economics or they'd wither on the vine. If Raymond pulled out, there'd just be someone else to replace him. Maybe someone worse.

Hermes was incandescent. "You utter, utter cunts. You sellout pricks."

Athos wheeled on him. "Listen, Hermes. You're upset. OK. But get a grip and get it now. This is a self-organizing system in action. People don't want to pay subscriptions. They don't want ads. This is how the system responds in order to stay alive. You can't hate the system you created because it's doing things you don't like. Jesus – think of it as a moody adolescent."

Hermes ignored him. "Fuck you," he whispered and walked coldly out of the room.

CYCLES

"FREELAND!"

Athos poked his head around the corner, tiptoed into the kitchen, and enveloped Trinity from behind. "Yes, ma'am," he breathed into her ear. He brushed his hands over her breasts, cupped them gently, slowly slid down to her elliptic belly, and squeezed it tenderly.

Trinity giggled softly and continued dicing the apple in front of her. "A month to go," she said. "I just wish I didn't have to pee every five minutes."

"We've had it pretty easy," smiled Athos. "No morning sickness – nothing."

"What's this 'we' business," chuckled Trinity.

"Sorry, boss. I thought gaining five kilos would count as sympathy."

"Yeah, come back when you've got twenty-four-hour reflux and sleeping becomes an engineering project."

A warm yellow light bathed the couple. Athos's parents had come over for a visit, opting to stay until the birth. Phillip had developed prostate cancer over the past year and was determined to meet his grandchild before finality took hold. He was gaunt and gray, but his eyes still shone and he still told the same five jokes as if he was a teenager again. Leila too had creased somewhat, but was settling nicely into grande-dame status and remained a major force to be reckoned with. Against all archetypal odds, she and Trinity got on like old friends, with none of the usual jabs and grinding smiles. Trinity had been particularly worried about a Middle Eastern mother-in-law, having visions of lacerating cooking critiques and assorted tutting, but her fears had been allayed within a day of Leila arriving. They bonded over mocking Athos, and he had been more than happy to take one for the team. Domestic harmony. He just hadn't seen it coming.

It was a good deal more than could be said for the state of his relationship with Hermes. Hermes had grown slightly erratic and spent more and more time away from the office. Militant bachelorhood had put lines on his face and bags under his eyes, and Athos couldn't help wondering if he'd be less tumultuous if he had a solid relationship in his life. They didn't see much of one another: board meetings and formal events, but they didn't hang out anymore – no shooting the breeze. When Friction married Javier in 2013, an unfortunate scene descended into blows and Hermes ended up spilling red wine all over Javier's grandmother, who was struggling enough with her beloved Javier marrying a man. The red wine just seemed like punishment by Communion.

Atalanta had finally met Mr. Right, and he was the last thing anyone had expected. A bookish, bespectacled sort, Ambrose was two fingers up to expectation. He loved her with a stammering passion – that much was clear – but just as people started to think she was in sole possession of the trousers, he began exhibiting a magic ability to restrain her most outrageous excesses. Then everyone wondered if she was having an identity crisis, but when the dust settled and everyone stopped with the pop psychology, a couple very much in love stood together in the hearth.

Chiara and Ben had unexpectedly got it together over the past eighteen months too. Both had their fun outside the Syndicate bubble, but Ben got tired of gold diggers, and Chiara realized the whole endless festival vibe wasn't really her. Both sought stability and both needed understanding, and they found it in each other's arms. It wasn't the kind of romance racy French novelists would have licked their lips at – no, it was a loving friendship, sexual on the margins, but essentially one long snuggle.

The IPO was scheduled for 2013. Valuations had increased dramatically since the market grasped the Syndicate's swing toward fully targeted advertising, and silly sums were being bandied in investor boardrooms. Goldman Sachs had become something of a fixture at HQ, and Ben was assigned to nanny their liaison team. They were "advising" on the float, but from what anyone could work out, they were fattening the calf while positioning themselves to make as much money as possible from both sides.

Hermes had turned into a bit of a Tony, much to the sadness and frustration of the others. He saw conspiracy in every shadow and got increasingly ranty about the "plot" to hijack the Syndicate. He had come to the conclusion that they wanted all their data, though in true Tony fashion, he wasn't being too specific about who "they" might be. Athos was pretty sure he meant capitalism in general, but the

Goldman guys were taking the brunt of it. In the end, Ben had to conduct secret meetings in undisclosed parts of the building lest Hermes come charging in to spit venom.

For Athos, it was pretty simple. Yes, they were swimming with sharks, and yes, the water was murky. But it was still their pool. Raymond had strong-armed them a fuck of a lot, but the company had grown as a result. All the changes he'd forced had proven liveable with, and the reality was that you couldn't have hundreds of millions of people using any service without it reflecting political, social, and economic pressures. To Athos, Hermes had confused a self-organizing system with a macrocosm of subculture – he was trying to apply purist principles to a global society, and in doing so, became increasingly ideological. He was contradicting his own core beliefs and trying to shape the parameters – resisting spikes the system itself sent up.

It was LSD thinking in a cocaine world. Society didn't just change because of a medium, and nor should it. But it was tragic seeing him so bitter. Athos was sorry to be losing a brother, but he couldn't hold onto him without betraying his own beliefs. He had a family now, a company, a charitable foundation. All of that mattered.

There was other shit going on too. He'd done a couple of spreads in *GQ* and *Vanity Fair*, and his blazer and chinos had become something of a fashion statement. He'd never really bothered wearing anything else since his teens, finding camouflage in neutrality, but now there was a Freeland range of navy blazers that he'd backed and put his name to. He wondered if he was merchandising his identity, but then realized he didn't care what label anyone stuck on it – they were all designed by his London tailor and no sweatshops were involved.

Athos and Trinity's daughter, Yasmina, was born on April Fool's Day, 2013. They did pregnancy their own way, buying all the books before deciding they were one long guilt trip. Looking at all the shit they were expected to buy, all the things they were expected to do, and all the feelings they were expected to have, Trinity bequeathed the books to Athos to roll joints on. Human beings had managed perfectly well for millennia, and with disease under control, did they really need a room full of products and a cupboard full of supplements they'd never use? The fear economy could look elsewhere for a mark.

They got a nanny, of course – not to abrogate parenthood, just to minimize the red-eyed psychosis. Yasmina herself was consulted at three days old and gurgled her assent, which settled it. A Brazilian spinster called Beatriz was brought into the fold, and she loved the child like her own, becoming a surrogate grandmother and part of the family within a few months. Life was stable, life was good, and he gave millions away each year, trying to avoid the NGO behemoths and researching smaller organizations he could really make a difference to.

As 2013 advanced, the IPO drew nearer. It was set for May. The Goldman tribe had multiplied and the executive wing at Syndicate HQ was now stuffed with transatlantic accents, analysts speaking in tongues, and swaggering frat boys who'd been to the strip club via the opera.

Unbelievably, his old friend from Eton, Harry Bradley, turned out to be one of the Goldman Sachs team. He'd flown in from New York for the final push, and as Athos got his head round the coincidence, he couldn't help feeling a touch disappointed. Athos had once held out great hope that they'd break out of the bubble together, and Goldman Sachs was the bubble incarnate.

They got on like a house on fire though, and the Freelands even went out to the Hamptons for a weekend to stay with the Bradleys. High society is full of plural nouns it seems.

Harry had married a Swiss heiress, and despite early apprehension, Vanya turned out to be a cracking laugh who could hold her booze with the best of 'em. Elegant, irreverent, and kind, she made Trinity feel wonderfully welcome, and the two became firm friends. It was comfortable to have another couple in their lives, and a rare thing to find two people with whom they both connected equally. Weirdly though, even as Athos was genuinely enjoying spending time with Harry, he wasn't at all sure they'd be friends if they met for the first time. But they'd been witnesses to the formative years of each other's lives, and in an ephemeral world, those anchors matter.

SNOWCAPPED PEAKS

"Holy fucking shit. It's still going up."

The conference room was agog with excitement. It looked like the Situation Room during the bin Laden mission: the Goldman Sachs team, Raymond, his new Uzbek wife, and every senior Syndicate executive was staring fixedly at the bank of screens. Flicking between Bloomberg and MSNBC with real-time stock prices rolling across computer screens, they watched the tides unleash. It was such a surreal moment: seeing everything they'd worked towards and everything that the hundreds of millions of Syndicate users had breathed life into be priced up on chaos's ticker.

One self-organizing system was marrying another – social network, meet financial markets. The market is arguably the most prevalent self-organizing system on the planet, using millions of trades to establish value points. The fact that it was wrong a lot of the time didn't make any difference; the market would always self-correct. Or so Goldman insisted. Looking at it from a purely metaphorical perspective, there was an undeniable beauty to the marriage.

There had been a flurry of changes at the Syndicate as they put their house in order for the float. Their governance structure hadn't survived contact with Goldman Sachs, and the notion that a company could be run by six people was laughed out of the building. Hierarchy was a language they needed to learn if they wanted investors to understand, and roles were doled out accordingly. Hermes point-blank refused any formal position, which was lucky because no one wanted to give him one in his current state of mind. Ben became CFO and Athos was voted CEO for his ingrained ability to speak "elite." The others stayed directors.

The acid test of any IPO is how the stock price behaves after trading begins. If it goes up too much, accusations of price fixing aren't far behind, but if it goes down, the market's pronounced it overvalued. Syndicate stocks rose and kept on rising, so for the moment at least, they had survived embarrassment.

When the initial frenzy wound down to a steady flow, they surveyed the terrain. The six of them had diluted their stock only as far as they could retain 51 percent of the company. Each held 8.5 percent, and it had been a precondition that together they still held a controlling interest. Some small investors bought Syndicate stock, which was refreshing to see, but when all was said and done, two major funds now had substantial stakes: TWI Capital Partners and Uranus Capital.

Shareholder meetings were called, bureaucracy doubled, and the whole thing was looking a damn sight less fun than once upon a time in the Tenderloin. Athos even wondered to himself why he didn't just jack it in and move to a beach somewhere; if he cashed out his shares, he'd have more money than he could spend in a lifetime. But having a founder liquidate equity just as a company floats would tank the whole offering. People would demand to know why they should invest when the CEO himself was bailing. At most, he could sell stock slowly over a few years, which seemed rather laborious, so for the moment, he did nothing at all.

Six days after they floated, all hell broke loose. Stock prices tumbled, investors bayed for blood, the press mobbed the building, and in the boardroom, the hatches were battened. Edward Snowden was on the loose.

The NSA had gone full-spectrum hijack. As revelations cascaded about just what Uncle Sam had been up to, the entire tech sector froze with fear. Athos had always imagined their surveillance operation to be patchy at best, but *The Guardian* and *The Washington Post* painted a picture more comprehensive, more ambitious, and infinitely more sinister than he'd ever imagined. The NSA had been hoovering up global communications wholesale, harvesting hundreds of millions of emails, telephone metadata, and vast banks of personal information. A phalanx of spying programs were described in terrifying detail by the conscience-stricken Mr. Snowden, and the first casualties were the big tech firms who'd been handing over user information.

Kafka would have nodded approvingly at the convoluted layers of circular secrecy. The major players had been forced by the federal government to comply with the PRISM program. Any communication that contained a worryingly broad range of terms and phrases was handed over, and it was in no one's interest to publicize what was going on. None of the tech firms had anything to gain by alerting their customer base to NSA data sharing, and the NSA were still trying to pretend they barely existed at all. Meanwhile, data kept pouring into government mainframes.

Athos shredded the internet looking for any mention of the Syndicate, praying to any deity who'd listen that they weren't caught in the crossfire. The first wave of revelations mercifully didn't mention them, but the second – oh shit, the second.

It turned out that their renegade reputation had been quite the talking point at Fort Meade. When the NSA started putting tech companies into a half nelson, they gazed uncertainly at the Syndicate with its hacking background, its random governance, its unpredictable founders, and its gangland roots. Risk assessments were conducted, and the results weren't encouraging. Put simply, there was no guarantee they wouldn't go public if approached – warrant or no warrant. The stakes were so high that it risked a constitutional crisis. If the Syndicate did go public, they'd be in breach of multiple laws, but those laws had been quietly smuggled onto the statute books without a sturdy public consensus. The 2008 FISA Amendment Act had a lot to answer for.

So even though the Syndicate would have been defying the law by going public, the resulting landslide would take everyone down. The other companies were more rational entities, paying their protection data to the star-spangled Mob. They knew how to be pragmatic. But those dangerous hippies over at the Syndicate were a fucking powder keg.

There was no question of leaving Syndicate data untapped though. They would just have to find another way. And from what Snowden was saying, they had. If he was to be believed, the NSA had opened a back door into the Syndicate network in 2008, and from that moment on, accessed every single communication channeled through it. It didn't make any sense though. There was no way they could be hacked like that. Either this was total bullshit, or else … Or else they had help.

Athos rang round the others and set a meeting away from the Syndicate building. It was crawling with journalists, and anyway, they didn't know who to trust. Athos was convinced that they'd been betrayed, served up on a fucking platter to the federal government, and as he sped to the nondescript diner they'd agreed to convene at, he cursed Obama's name. Fucking asshole – all that hope shit and here he was, letting this happen on his watch.

If you'd tried calmly explaining the calibration of privacy and security to Athos at that moment, he'd have bitten your balls off. Now was not the time. The fucking state was stealing citizen's data from a private company. And data is such a depersonalized word – they were stealing their lives, their loves, their hopes, their dreams, their secrets, their lies, their insecurities, their cries. They were stealing identities. Robbing them fucking blind and using them to better control their population.

The terrorists had not only won, the United States had bent over and invited a jackhammer fucking. This kind of galactic empire shit was gold dust for recruitment. That is if anyone believed it was about terrorism. This was where the line between conspiracy theory and realism blurred.

The reason the TAZ movement had provoked such ire was the inability to either understand or predict it. If you sat down with MI5 and asked them why they had devoted such resources to the TAZ, they would most likely have been stumped for a coherent answer. Ultimately, people dancing, painting, and reading poetry was hardly an overt threat to the public, but public and state aren't the same thing, no matter what the state says. And they believe it themselves. In the same way that an Arab dictator sees himself as the embodiment of the nation, state organs in democratic countries genuinely believe their machinations are in the public interest.

The state is by nature nervous about what it doesn't know. To paraphrase Sir Humphrey Appleby, if it doesn't know, then how does it know what it needs to know? Not knowing is a cancer. They need to know.

So if the state can't figure out how a subcultural mass movement operates, how it assembles, how it communicates, why it seems to command such devotion, and what its endgame is, then they need to find out. If that endgame doesn't make any sense to them, the need for information only escalates.

It was the same with the NSA. Take the fucking lot, and then see what was pertinent. Deciding what they needed to know when they didn't know everything seemed ridiculous. And of course, they all trusted themselves to have the public interest at heart.

So while the NSA weren't gearing up to use the data to start interning people, they felt entitled, nay obligated, to collect it. The problem is, once you legitimize that kind of spying operation, its mechanism can be used for pretty much anything. Those at the NSA might trust themselves, but what about in ten years? What if a fascist became president?

So just as the state will always legislate the broadest laws possible, its DNA demands that it collect information on its citizens. It's not a plot as such; it's like asking why a tiger mauls people. It's just wired that way. To call it a nefarious conspiracy is to let it off the hook, because this isn't about bad apples – it's systemic.

Athos was the first to arrive at The Happy Hotcake. The rest filtered in slowly, but with Friction not having arrived yet, they decided to wait. They ordered a round of juices. Then breakfast. Then coffee. No Friction. By midday, they were starting to think the unthinkable. Had Friction fucked them all?

REFORMATION

"It's a privilege and an honor to be working alongside you all. There's been some amazing highs and some unfortunate lows these past months, and I hope that together, we can steady the ship, sail new seas, and unlock new synergies."

Athos grimaced from the side of the stage. This guy was a real fucking asshole.

When Friction disappeared, the remaining five did everything they possibly could to obfuscate. First, they claimed he was on holiday, then that he was seriously ill, but in the end, the lack of either Friction or explanation did for them. With stock prices hemorrhaging, shareholders had gone into damage-limitation mode and applied intense pressure. How had they been hacked? Was their security hopelessly inadequate, or were they in a warrantless bed with the NSA? The moral questions were irrelevant; this was about consumer confidence.

No one threw Friction to the lions, but it wasn't looking good. Markets abhor uncertainty, so when shareholders couldn't get a straight answer, they moved for new management. Raymond cut them loose within minutes, and set about leading the charge for a new CEO. The candidate the board settled on was Luther Durant, a former hedge-fund manager and asset stripper who'd built a fearsome reputation whipping ailing companies into the black. He had a solid grounding in the digital economy, partnering in a new online payment system and backing a mercenary dating app that judged on appearances alone.

As Luther was touted to take over, Athos hired a New York risk-management firm to dig up any dirt they could find, and despite the dossier they proffered, no one seemed to care. Luther was notorious for cutthroat tactics, and while the files revealed worrying ties to foreign intelligence agencies and a series of date-rape allegations, shoulders just shrugged. In the end, Athos ended up looking petty – a drowning man.

It headed to a vote, and they were short on allies. Even Errol had flown over to back the changes, flush with his new billions. *Et tu*, Errol? Friction had given a proxy to Hermes a while back that meant he could vote on his behalf if Friction was indisposed for whatever reason. No matter what the consensus on Friction's collusion, his vote still counted. The only problem was that Hermes was AWOL too. He had taken the news calmly, as if he'd been expecting something like this. The rest of them hadn't seen him since the crisis meeting at the diner, and there was no clue to his whereabouts. Terra Byte thought he may have gone to an ashram in India they'd discussed, but when Athos sent a team, there was no sign of him. Sandalwood, the security company who'd prepared the Durant dossier, were tasked with tracking him down, and despite leads on three continents, they came up empty.

As the day of the vote neared, the four that were left grew increasingly desperate, hiring more and more investigators to try to find Hermes, but even though they found a recent telephone number, nothing came of it as it was traced to a rubbish bin in Amsterdam. Friction could stay gone for all they cared, but Hermes... they needed him back urgently.

Atalanta even called in a bomb threat on Syndicate HQ to get the vote delayed, but it only bought them forty-eight hours. The shareholders could smell the panic, and nothing about Athos's demeanor gave them any confidence. There had been one chance to diffuse the revolt: lay the Friction situation on the table, eviscerate him mercilessly, roll out a statement to restore confidence, and craft a new governance system to show "something had been done." But they didn't do any of that. They just stalled for all they were worth and tried to find Hermes. It was a doomed strategy.

So there stood Athos, the former CEO, as new CEO Luther Durant greeted his public. The company was renamed Syndicate Enterprises, though of course the site retained its original name. An avalanche of press releases sluiced out from the PR agency Luther brought on board, and the hack wasn't even mentioned. They stuck to a dementedly positive party line that heralded security upgrades and a dynamic multimedia future, and people seemed to swallow it. Those that were still paying attention, that is. User numbers had dropped slightly, but as Luther assumed office, the stock price began to rise again. And then the user stats followed suit.

As Athos looked around him, he had to admit he was surprised. After a frantic period obsessed by finding Hermes, he finally examined the fallout, and the first thing that struck him was the total lack of fallout. Yes, there had been a hurricane of headlines, yes, there had been a shareholder revolt, yes, they had been savaged on their own site, and yes, the stock price had swan-dived off a bridge. But just a few weeks later, there was no evidence that any lasting damage had been done.

He couldn't work it out. Maybe it was the fact that every major organization was implicated, but users kept right on using the site, and in time, the headlines evaporated. It beggared belief. How were there not protests in the streets, how were other start-ups not challenging their dominance, and how was the federal government casually moving on? Again, interests aligned and few institutions made much of a fuss. Google, Yahoo, Microsoft, and the rest of the big guns made gung-ho noises about standing up to the state, but in essence, they waited for it to blow over, and sure enough it did. The government hid behind national security, deflecting onto Snowden's "treason," while even newspaper editors, who'd been convinced the story would run and run, were astonished by how quickly the majority lost interest.

So basically, they had surrendered control of their company over a phantom crisis. It had seemed so viscerally real at the time, but here they were three months later with a record stock price and a record increase in user numbers. The management change had contributed to the bounce-back, but Luther was so obviously a *condottieri* that Athos couldn't believe people weren't more concerned. This was their personal information. This was their communication network. This was their lives.

"People don't give a fuck about data."

Such were the first words out of Luther's mouth once the cameras departed and the new-look board assembled.

"The biggest fallacy is that they do," he continued. "They don't. Don't take my word for it, just look around you. As long as they don't have to pay for shit, they couldn't give one single, orphan fuck. So, ladies and gentlemen, we're going to take them at their word."

Athos winced. Atalanta walked out. Luther smiled, jumped up, and opened the door for her like a triumphant *chevalier*. Sitting back down, his gimlet eye invited any other malcontents to do the same. Athos thought about it, but clung to his temper, knowing that if he left, any thought of keeping a hand on the tiller would go with him. Luther had clearly spoken to the Goldman guys, because the first order of business was to greenlight the microphone idea. No one objected – not even Athos, who knew what everyone was thinking: if the NSA can do it and no one cares, why shouldn't they? Luther followed up with a host of advertising initiatives and vowed to start selling data packets to third-party businesses. The argument with Goldman over letting advertisers target users suddenly seemed so trivial. This really was a brave new world.

RELATIVITY

Athos, Atalanta, Ben, and Chiara fought the reforms tooth and nail, but they were powerless in the new reality. They had influence and a voting block, but without the controlling stake, their power was limited, and their influence had been undermined by the NSA hack. Friction might be gone, but suspicion lingered over them all. If they'd been having an extramarital affair with the NSA, then maybe they'd do the same with a competitor. The less power they had, the less anyone else trusted them, fearing they might scuttle the ship to regain control.

Meanwhile, Hermes's founding precept that "good" and "bad" content would self-organize was looking more naive by the day.

Celebrity culture. It was the perfect balance of mediocrity and aspiration, where people could revel in glossy mystique while thinking, "That could be me." Athos always wondered why talent had stopped being a prerequisite for fame, and the simple answer was that talent alienated. If you actually needed to be prodigiously good at something, then chances were you'd never be famous. But if *that* chick can have five million Syndicate followers based on posting photos of her ass, well maybe I'm in with a shot too. It was the democratization of aspiration, the American Dream through an Instagram filter.

When soap operas peaked in the 1980s, they offered a fascinating insight into national psyches. British soap operas were grotty and miserable – a Larkin-like dirge of kitchen-sink banality. The reassuring gloom tapped into the Blitz spirit, and for a country that was suspicious of success and traumatized by the postwar decline, the bleakness proved cathartic. The world was shit all round – not just from where you're standing. Best we can do is muddle through with a cup of tea.

In American soap operas, however, everyone was wealthy, attractive, and successful. Families fought over companies, divorces came gilded with intrigue, and the sun was always shining. It was an aspirational medium, where being able to identify with certain emotions also allowed the viewer to identify with the onscreen lifestyle. There in a couple of years go I.

Reality television brought the two strands together. It was still on TV, so that made it instantly sexy. Yet the people on it were average. They weren't stars. They were everyman. Reality shows became the new soap operas, and with the internet mirroring and catalyzing culture, it wasn't long before the networks churned with gossip. Reality TV and celebrity culture were interchangeable, and pretty soon, the life of a celebrity had turned into a reality show of its own as the selfies stacked up.

Vacuous content was increasingly rewarded by the Syndicate algorithm, while serious stuff foundered in the shallows. With most sites furiously looking for new ways to squeeze revenue out of advertising, eyeballs became collateral. If you could go to an advertiser and say a million people a week visited your site, then that gave you value. So with the Syndicate in the middle, how could they lure people onto their own site? Clickbait, that's how.

Cliffhangers were another borrow from the soap-opera format as headlines ramped up expectation and hinted at outrageous scandal to extract clicks. Once people were logged as a visitor onto the fisherman's site, who cared if they didn't stick around? The stats were in the bag and clicks were currency.

Luther noted this trend and drew up plans to keep all content on the Syndicate. It was a secret document Athos was never meant to see, and while it was a ten-year plan, the conclusion was inescapable. He wanted to force independent websites to publish all their content on the Syndicate in return for a share of ad revenue. No more external links. Everything in-house. That was more ambitious even than the Google monopoly – the Syndicate as virtually the entire internet.

And while aspiration was being democratized, so too was truth. The Syndicate had certainly created an individualized experience for its users, but in doing so had insulated them within a dangerously self-referential bubble. The more enterprising content creators factored this in and moved further from objectivity, calculating that confirmation bias sold a fuck sight better than a measured dialectic. The more strident content sounded, the more it was "telling it how it is."

In an individualized medium, blue-chip media no longer held the same sway. There was no Walter Cronkite voice of

America – this was an atomized nation now and everyone had a voice. Individuality bred contempt of collectivism – tribes, yes, but a national consensus? No way.

It was a bitter irony: the Syndicate had been born from subculture, creating global communities where once they were local. Before the internet, you might be ostracized in your local town if you thought differently, but the World Wide Web put you directly in touch with others just like you. So subcultures got a turbo injection, but that didn't stop at happy-go-lucky hippies – subcultures could be anything. And while on paper, democratization and connectivity had seemed like the ultimate liberty, they had been used in wholly unforeseen ways. People were forming internet tribes to plot the destruction of other internet tribes. The paradoxes spun ever faster.

Luther pressed on with the commodification of Syndicate users. They were a remarkably evergreen crop, permanently updating their data points through daily interactions and meticulously tending their own consumer profile. The analysis department was expanded and a series of new metrics introduced: a Conversion Index ranked users by their propensity to click on native advertising, a Privacy Index charted how jealously users guarded sensitive information, and a Gullibility Index measured the credulity of every single person on the site.

"No one ever checks Google to cross-reference information. It's two seconds too many," rhapsodized Luther, who adopted the phrase "Two seconds too many" as something of a mantra.

Russia had started doing a Tony, realizing psy ops had a fresh lease of life. Manufacturing disinformation proved fruitful as they drove a wedge between populations and governments through "knowledge." With the social contract fracturing, they piled on the breezeblocks with an endless stream of semi-plausible, "independent" news reports, and before long, Kremlin-funded media was a bastion of integrity to those corroborating existing worldviews.

Whole industries sprang up, and Luther made damn sure the Syndicate could piggyback a profit. Macedonian villages proved an unlikely source of American political news, but the bullshit economy was global and the English was passable enough to swallow. Luther built community centers and hospitals in villages across Macedonia to show solidarity with the tide, and in doing so, took percentages in the most active sites. The brasher advertisements were seeded into the fake news sites as Luther noted parallel patterns between the Gullibility Index and the Conversion Index. "If they'll buy that shit, then they'll buy anything," he maintained. And they did. Fake news was a growth engine.

If Orwell's *1984* was the apex of totalitarianism, then 2016 was the apogee of relativism. Mendacity was flying off the shelves and despite the glut of supply, demand seemed insatiable. Two events above all symbolized disinformation's triumph: Brexit and the election of Donald J. Trump.

Brexit had been percolating for a couple of decades. When the ludicrous Boris Johnson waddled into Brussels as a correspondent in the early '90s, he soon tired of procedure's turgid grays. Finding nothing of fishnet-wearing note in the ruminations of European administration, he looked for stories that might make amusing dinner-table conversation. Sourcing and indeed fact were rather bourgeois preoccupations and he soon cast off their plodding yoke. Cobbling together unguarded comments by junior staffers and blue-sky policy documents that would never see the light of day, he crafted two central narratives. "Unelected bureaucrats" were plotting a European superstate, utilizing stealth to achieve what Napoleon and Hitler couldn't commandeer by force. Furthermore, said bureaucracy had gone mad, trying to straighten bananas and rename sausages. Both struck a chord back home and both were hamstrung by only a kernel of truth.

Correspondents who followed Boris were astonished to discover editorial resistance to serious reporting, and Fleet Street looked askance at anything that didn't meet the dinner-table standard. The EU was boring. So sex it up, if you please.

Twenty years later, these themes had grown so ingrained in the British perception of the EU that the only surprise was how close the referendum actually was. The Eurosceptic press went into overdrive, and a potent fear of "the other" pushed Brexit over the finish line. No matter that none of the facts added up. Fear of crime was the perfect template for reality inversion. For years, the actual crime rate had been decreasing, while the fear of crime soared. The press had proved adept at prizing people from fact using fear, and here they were repeating the trick with migration. Unemployment at historic lows, migrants proving net economic contributors, and yet "they come over here and sponge off our benefits." Britain took fewer refugees than most in Europe and yet they were "swamped." The single market was a burden rather than a boon.

But Brexit was a stately game of croquet compared to the mind-boggling lunacy playing out in the US. Reality turned inside out. Lies were truth, truth was lies, and if you just kept shouting, people started to believe you.

You had to hand it to Trump: he had some balls. Incoherent, rude, vain, boorish, uninformed, and with a steroidal arrogance usually only seen in the wrestling ring, he wiped the floor with every establishment in America. He was the inheritor of a virulent anti-intellectualism in the United States, where knowledge and competence were taken as evidence of corruption and manipulation. Just as the frontier settlers had once rankled at Washington edicts, so now did many resent the implication that their leaders knew more than they. The financial crisis didn't do much to disabuse anyone of this, as elites were exposed as either incompetent or criminal, while the Iraq War debacle leached into the topsoil, painting a farcical picture of pan-governmental ineptitude.

Intelligence wasn't to be trusted and science was just a point of view. Enough lawmakers had pandered to this notion to help institutionalize it, and the bullshit news industry went on the rampage, dismissing talk of fact with accusations of elitism. And then, as satire finally ate itself, one of the arch bullshit merchants was appointed senior White House advisor.

Lying just wasn't a deal breaker anymore, it was a sign of honesty. The more you lied, the more you were a "straight shooter." And when caught out by pesky facts, just call it an elitist plot and keep lying. It was genius really.

Even after the shock of Brexit, the rest of the world couldn't believe the Americans elected Trump. It felt like an imperial swansong, as no one could possibly take them seriously after this. From what Athos had heard on the grapevine, the Chinese even thought it was an elaborate CIA sting. When Trump started governing by tweet and undermining his own intelligence agencies, they simply couldn't believe it was real and redoubled their vigilance lest they were being played.

Luther voted Hillary and contributed to her campaign, even though he was a Trump man at heart. The way he saw it, Trump might burst the bullshit bubble by taking it too far; if Clinton was elected, there'd be far more scope for conspiracy theory and most likely a longer lifespan.

Trump took a sledgehammer to institutions, pummeling away at their legitimacy – the press, the intelligence agencies, the political system; he was running a scorched-earth policy from the very start. And good old America managed to crown internet culture's pinnacle by electing a fully fledged troll as president.

Phillip died three days after Brexit. He'd held on a lot longer than anyone had expected, but multiculturalism's collapse pushed him over the edge. Trump was barracking from the bully pulpit, Nigel Farage was grinning ear to ear, and in the end he just gave up the ghost. The way Leila saw it, the news had been his lifeblood, and CNN probably kept him alive another few months. Now it had helped kill him. There was a weird balance there, and she somehow managed to be thankful for the time it bought them rather than the time they lost. Trinity was shocked – she couldn't believe someone let go because of politics when they had a family to live for. But if 2016 had proved anything, it was that irrationality reigned supreme.

The Freeland family flew back to London for the funeral, burying Phillip in Kensal Green cemetery. He hadn't left any specific wishes, having always avoided the subject, but Athos insisted on burial rather than cremation. He remembered smoking pot in cemeteries as a kid and wondering about the people whose headstones he read. Maybe Phillip Freeland would touch a stranger too one day.

Athos and Trinity gave serious thought to a London move. They were both at a loose end and needed a project, so maybe they should buy a huge house and renovate it together. It was tempting, but even as he gushed about bay windows, Athos sounded unconvincing. His heart wasn't in it, and truth be told, Trinity wasn't sure about London either. She'd met all Athos's old TAZ mates, and while she had no doubt they were lovely people, it never fully clicked.

Neither the US nor the UK felt like home anymore – the cosmopolitan dream of global unity was a smoldering carcass, and it was difficult to look a stranger in the eye without wondering, *Which way did you vote?* Athos's entire life had been devoted to inclusion, and no matter how big his bank balance got, his essence had been trampled into the embers. He was savvy enough to know that the wheel would turn again; he just didn't know if he'd have enough left in the tank when that day came.

In the end, they bought a rambling art nouveau villa in the South of France and a house in Berlin, but both fronts proved half-hearted. Footloose yet weighed with care, they concentrated their attentions on Yasmina, but even as Athos tried to channel his childhood lessons, his mind kept wandering. After a year abroad, they settled back in California and Athos started back at the office, a slow slide toward despair that offered little but "what ifs?"

Chiara and Ben started firing out children like smallpox was still a threat and opened the biggest animal shelter on the West Coast. Ranching it, they abandoned city for wilderness and tended to their ever-growing flock in rustic meditation, red cheeked, ruddy faced, and if we're honest, rather dull. Ben grew his own lettuces with a fevered pride, and would hold forth at dinners about their watering cycle until Chiara threatened to divorce him. Pulling himself together and realizing the lettuce thing was a concern, he started therapy, had an affair with his therapist, and was then beaten to within an inch of his life by her irate husband. Chiara forgave him in traction, and neither lettuce nor liaison was ever mentioned again as they set their sights on a permacultured tomorrow.

Errol bought an island in the Caribbean and founded a treasure-hunting fleet called Poseidon. Convinced that Spanish galleons awaited him, he poured money into expedition after expedition, but always managed to come up short. Judged from a business perspective, it was a total failure and it looked like his Midas touch had abandoned him, but he really didn't give a shit. This wasn't about money, it was about defying time, and when his doctor diagnosed him with a degenerative nerve condition, he redoubled his efforts, digging deep for a final doubloon. At long last he found love too, in the shape of a rather aggressive old harridan called Alice, who treated him like an inconvenience. Errol couldn't get enough of her admittedly witty abuse, and with enough paid nurses to get him through the day, he sat back with leather-bound, seventeenth-century shipping records and basked in the pasting he took. When he finally died, he left Alice his entire fortune and she still called him a cunt, but as if karma was balancing the scale, his fleet struck gold the day he slipped away, and the find was given to the Smithsonian as part of the Johnstone Collection. Errol Johnstone – you fucking legend.

Terra Byte reverted back to Terra Baba, lamenting the abject failure of the internet to deliver a holistic new consciousness. He toyed with the idea of another commune, this time without any men, but he was a forward-looking sort and that smacked of repetition. Scanning the horizon for spiritual possibility, he found the answer in solar energy, renamed himself Helio Baba, took a shit ton of acid, and bought a panel manufacturer. The TV commercials weren't far behind and by 2018, he was the Sun Guru, preaching the solar gospel with a heady blend of half-naked women and verses from the Bhagavad Gita. The merchandise section of his website was a surreal playground of lunacy, featuring everything from clocks to hose reels with rays beaming out from behind his head like a halo. He was arrested for tax evasion as his empire took hold, but the authorities were way out of their depth. The entire jury had bought solar panels by the end of the trial, the court reporter invested her pension in the company, and the judge sacked off jurisprudence to take up yoga. Needless to say, he was acquitted, despite incontrovertible book-cooking evidence, and he hit the lecture circuit in the Sunmobile: a solar-powered limousine driven by a bikini-clad model in a chauffeur's cap. The mad bastard seemed to be getting younger with every passing year, despite drinking vodka like a parched Cossack and chugging through a cornucopia of pharmaceuticals. He just kept on shining.

Atalanta and Ambrose upped sticks and traveled the world building schools. Starting in the tribal regions of Pakistan, where Wahhabism ruled the educational roost, they made secularism their cornerstone. Early results were promising, and they expanded their operations across Asia to fly reason's flag. But the honeymoon didn't last, and accusations of colonialism started to chip at their resolve. When they realized kids in Pakistan were finding rebellion in religion after a secular schooling, they were torn between their own principles and what people actually wanted. In the end, they swallowed their secularism and let the schools evolve how they chose. They never quite recovered the same passion though, and only perpetual motion kept their spirits above water. They kept trying for a baby, but after the fourth miscarriage, they accepted the inevitable and adopted a rainbow brood.

On Yasmina's fifth birthday, Athos left the office brandishing a new telescope and headed home for the festivities. Pulling into the drive, he noticed an unfamiliar vehicle poking out of the garage, and wondering what heathen would turn up this early for a kid's party, he trotted quizzically inside. Trinity greeted him with a rushed kiss and scanned his face uncertainly. Satisfied his mood was viable, she pulled him into a corner.

"There's someone here to see you," she hissed.

"OK," replied Athos. "What's with the secrecy?"

"Promise you'll be nice? Hear him out."

"What are we talking about here?" asked Athos, his voice pitching higher.

He looked up. Standing in his hallway in a pair of slacks, a battered flat cap, and a hedgerow beard was Friction.

Athos dropped the telescope and lunged toward him. It clattered across the marble floor and Trinity went with him, blocking homicide's route and pleading for calm. Phosphorescent with rage, Athos made another break for it, but Trinity was too quick for him, pirouetting lithely between hunter and prey.

"I can explain everything," ventured Friction.

"You fucking cunt!" screeched Athos, tearing at his own shirt.

"Five minutes," begged Friction.

"You treasonous fuckbag!" yelled Athos. "How dare you come here with your traitorous fucking beard!"

It was an unexpected choice of insult and they all paused to appreciate the randomness. Then it kicked off again.

By the time Athos finally calmed down long enough to even consider a hearing, they were halfway down the garden, having played cat and mouse through hallway, living room, study, and terrace.

"One minute!" bellowed Athos.

"They blackmailed me!" cried Friction.

Athos peered at him suspiciously. "Two minutes."

"I don't know how they found out I was gay, but they honey-trapped me."

"What do you mean, they honey-trapped you?"

"I was using a couple of websites – fake name, the works. Anyway, I met this biker through it, and he was in the same boat as me: totally on the down-low. We met in a park and, well, we had some fun, and then the next day, photos were emailed to me."

"Are you telling me that you fucked us because you didn't want to come out of the closet? In the twenty-first century?"

"It's not as simple as that. I was really struggling with it. I wasn't ready to tell anyone shit, and if you must know, I was abused by my priest as a child."

"What the fuck has that got to do with it?" snapped Athos harshly.

"I didn't know if I was really gay or if it was a reaction to that. I was totally ashamed of my sexuality – it felt dirty, weird, and I wasn't ready to face it. I was seriously fucking confused, and it wasn't until I met Javier that I realized who I actually was. Gay and proud – that fucking priest hadn't stolen that from me, but it took a long time to separate out my sexuality from what happened."

Athos wasn't convinced. Friction could be playing him again, for all he knew. "So what happened with the NSA?"

"They never said they were the NSA. They just said they were federal agents. They said that a terrorist cell was active on the Syndicate and they needed urgent tabs on them to prevent an attack. I offered to get them data on the names they were looking for, but they kept pushing for a wider net. They said we were facilitating terrorism, that if I didn't help them, they'd leak our involvement with Al Qaeda to the press. They said I'd be doing the Syndicate a favor."

"With all due respect, Friction, you weren't a wide-eyed college kid. You were a hardened fucking pirate. This sounds like government pressure 101."

"I know, I know. I can't believe I was so vulnerable. I was so desperate to keep my secrets that I was looking for an honorable way out, I guess."

Athos snorted. "Honorable, my ass. If you really thought that, you'd have told us."

"I'm sorry."

"Sorry... Sorry... Jesus." There was silence.

Friction had the good sense to stay quiet, and Trinity looked on from behind a chewed fingernail.

'For fuck's sake. Suppose you'd better stay for cake."

DEMOCRACY

Friction's return posed several questions, the first being whether he still had links with the NSA. Athos had reluctantly taken the first step to forgiveness, but there was a long road ahead. He still couldn't quite believe it had been about keeping the closet bolted, but he was just prepared to give Friction the benefit of the doubt. Javier was far less ready to forget – his husband had disappeared for six years without so much as a fucking Post-it note. Rage had subsided into icy contempt, and despite Athos's efforts to mediate, Javier flatly refused to set foot in the same room as his prodigal partner.

Friction's shares had been frozen by the board after his disappearance. They would've confiscated them altogether had they been able to prove malfeasance, and by laying his cards on the table, he risked exactly that. His disappearance had proved mighty useful to the new order, allowing as it did for the defenestration of the founders. But he had nothing to lose, and calculated that he had enough compromising knowledge to prove awkward if they wanted to play hardball. It was hardly the most conciliatory step – apologizing for being blackmailed while doing a bit of blackmailing – but relying on their mercy was a risky tactic because they'd never shown the slightest sign of having any.

In the end, they allowed him his stock as long as he gave up voting rights and didn't set foot in the building again.

None of it did much for his dignity, but there was a billion dollars at stake. Luther reasoned that a fight would be messy, and they didn't need that kind of attention. Not when his innovations were on the cusp.

The Syndicate inexorably advanced toward content hosting and external links were phased out. Partners received a share of the ad revenue their content generated and were paid in a similar way to artists on streaming sites. Brand identity could be preserved on the new-style content pages, but the content all lived within the Syndicate. It had been a voluntary rollout thus far, but the tipping point was approaching.

Cometh the hour, cometh the man, and while Donald Trump may have been the relativist messiah, Luther was St. Paul and St. Peter rolled into one. He instinctively sensed which way the wind was blowing, and while others struggled to hold back the tide, he built a surfboard to ride it.

The genie wasn't about to jump back in the bottle, whatever editorial filters were applied. Trying to screen content for veracity was a fool's game; it wouldn't work, and there would simply be a succession of embarrassing mistakes. Luther wasn't keen on losing the revenue it generated either, and had quietly taken positions in the main bullshit manufacturers. The development of the bullshit industry mirrored the early years of the internet and indeed the Syndicate – starting open source and then consolidating into conglomerates. The main state actors like Russia, Turkey, and indeed the United States were still denying everything, but most of the private boiler rooms had given Luther a piece to keep trading.

No matter how much organizations like the *New York Times* banged on about multiple sources, they had no more authority than anyone else. Millions still followed them, but they were just another tribe with just another sales pitch – everyone else arbitrated truth too. Luther's genius was to realize objective truth and undisputed facts had gone the way of the steam engine, and while others scrambled to put Humpty Dumpty together again, he was wiring up Frankenstein.

His greatest innovation was the introduction of voting. Positioned alongside the usual "Like" and "Repost" options, there came the "True" and "False" buttons. These allowed users to have their say on whether a story was true or not, and they proved an instant hit. News organizations prided themselves on their ratios, and despite some early click-farm scandals, the process was deemed to have great integrity – especially by Luther himself. What better way to establish truth than to let the public vote on it?

In many ways, it was the logical extension of Hermes's original vision. He probably wouldn't have seen it quite that way, but fuck him, he was missing in action.

Buoyed by the success of the truth buttons, Luther began to think big. With direct democracy in the ascendancy, more and more propositions were submitted by state authorities to the public vote. Schlepping to a polling station seemed rather backward in this day and age, and he wondered whether the decline of representative government didn't synergize with the Syndicate.

There was a monumental irony in lobbying Congress for direct democracy, and in any other age, self-preservation would have killed the bill. But the new wave of senators and congressmen were a post-Tea Party vintage; they weren't professional politicians and they thirsted for a people's democracy. They had gotten elected to change the system, and now Luther was giving them the tools.

Put simply, he offered the Syndicate as a voting platform. Referenda could be put to the user base and voted on, with results in real time. Naturally, the first question concerned fraud prevention, but Luther had an answer. DNA and a retina scan would be taken from online voters. Both would be cross-referenced through a central database at the point of voting to confirm identity and register that person's vote. Manufacturers were already phasing retina-scan technology into webcams, so they were halfway there, and if this could be made to work even on a state level at first, soon it could go national and then get traction in countries around the world.

It was an awful lot of trouble to go to in order to facilitate digital democracy, and questioned on Capitol Hill, Luther was frank about the payoff. The Syndicate would retain the right to map and exploit the DNA samples provided. They could then be used to target ads at genetically, pinpointing medical conditions, predispositions, and traits alike. Customer profiles would no longer be limited to a history of their actions, but go straight to identity's source.

It was a masterstroke. Lobbyists were outraged at the loss of influence and vehemently fought the proposals, but Luther picked them off by explaining they could lobby the voter directly. It wouldn't even look like lobbying in some cases – "gentle persuasion," he called it. They could either lobby for a specific law or else shape content streams to subliminally advance a point of view. Vegetarians could gradually be shown "independent content" that proved the health benefits of meat. Environmentalists could be presented with persuasive "independent arguments" that global warming didn't really exist.

Concerns remained – pressure groups were far more comfortable leaning on individuals than millions of people, but when Luther produced the Syndicate indices, he categorically demonstrated the hive mentality of large groups. Targeted right, millions of people could be influenced in a very similar way to just one, and the scale of numbers offered a greater legitimacy than a single representative's vote.

Stock prices rocketed as the news broke. Being an official voting platform had immense value, but the real prize was the human genome. Some investors questioned whether people would consent to having their DNA stored and monetized, and street protests detonated across the country. But no one would be forced to comply, and that seriously blunted the backlash. This was an opt-in scenario. Luther knew people didn't give a fuck about privacy as long as services came free. DNA was just another step in the same direction.

The only unresolved question was how the initial swab could be taken without feeling totalitarian. It was the final piece of the puzzle, and the answer wasn't long in coming. A young start-up created an elegantly simple bit of technology that analyzed DNA from skin cells. Developing a prototype, they built it into touch screens and keyboards, allowing devices to identify a genetic profile through skin contact alone. Marketed as a security feature, it was doing the consumer a favor, and when it came to DNA submission, no specific action was needed.

This nailed the "out of sight, out of mind" principle. If every bit of data the Syndicate held needed to be directly submitted by the user, no one would have surrendered shit. But let it happen by osmosis… and people barely noticed.

The Syndicate was now the biggest company on the planet, and even though revenue still didn't match valuation, the DNA advertising model was every hedge fund's wet dream. The Digital Voting Bill still had a way to go, but it was looking mighty promising.

Athos didn't know whether to laugh or cry. In the end he had to laugh. It was so far past the realms of sanity that hysterical laughter and a wry tip of the hat to Luther were the only possible responses. And who judged sanity anyway? Maybe it should be put to a public vote.

He'd been divesting his stock for a while, unable to bear the dystopian clusterfuck. He'd become something of a recluse, and only really focused on the charitable foundation, working with Trinity on an ever-growing spectrum of projects. He'd even deleted his own Syndicate account. Their home was their office now, and they would wade through proposals and funding applications late into the night. One October evening, with Yasmina asleep and Trinity out at a homeless shelter, the phone rang in his study.

"Hello, sir, this is Fred Hawthorn from Sandalwood. Sir, we think we've found him."

Athos was momentarily baffled.

"Found who?"

"Damian Anderson, sir. We believe we've traced him to an address in New York City. Identification has been confirmed and we've got a team on him, sir."

Fucking hell… Hermes.

CATCH TWENTY-TWO

The rain smacked down like a lobotomized Mongol horde. Pulling his overcoat tighter, Athos pounded up Lenox Avenue and swung left into 123rd Street. Then he stopped, realized he was getting soaked, and dipped into a doorway. Gazing out, he watched the street lights ripple through the puddles and locked onto the falling droplets. There was an order to the rhythm and yet a chaos too.

What the fuck was he going to say? What was he going to do? Did he even want to be here? Hermes clearly didn't want to be found. Or did he? After nine years, suddenly Sandalwood had found a clue. Hermes was a lot of things, but sloppy wasn't one of them, so maybe this was a subconscious cry for help.

In fact, Athos had forgotten about the search altogether. Back in 2013, when Hermes first went missing, he'd thrown every resource at it. Retainers had been agreed upon, papers had been signed, and it seemed that Sandalwood had been paid ever since. At least they'd been earning their keep. But had it occurred to him, Athos would have called off the dogs years ago. He wondered why his accountant hadn't at least flagged it, but this wasn't the time to wonder what other bills he'd been unwittingly paying.

He poked his head out of the doorway and looked at the brownstone. Harlem sure as hell wasn't the hood anymore;

it was mostly mid-level bankers and service-industry executives – anything south of the Park was pretty much jet-set territory now. All these years, Hermes hadn't touched a credit card that linked back to his old identity or they'd have tracked him down like a shot. No phones, no internet accounts – nothing. He'd taken a shit ton of cash with him when he disappeared, but that could never have lasted nine years. Athos had to wonder how he'd been supporting himself, but then Hermes had always known how to rustle up a few bucks. He was calling himself Ingmar Daschle these days, according to Sandalwood.

Athos stepped out from the doorway. Steam from a nearby grate enveloped him. He pulled back. *Fuck it*, he thought. *Let's do this.*

He stalked out with steel in his stride, crossed the road, and quick-marched up the stone stairway. Taking a deep breath, he pressed the bell. Nothing.

He pressed it again. Silence. There weren't any lights on either. It was 10 p.m. He gave the bell a few more tries and turned to face the street once more. Bollocks.

Well, he was here now – may as well go for a drink, then try again in a while. He spotted a flickering neon sign a hundred meters or so away that gave every impression of alcohol being available, and set off in search of solace.

Arriving at a wooden door, he pushed it open and stepped into a hipster relic. All brushed woods and rust porn, it had seen better days. None of the touch-screen chic you saw downtown.

He walked up to the bar and sank his elbows down, scanning the whiskey selection for a decent bourbon. And then, as if in slow motion, he realized frame by pixelated frame that Hermes was sat next to him, hunched over a drink. He appeared to be unconscious.

The barman shrugged his shoulders. "Guy's a regular," he offered by way of explanation.

"He's an old friend," said Athos.

The barman perked up. "Can you get him home then? I'm looking to close early tonight."

"Sure," smiled Athos.

He carried Hermes out in a fireman's lift, and despite some abstract grunting from the patient, they made it halfway up the street before Athos collapsed under the weight. Tumbling into a tangled pile, Hermes yelped like an angry hamster and opened a bloodshot eye.

"Shit," he mumbled. "Athos."

"You fucking liability."

They were getting drenched, so they ducked under the awning of the community theatre behind them. It took Hermes a while to conjugate complete sentences and the first thing he asked for when coherence had been restored was a drink. Luckily Athos had bought a bottle of bourbon before leaving the bar, and he cracked it disapprovingly. Still – who was the ex-junkie to talk?

A decade dissolved in the twilight. Hermes had spent the first few years of his wanderings on a boat in Kashmir, cutting himself off from communications in any form. It had begun to grate after a while though, and he returned to Europe, replenishing his resources by running an Amsterdam coffee shop under the name Siegfried Johnson.

From there, he kept a mortified eye on the Syndicate and descended wholeheartedly into alcoholism, drinking away the pain and fornicating with oblivion. He knew he was being hunted, just not by who, and paranoia kept him moving: Paris, Prague, Sarajevo, Odessa, then finally New York.

Athos asked him how much he knew about their baby – all grown up and holding the world to ransom.

Hermes looked at him with an intensity Athos didn't think he'd be able to manage.

"It was the fucking ketamine," he said.

Hmm. How coherent was he? Was he still litigating the first Syndicate? Gently, Athos said, "Yes, yes it was. But I mean the website."

"So do I," said Hermes. "It was a carbon fucking copy. We thought we had a magic potion and it turned everyone into a fucking zombie. We thought we were opening up an astral plane and instead everyone got trapped in their own, anesthetized fucking bubble."

Athos nodded. Didn't get much more lucid than that.

"How did we manage to fuck it twice?" asked Athos. "How did we not learn?"

"It's the wave particle duality," said Hermes softly. "Human patterns are both linear and cyclical. So while there's continuous progression, there's also a series of cycles. Which I suppose is why we never learn from history. It's like we're doomed to keep repeating the same mistakes, but advance a bit each time too."

"Sisyphus," reflected Athos.

"Yeah, but the stone doesn't roll right the way back down to the bottom. Each time, we gain a few inches on the last. And every time, it's a different-looking hill."

"But we still gain those inches," pointed out Athos.

"Aren't you Mr. Glass Half Full," spat Hermes. "Here, give me that bottle."

Athos took a swig and passed it to him. "I've been thinking," he said.

"Oh dear," said Hermes.

"You're a paranoid drunk and I'm a depressed recluse."

"You're really selling this."

"I'm serious, Hermes. The fucking rush we felt, the buzz we had on the up both times. It was fucking magic, man. Even though it all came crashing down, does that take away from how alive we felt when we believed?"

"Um. Yeah."

"It doesn't though. Half the reason we're so fucked is because there was nothing left to build. Even if it had all stayed above board, we'd still have ended up lost."

"So what's your point?"

"That we should keep trying. Doomed or not."

"This really is quite a pitch."

"For fuck's sake, Hermes – we've got a few billion and some brain cells left between us. And there's one more space out there to take. We did physical space, now we've done virtual space. What's left?"

"You tell me."

"Space."

"What space?"

"Space space. As in other planets."

"Oh Jesus, you've got to be joking. For starters, our billions wouldn't get us past the fucking moon. And anyway, I don't want to be responsible for fucking up the galaxy. Maybe there's an intelligent species out there who'd do a better job than us."

"We could build in safeguards though. Create cast-iron institutions and have fixed-term stays on Mars. That way, no one person or faction can ever build a power base. You ride that fresh wave of idealism each time before people get jaded and their worst instincts come out. If we keep shuffling the deck, it can never be stacked."

They chattered on the theatre steps. The rain slowed to a drizzle and a creeping allegro filled the mist. A man walked past to check the program, and as he pressed on into the onyx night, the playbill flapped in the breeze.

Now Showing:

Catch-22

Lightning Source UK Ltd.
Milton Keynes UK
UKOW04f0601180917
309391UK00001B/109/P